"Until this mission is over, consider me your shadow. Do you have a problem with that?" asked Flynn.

Abbie decided to clear this up right away— before it could go any further. "Not as long as you understand that our relationship isn't personal. I don't want to repeat what happened at my apartment the other night."

"Check. No kissing or fooling around in bed. Got it."

His blunt comment startled her into meeting his gaze.

Flynn watched her intently, his eyes gleaming. "Did I misunderstand what you were referring to?"

"No, you understood perfectly."

"Too bad, Abbie. I enjoyed kissing you and being in your bed. I think you enjoyed it, too."

Dear Reader,

This month we have something really special in store for you. We open with *Letters to Kelly* by award-winning author Suzanne Brockmann. In it, a couple of young lovers, separated for years, are suddenly reunited. But she has no idea that he's spent many of their years apart in a Central American prison. And now that he's home again, he's determined to win back the girl whose memory kept him going all this time. What a wonderful treat from this bestselling author!

And the excitement doesn't stop there. In *The Impossible Alliance* by Candace Irvin, the last of our three FAMILY SECRETS prequels, the search for missing agent Dr. Alex Morrow is finally over. And coming next month in the FAMILY SECRETS series: *Broken Silence,* our anthology, which will lead directly to a 12-book stand-alone FAMILY SECRETS continuity, beginning in June. In Virginia Kantra's *All a Man Can Be*, TROUBLE IN EDEN continues as a rough-around-the-edges ex-military man inherits a surprise son—and seeks help in the daddy department from his beautiful boss. Ingrid Weaver continues her military miniseries, EAGLE SQUADRON, in *Seven Days to Forever*, in which an innocent schoolteacher seeks protection—for starters— from a handsome soldier when she mistakenly picks up a ransom on a school trip. In *Clint's Wild Ride* by Linda Winstead Jones, a female FBI agent going undercover in the rodeo relies on a sinfully sexy cowboy as her teacher. And in *The Quiet Storm* by RaeAnne Thayne, a beautiful speech-disabled heiress has to force herself to speak up to seek help from a devastatingly attractive detective in order to solve a murder.

So enjoy, and of course we hope to see you next month, when Silhouette Intimate Moments once again brings you six of the best and most exciting romance novels around.

Leslie J. Wainger
Executive Senior Editor

Please address questions and book requests to:
Silhouette Reader Service
U.S.: 3010 Walden Ave., P.O. Box 1325, Buffalo, NY 14269
Canadian: P.O. Box 609, Fort Erie, Ont. L2A 5X3

Seven Days
to Forever
INGRID WEAVER

Silhouette®

INTIMATE MOMENTS™

Published by Silhouette Books

America's Publisher of Contemporary Romance

SILHOUETTE BOOKS

ISBN 0-373-27286-3

SEVEN DAYS TO FOREVER

Copyright © 2003 by Ingrid Caris

Visit Silhouette at www.eHarlequin.com

Printed in U.S.A.

Books by Ingrid Weaver

INGRID WEAVER

admits to being a sucker for old movies and books that can make her cry. A Romance Writers of America RITA® Award winner for Romantic Suspense, and a national bestselling author, she enjoys creating stories that reflect the adventure of falling in love. When she and her husband aren't dealing with the debatable joys of living in an old farmhouse, you'll probably find Ingrid going on a knitting binge, rattling the windows with heavy metal or rambling through the woods in the back forty with her cats.

To Mark.
The adventure continues....

Chapter 1

Out of the hundreds of tourists who had passed by his post in the past hour, why should Flynn notice this one? Even if he wasn't on duty, he shouldn't have noticed her. Sure, she was attractive enough, in a compact, earth-mother type of way. Soft-brown hair, eyes the color of caramel, a hint of freckles on the tip of her small nose and a quick, coiled-spring energy to her movements. But she was the kind of woman who would want to meet a man's parents. She had probably picked out a china pattern and two names for her firstborn. She was the kind of woman who usually made Sergeant First Class Flynn O'Toole of Eagle Squadron, Delta Force, break out in hives.

A spot just under his left shoulder blade developed a sudden itch. Flynn rubbed his back against the wooden bench. "I don't think she's our target."

He barely moved his lips as he spoke. His words wouldn't have been audible to a person sitting beside him, but the microphone under his collar had no problem picking up everything he said.

"She would be a good decoy." The voice of Captain Sarah Fox, Eagle Squadron's intelligence specialist, came through the pea-size receiver in his ear. "I wouldn't underestimate her."

Sarah had a point, Flynn thought. The brunette with the freckles would make an excellent decoy, since no one would suspect someone who looked that wholesome and innocent to be involved with a group of terrorists who were dedicated to the overthrow of the Ladavian government.

Then again, no one would expect a group like the Ladavian Liberation Army to be using the National Air and Space Museum for a ransom drop in the first place.

The woman hurried past the bench without giving Flynn a second glance. She headed straight for a pair of boys who were paused under the biplane that hung from the ceiling. For a moment all three of them craned their necks, gazing at the Wright Brothers' 1903 Flyer with expressions of delighted awe. Then the woman herded the boys toward a group of more than a dozen chattering, fidgeting children.

Evidently, the woman hadn't come to the museum alone, she had brought a classroom worth of kids with her. Unless the LLA had dropped their height requirements and were recruiting fresh-scrubbed seven-year-olds now, it was unlikely that the woman was involved. She was probably exactly what she seemed, a teacher on a field trip.

"Heads up. Vilyas just passed the front entrance." The warning came from Flynn's friend, Master Sergeant Rafe Marek. He was positioned outside where he could observe the approach to the building without attracting undue attention—Rafe's scars tended to spook people who didn't know him.

Although his posture didn't change, Flynn's senses went on high alert. Ambassador Vilyas was carrying the ransom himself, as the terrorists had demanded. The man was adamant. He would do anything for the safe return of his son.

If it had been any other case, the FBI would have handled it—Delta Force normally didn't operate on American soil, and when they did, it was in the role of advisors to other law enforcement agencies—but this was no run-of-the-mill snatch.

Absolute secrecy was vital. Not only was Vilyas the Ladavian ambassador, he was married to the niece of the Ladavian king. If a child with royal blood was killed here, the delicate negotiations that were already underway to bring democracy to the strategic, oil-rich Balkan nation would be derailed. And if the media caught wind of what was happening, they might as well put on their silver suits because the political powder keg of Eastern Europe would blow.

So Ambassador Vilyas had demanded the best. He had insisted on nothing less than the legendary hostage-rescue expertise of Delta Force and the president had agreed. Which was why Flynn and the team of highly trained commandos from Eagle Squadron were spending the day scattered around one of the most visited museums in Washington, D.C., dressed in civvies to blend in with the tourists. The mission was straightforward: recover the Vilyas boy unharmed, hand the terrorists over to the Ladavians and keep the entire operation completely secret despite the few hundred bystanders with cameras who were wandering through the target zone.

Oh, hey, piece of cake, right?

A small, balding man Flynn recognized as Anton Vilyas walked past his bench. His features were sharper than they had appeared in the briefing photo. Exhaustion did that to people—the man reportedly hadn't slept since his kid had been taken three days ago. Poor bastard looked to be near collapse. The top of his head gleamed damply and his fingers were white where they curled around the strap of the green canvas backpack he carried.

How heavy was twenty million dollars? Flynn wondered. Even in the large denominations the kidnappers had demanded, the weight would be substantial. He'd heard the entire amount of cash had been provided by the U.S. government, an indication of how vital they considered Ladavian goodwill…and the mission of Flynn's team.

Vilyas reached the designated spot and stopped. It was hard to tell whether he intentionally dropped the pack or whether it simply slipped through his sweaty fingers. It hit the floor with a quiet thud, wobbled briefly, then slumped against the base of a trash can. The green backpack stuffed with twenty million dollars lay discarded like someone's forgotten lunch. The ambassador walked away without a backward glance, just as he'd been instructed.

"All right, people. Stay alert."

Flynn heard Major Redinger's voice and grunted an acknowledgment. Mitchell Redinger, the team's commanding officer, was stationed at the temporary base they had established in a vacant warehouse. He was monitoring the feeds from the surveillance equipment that was positioned around the target zone, watching everybody's backs. When this went down, it would go down fast.

And that's just the way Flynn liked it. He felt his pulse pick up. It didn't race. He was too disciplined for that. No, it was a steady, solid rush of blood to well-conditioned muscles that hummed in readiness.

He didn't know what the target would look like, or how many there would be. He didn't know what direction they would come from or how long he would need to wait. The odds of following the kidnappers without their knowledge, of assessing the best way to free the hostage, of bringing the whole incident to a quiet, successful conclusion weren't good. As a matter of fact, they were abysmal.

But Flynn's team had pulled off missions that had been far worse. When they did, there was never any recognition. No medals or official commendations, because the government wouldn't even admit that Delta Force existed. The hours sucked, the stress was incredible. He had to be prepared to go anywhere in the world on a moment's notice. His home was whatever base he was stationed at, his family was the soldiers of Eagle Squadron. He was expected to accomplish the impossible, continually challenging his brain and straining his body to the limit.

Flynn pressed his lips together and exhaled slowly through his nose.

Damn, he loved this job.

"Everything sure is old here, Miss Locke."

Abbie smiled at the boy on her left. "Yes, Bradley. That's because this is a museum."

The child on her right side leaned over to roll his eyes. "Boy, Bradley, are you ever dumb."

"You're dumb, Jeremy."

"Yeah, right."

"Uh-huh. As if."

The children were getting tired, Abbie thought. The squabbling was a sure sign. "But as museums go, the exhibits here aren't all that old," she said. "How can anyone think of space flight as old? Not that long ago it was science fiction. Look over here."

"What's that?"

"It's the space capsule that John Glenn used when he orbited the earth." She paused. "The first time, anyway."

"He went to space twice?"

"Yes, but the second time he was much, um, older."

"It looks burned."

"Yes, it heated up when it went through the atmosphere. That was before NASA developed the space shuttle. Astronauts were shot into space inside a little capsule like this that was fitted on the tip of a rocket.''

"Wow," the boys said, tipping their heads one way and then the other to study the capsule.

"That was more than forty years ago."

"Wow! That's older than my mom!"

"It's older than *my* mom."

"Is not."

"Is, too."

Abbie put her hands on their shoulders and gently guided them along with the rest of the class. "It's older than me, too, Jeremy."

The boys looked up at her, their mouths rounded. "Hey. Really?"

Abbie suppressed a grimace at their expressions of disbelief. She wasn't old, she reminded herself. Turning thirty didn't mean that she was over the hill. She was just coming into her physical and sexual prime. A woman's vitality peaked in her thirties, isn't that what people said? She had plenty of good years to look forward to.

But if she had intended to keep a positive attitude about her youth, visiting a museum on her birthday wasn't that great an idea.

"Miss Locke?"

She smiled at a plump redheaded girl. "Yes, Beverly?"

"I have to go to the bathroom."

"Me, too," another child said.

Abbie turned to the parent volunteers who had accompanied the class and efficiently divided everyone into rest room squads. It was time to call it a day, anyway. They had been on the go since the morning, and the bus was due to pick them up in half an hour. Well-accustomed to the vagaries of seven-year-olds, she knew enough to allow plenty of extra time to organize their departure.

The unfortunate reminders of her advancing age aside,

it had still been a good day. She was lucky to have a job she enjoyed as much as this one. She loved children and longed for the chance to have one or two of her own some-day. Yes, her ambition was embarrassingly old-fashioned: a home in the suburbs filled with the warmth of a loving family…and of course, a nice, stable husband to share it all with. Was that really too much to ask?

Perhaps it was, since she'd always assumed she would have been married by the time she was thirty. That's prob-ably what was causing her to be so conscious of this mile-stone of a birthday. But chances were that she wasn't going to find Mr. Right by the end of today…unless he jumped out of the cake at her surprise party.

For a moment Abbie imagined the scene in her parents' house. Her family always threw her a birthday party. She always pretended to be surprised. There was something wonderfully comforting about the whole thing, a sweet rit-ual that arose from her family's love. Her mother would fix her favorite potato salad, plates of fried chicken and egg sandwiches with no crusts. Her father would make the same joke he always did about how Abbie couldn't pos-sibly be more than two because her mother hadn't aged a year since her birth. They would hug and laugh and make toasts to the future while she opened her gifts.

She would bet a hundred, no, a million bucks that the gifts wouldn't include a cake with a man inside.

Abbie chuckled at the whimsical thought and scooped up a pair of discarded jackets from the rest room counter, then guided the children to the lobby where they waited for the stragglers. Of course, more jackets came off and backpacks hit the floor as they waited.

"Miss Locke, I lost my hat."

"What did it look like, Ricky?"

"It was blue."

Well, that narrowed it down. Abbie spotted a ball cap
on the floor and pointed. ''Is that it?''

''Yeah! Thanks, Miss Locke.''

She held out the jackets. ''Whose are these?''

Two children raced up to take them, then dropped more
of their belongings as they contorted themselves to put the
jackets on.

Once the whole group was assembled, Abbie did a head
count. As soon as she was assured that everyone was present and accounted for, she hurried them toward the door
before anyone could wander off or decide they needed
another rest room trip. Ricky's hat fell off as soon as he
started moving. Abbie picked it up as she passed by, along
with three stray backpacks, breathing a sigh of relief when
she saw the yellow school bus already waiting outside.

''What the *hell* just happened?'' the major demanded.
His voice was low, his words clipped, always a bad sign.
''O'Toole, report.''

Flynn stared at the empty spot on the floor, then looked
at the departing group of children. ''She took the backpack.''

''Who?''

''That teacher.''

''I told you not to underestimate her,'' Sarah said.

Flynn folded his museum guide, stuffed it into the back
pocket of his jeans and followed the woman to the door.
He deliberately kept his strides slow and easy, in case anyone was watching for a tail. ''I can't believe this,'' he said.
''She would have been my last choice.''

''It was neatly done,'' Sarah said. ''The children
swarmed the target zone while she lifted the ransom. We
never saw it coming.''

Flynn emerged into the crisp sunshine of the autumn
afternoon. The woman was making no effort to disappear.

In fact, she couldn't have chosen a more obvious mode of transportation. "You can't miss seeing her come now," he said. "Bright-yellow mini school bus with a whole bunch of screaming kids. That's going to stand out in traffic."

"I need a visual confirmation that she has the money," Major Redinger said.

"The bus is blocking my view," Rafe said. "Flynn, can you see the bag?"

Flynn ambled toward the sidewalk. The woman formed the kids into a line, then stood by the open door of the bus and counted heads as they climbed inside. She handed what appeared to be a hat to one boy as he passed her and held out a sweater to another kid, all the while balancing three backpacks against her chest with one arm.

"Affirmative," Flynn said. "The green backpack she's holding appears to be the one Vilyas dropped. Aren't the electronics we installed in the pack working, Major?"

"The mike's muffled."

"She's holding the pack to her chest," Flynn said.

"Clever woman," Sarah said. "Anything on the homing signal, major?"

"That's coming through no problem."

As the last child climbed on the bus, the woman's shoulders rose and fell with a sigh. She started after them, pausing on the first step to glance over her shoulder at the museum. And despite the noise from the squirming kids that Flynn could hear all the way over here, she was smiling.

Flynn took an involuntary step backward. If he had seen her smile before, he wouldn't have needed to wonder why she had drawn his attention. Despite the freckles, despite the wholesome demeanor, there was something…alluring about her smile. It was a private little tilt of the corners of her lips, not meant for display. It was the smile of a woman who knew what she wanted, and for a crazy moment it made him wish he could give it to her.

What the hell was he thinking? She had just walked off with twenty million dollars in cash. What more could she possibly want?

She turned away. The doors of the bus closed. Flynn snapped his attention back to the conversation that was coming through his earpiece.

"...the mike's working now. All I can hear are children's voices."

"...chase vehicles in position."

Flynn pivoted and headed for his motorcycle. He'd chosen to use it because of the advantage it would give him in the Washington traffic, but considering the nature of the getaway car—no, bus—there was little chance of losing track of the ransom.

"This doesn't add up," he said, unlocking his helmet from the back of the seat. "She can't be with the LLA. They wouldn't use a bus full of kids to transport the ransom. It's too obvious and it's not maneuverable enough."

"But it would provide excellent cover," Sarah said. "They know we wouldn't dare make a strike with all those children in the way."

"Come on, people. Can't you see it was an accident?" Flynn persisted. "She picked up that pack because she thought it belonged to one of the kids."

"That's a possibility, but—"

"She's not one of the LLA," he said.

"That's immaterial." At Major Redinger's voice, the radio chatter stopped. "Until we know for sure whether this was a legitimate ransom pickup or just bad luck, our only option is to split up. Team A follows the ransom, Team B remains in position to continue monitoring the museum."

Flynn kicked his bike to life, slid down his visor and

slipped into the line of traffic that inched along behind the school bus. He noticed Sarah's van waiting at the next cross street and heard the distant chug of a helicopter overhead. Much farther overhead, a satellite was beaming down second-by-second updates from the Global Positioning System that had been stitched into the pack.

Redinger was right. They had to cover all the possibilities. Considering what was at stake, they couldn't afford to make any assumptions.

Why was Flynn so sure that the woman was innocent? Simply because she didn't look like a terrorist meant nothing. Trouble came in all shapes and sizes. He'd seen old women in patched coats and kerchiefs lob hand grenades. He'd seen children act as spotters for assassins with high-powered rifles. He knew better than to trust anyone except the members of his team.

Besides, even if he was right and the pickup had been accidental, it was too late to put the ransom back in place. Boarding the bus now and retrieving the money would attract too much negative attention, to say the least. And the LLA had ordered Ambassador Vilyas not to alert the authorities about the kidnapping. No one, especially not Delta Force, was supposed to have been at the ransom drop, so how would they have known of the bungled pickup? The LLA could be following the ransom as easily as Flynn was, and they would be sure to spot any attempt at interference.

Oh, hell. For the sake of the mission, he should hope he was wrong about the woman. It would be far easier if she really was a clever terrorist in disguise who had just pulled off a brilliant plan.

Then again, since when had Flynn liked things easy?

Flynn dropped back, allowing more traffic between his bike and the bus as he followed it. Terse, one-line reports came over the radio link as Sarah Fox and her friends in

Intelligence scrambled to keep up with the situation. Information began to build. The licence plates of the school bus were registered to a local bus company. According to their log, this bus was booked by Cherry Hill School for a field trip. Contact name at the school was a Miss Abigail Locke.

Abigail? It was an old-fashioned name, perfectly suitable for a wholesome-looking schoolteacher. He wondered if her friends called her Abbie.

As if following the script that Intelligence had written, the bus pulled into the parking lot of Cherry Hill School. Flynn coasted past, did a U-turn and let the bike idle in the shade of the trees at the corner of the schoolyard.

The teacher—Abigail—got off the bus first but she was unable to stem the flow as the kids burst out after her. She did manage to hand out a few jackets and two of the backpacks before the children met up with their waiting parents, but the kids were eager to be gone. The whole thing was over in a matter of minutes.

A strange woman's voice came over the radio. It was soft and tinged with humor, and somehow Flynn knew it had to be hers.

"...good thing their heads are permanently attached."

"I've patched in the feed from the mike in the backpack," the major said, confirming Flynn's suspicions about who was speaking. "The woman's been trying to give the ransom away for the past ten minutes."

"Could she know the mike is there?" Sarah asked.

"Possible, but unlikely."

"What's going on at the museum?" Flynn asked.

Rafe's voice replied. "Nothing. If the LLA is here, they're not making any moves yet."

Flynn leaned forward and crossed his arms on the bike's handlebars, straining to see across the schoolyard. Miss Abigail Locke waved at a few of her departing students, then turned away. "Geez." She gave a breathy grunt as she hitched one strap of the green backpack over her shoulder. "How many Pokémon cards can they cram into these things?"

"Abigail Locke has brown hair, brown eyes, is five feet four inches, 103 pounds…" Sarah's voice droned in the background, describing the details of the woman who was walking across the parking lot toward a beige subcompact. "She's the registered owner of a beige Pontiac Firefly, license number…"

Flynn's lips quirked. Well, either this particular terrorist had established an exceptionally solid cover and was so clever that she was deliberately acting innocent for the microphone she knew was in the backpack…

Or she was exactly what Flynn hoped she was.

Wait a minute. He'd been through this already. He had no business being pleased. Her innocence was going to increase the difficulty of this mission by a factor of ten.

They had to get the money back before Abigail discovered it—along with the surveillance devices in the specially designed pack—and decided to be a law-abiding citizen and turn everything over to the police. Once that happened, it would be next to impossible to contain the damage. The secrecy of the mission would be compromised. Rumors would get started, questions would be asked and the LLA would cry "double cross" and kill the Vilyas kid.

"She's twenty feet from her car," Flynn said. "With this bike, I can reach her and take the backpack before she gets her keys out. Few if any witnesses. She'll think it was a random mugging."

"Negative," the major said. "We can't make a move on her in public. If the LLA did tail her and are watching, they'll know Vilyas talked."

And cry "double cross" and kill the kid, Flynn repeated to himself. "Tell me where she lives," he said, easing his bike into gear. "I think it's time we meet."

Chapter 2

Abbie flicked another glance at her watch as she dug her keys out of her purse. The traffic had been worse than usual. Every direct route to her apartment building had been blocked by stalled cars or minivans. Why couldn't everyone simply follow their vehicle manufacturer's recommended maintenance schedule? She always did, and she hadn't had any problems with her car yet. Still, it was odd that the car trouble seemed limited to her neighborhood. It was almost as if there were some grand conspiracy out there to delay her from reaching home.

She shook her head at the ridiculous thought. Washington was undoubtedly full of enough conspiracies, but they wouldn't be targeting her. No, she was about as ordinary and law-abiding as a person could get. She understood the value of structure. Maintenance schedules, school timetables, to-do lists, these gave a lovely framework on which to build a life.

Of course, sometimes timetables did require adjustment.

She'd have to pencil in thirty-five as her next target date for the husband, family and home in the suburbs.

"Oh, for heaven's sake," she muttered, fitting the key into the lock. "Get over it. Thirty is only a number."

The phone was ringing when she opened the door. She bolted the door behind her and flicked on a light just as the answering machine picked up.

"Hi, dear." It was her mother's voice. "I hope everything's all right. I thought you'd be home by now."

Abbie hurried through the short entrance hall to her living room, dodged around the avocado plant and reached past the fig tree to grab the telephone. "Hi, Mom."

"Oh, you're there. How was your day, Abigail?"

"Great. The kids loved the museum." She started to shrug off her jacket, belatedly realizing she was still holding on to the stray backpack she'd picked up. She'd meant to leave it in the car so she could take it in to school tomorrow, but in her rush to get home she must have brought it upstairs to her apartment without thinking. She was getting as absentminded as her students.

On the other hand, wasn't forgetfulness a sign of advancing age?

She grimaced, dropped the pack and her purse beside the fig tree and sank into a chair. "How are you, Mom?"

"Just fine." There was a spurt of conversation in the background that was quickly muffled. "Are you still going to come over tonight? You haven't forgotten, have you?"

"No, of course I didn't forget. I was late getting in because the traffic was horrible. If I hadn't used all my shortcuts, I'd still be sitting in it."

"Well, I hope it clears up before you set out for our place." The sound of a doorbell came over the line.

"I'll be over as soon as I can. Is someone at your door, Mom?"

"Oh, that's nothing. Just your dad fidgeting with the bell again."

"Mmm." She was sure she heard more muffled conversation in the background. It sounded like her older sister's voice. "Are you sure you aren't expecting any visitors?"

"Now, why would we be expecting anyone but you, dear?"

"I don't know. Are you making fried chicken?"

"Yes, as a matter of fact. How did you guess?"

Fried chicken, potato salad, egg sandwiches without crusts, just like every year. The surprise party was on. "I could smell it from here, Mom."

"Oh, you." She laughed. "We'll see you in a little while, then. Drive safely, dear."

Abbie put the phone down and leaned her head against the back of the chair. She had to try to think positively about this birthday, she thought as she studied the ceiling. Apart from a different digit at the start of her age, it was the same as all the others.

She looked at her watch and did a quick calculation of how much time she would need to drive to her parents' house if the traffic didn't improve, then pushed to her feet and hurried toward the shower. She'd better get moving or she was going to be late for her own party. She just hoped she would be able to act surprised. It was going to be tough. She had never liked surprises.

"Twenty-nine years old," Sarah said. "No, make that thirty. Birthday today. Single. Has worked at Cherry Hill School for the past seven years. Four hundred and sixty-one dollars in her savings account, seven thousand dollars in government bonds. Want her credit card balances?"

Flynn buckled on the electrician's tool belt as he swung around another turn in the stairwell. Sarah was on the radio, feeding him information about Abigail Locke as it came in. He was thinking on his feet now, making up the action plan as he went along; so, any fact, even a date of birth might prove to be useful. "Does she have a debt problem?"

"No, she has a good credit rating. No debts apart from a car loan. She's a nonsmoker, according to her insurance records," Sarah continued. "No outstanding traffic fines. Three library books on loan. History texts, judging by the titles."

Flynn wasn't surprised at the depth of detail Sarah could obtain on such short notice—all it took was a little know-how, and nothing that had ever been entered into a computer was secret. If the public became aware of how easily the privacy of a private citizen could be breached, the conspiracy theorists would have a field day.

One detail that hadn't shown up on the records, though, was the fact that Abigail could drive like a New York City cabbie. If Flynn hadn't seen it for himself, he never would have believed what she could make that little beige Firefly do. She'd gotten past every one of the obstacles they'd set up. It was a good thing he'd been on his bike, or she would have lost him back at Sarah's "stalled" van.

He clipped a fake power-company ID card to his shirt pocket. "What about boyfriends?"

"No data about that so far. I could get into her prescription records and find out if she's gone to a doctor for birth control."

"No," Flynn said immediately. He didn't know why, but he didn't like the idea of Intelligence digging quite that deeply into Abigail's life. "I only wanted to know whether she might have company with her at her apartment."

"Sorry, prescription records wouldn't help you there. She has her mother, Clara Locke, listed as her next of kin.

Parents live in Maryland. One older sister named Martha, a younger one named Eleanor, both married with kids.'' Sarah paused. ''Abigail and her sisters are named after first ladies. Seems like she's not the only history buff in the family.''

Flynn reached the next landing just as the lights went out. The power failure didn't startle him—evidently Specialist Gonzalez had located the main breakers in the basement and had done his job right on schedule. This was the reason Flynn was using the stairs to get to the seventeenth floor instead of the elevator. He waited where he was until the emergency light clicked on, then continued climbing.

''Vilyas has just received word from the LLA.'' Redinger's voice replaced Sarah's. His words were even lower and more clipped than earlier—definitely a very bad sign. ''They claim they were double-crossed, that he never left the ransom as he had agreed.''

''What did he tell them?'' Flynn asked.

''Vilyas said he left the money but it was picked up by a schoolteacher.''

Flynn increased his pace, taking the stairs three at a time. Great. If the terrorists hadn't followed Abigail from the museum, they'd be able to find her for sure, anyway, now that Vilyas had told them the ransom was picked up by a schoolteacher. They wouldn't need the resources of Delta Force to be able to trace which schools had field trips at the museum today, all they'd need would be a telephone. It was only a matter of time before they narrowed it down and decided to come after Abigail and the money themselves.

''Wasn't anyone with him when he took the call?'' Flynn muttered. ''Couldn't they have stopped him from talking?''

''He was advised not to say anything, but the LLA put

his son on the line and then struck the child. When Vilyas heard his son scream, he disregarded our instructions.''

Flynn felt a surge of adrenaline. The LLA had abused a helpless child. They would stop at nothing to get what they wanted. They wouldn't care how many innocent people were hurt or how much collateral damage they did in the process.

Miss Abigail Locke, who turned thirty today, with her three library books and her little beige car was a sitting duck. He had to get the money away from her—or get her away from the ransom—as soon as possible.

''Is the kid okay?'' Flynn asked.

''We have no way of knowing,'' Redinger replied. ''All we know is that he was alive and conscious ten minutes ago.''

''How long do you estimate I have before the LLA gets here?''

''We're keeping our units in place to gridlock the traffic in the immediate area, so best-case scenario, you'll have thirty minutes.''

He didn't need to ask what the worst-case scenario was, Flynn thought, hearing footsteps in the stairwell below him. He waited until he could be sure the footsteps were retreating—probably one of the building's tenants, nervous about the power failure. He placed his hand on the door to the seventeenth floor. ''What's the latest from the electronics in the pack?''

''The pack is stationary, somewhere in her apartment.''

''Has she opened it?''

''Unlikely. The mike didn't pick up any sound to indicate the buckle was being unfastened.''

''Did it pick up anything?''

''Only a phone call from her mother. They're expecting her for dinner.''

''Maybe I should wait until she goes out.''

"The LLA won't wait if they find her first."

"Right. What's she doing now?"

"Nothing on the mike except some shuffling sounds. Probably trying to find her way around in the dark."

"Okay. Keep me posted. I'm going in."

Abbie balanced on one foot to put on her shoe as she peered through the peephole in the door. She tried to make out the features of the man who stood there, but the beam from the emergency light at the end of the corridor didn't reach this far. All she could see was a tall, broad-shouldered figure with some kind of tool belt strapped around his hips.

"Who is it?" she called through the door.

"I'm with the power company, ma'am."

She buttoned her blouse and tucked it into her skirt, thankful that she'd finished her shower before the lights had gone out. The bathroom had no window, so it had been pitch-black, but at least there had been enough light from the dusk filtering through the other windows for her to find some clothes. "That was fast," she said.

"There's a problem with the wiring in the building. We've traced it to a circuit in your apartment. I need to check it out."

Water dripped from the ends of her hair onto her shoulders. "What?"

"Do you mind letting me in?"

She opened the door to the limit of the security bar. "Do you have any identification?"

There was a rustle of fabric as he reached for something on his chest. "Here's my I.D. card."

She squinted at the card, but all she could make out was a pale rectangular blur. "Sorry, I can't—"

"Hang on." He took a flashlight from his belt, clicked it on and directed it toward the card. "This should help."

The suddenly bright beam made her blink. She looked at the printing on the card. Flynn O'Toole. Sure enough, he was an employee of the power company. She glanced at the small color photo in the corner. Her grip on the door tightened.

Who had ID photos that turned out like that? Even the stark head-on flash couldn't hurt that square jaw and those high cheekbones. A picture like that should be gracing an ad for designer cologne, not an identification card for the electric company. She raised her gaze to his face.

The photo wasn't that good after all. He looked far better in the flesh.

Good Lord, but he was gorgeous. Not in a pretty, cover-boy way, but like a man. All man. Those deep-set, thick-lashed blue eyes gleamed with quiet male confidence. His nose was bold and straight, his lips framed by twin lines that etched their way down from the hollows of his cheeks. His hair was black, curling over the tips of his ears and the back of his collar in a way that invited a tousling. In his plaid flannel shirt and his snug-fitting jeans, he looked rugged but approachable, a natural-born heartbreaker.

Abbie wanted to slam the door in his face.

"Ma'am? Would you like to call my supervisor? He'll verify my ID for you."

"No, I—" She cleared her throat, thankful for the lack of lighting so he might not notice how she was staring. On the other hand, a man who looked like that would be accustomed to attracting plenty of female attention. Yes, he probably reveled in it, drawing women like mindless, doomed moths to a flame.

It was a good thing she was immune to men like that. That was the advantage of being infected before—it served as a vaccination against future bouts of the same affliction. "Are you sure the problem is in my apartment? I haven't had any trouble with the electricity until now."

He took a slim, rectangular device from the pocket of his jeans and held it toward her. "The readings I'm getting on this gauge pinpoint your place."

She made a show of studying the numbers that were flickering across the screen of the instrument, but it could have been a pocket calculator for all she knew. "I see."

He hesitated for a moment, then lowered his voice and bent his head toward her. "Please, ma'am. I'd like to get this job finished and get home. You see, it's my birthday."

The door wobbled as she jerked. More water dripped from her hair to her shoulders and trickled down her blouse. "Your birthday?"

"Uh-huh."

"You're not serious."

"'Fraid so. I hit the big three-oh today."

"That's…odd."

"Sure is, according to my folks. They claimed I'd never make it this far."

"That's not what I meant."

"They're expecting me for dinner tonight, but I have to finish this job before I can leave, so if you don't mind…"

She gritted her teeth and forced herself to return her gaze to his face. He was smiling. A hopeful tilt at the corners of his lips. She could almost hear moth wings sizzling. "I meant I can't believe it's your birthday today. It's mine, too."

His eyebrows rose. "Really?"

"Yes."

"Now that's a coincidence." The lines beside his mouth curved as two dimples appeared in his cheeks. "What are the odds?"

Yes, indeed. What were the odds? Having a man who looked like Flynn O'Toole show up on her doorstep was unlikely enough, but sharing something as personal as a birthday with him was beyond strange. It bordered on bizarre.

Was this some kind of cosmic joke? she wondered. Was this fate's way of pointing out the road she'd almost taken, the very thing she used her schedules and her timetables to guard against? Just as she was about to adjust the best-before dates on the plans for her life, instead of Mr. Right, Mr. Flynn O'Toole shows up at her door with his blue eyes and his dimples like some karmic birthday present....

Oh, for heaven's sake, she thought sternly. He was only here to do his job. He couldn't help how he looked.

Abbie tucked her hair behind her ears, then wiped her wet fingers on her skirt. "Did you say your parents were expecting you for dinner?"

His budding smile disappeared. "Hey, just because I'm thirty and spending my birthday with my parents is no big deal."

Her conscience twinged. He couldn't help how he looked, she repeated to herself. She had learned the hard way not to trust handsome men—or to put it more accurately, not to trust her reaction to handsome men—but she really shouldn't be letting her personal prejudices color her judgment. Who knew? If he actually did plan to visit his parents, maybe there were a few ounces of human decency behind that pretty face, after all.

Not that she would be willing to bet money on it.

Not that his character had any bearing whatsoever on the current situation, she reminded herself firmly. "Excuse me, I didn't mean to imply there was anything wrong with that. I was getting ready to go over to my parents' place for dinner myself when the power went off."

He was silent for a moment, then shook his head and chuckled. "Go figure. Guess you're in as much a hurry as I am, then."

"Yes, I believe I am."

He clipped his ID back on his shirt pocket and gestured toward the door. "Well, the sooner I get started, the sooner both of us can leave."

She hesitated. The logical side of her brain waged a brief battle with the dark little corner where she kept her instincts. As usual, though, logic won. She had to get organized and get out of here within the next thirty minutes or she was going to disappoint her family. She eased the door shut to unlatch the security bar, then stepped aside to let him come in.

It would be all right. She was just letting him into her apartment, not her life.

Flynn kept his light aimed at the floor as he walked into Abigail's apartment. She pressed herself against the wall, giving him as much room as possible, then closed the door behind him.

Miss Abigail Locke was a cautious lady, he thought. It was a good thing he'd hit on the idea of making up that story about today being his birthday. That seemed to have smoothed his way inside.

Flynn was good at saying what people wanted to hear. It was a useful talent to have in his business—talking his way out of a situation was often preferable to using force. In spots like this, people called it quick thinking. When he was off duty, people called it charm.

The technical word for it was lying.

But it wouldn't have accomplished his objective if he'd told Abigail that he'd celebrated his thirtieth birthday more than two years ago. And it sure as hell hadn't been with his parents. He'd been six years old the last time he'd seen his mother, and as far as he knew, his father was somewhere in Brazil with wife number four.

"What exactly are you looking for?" Abigail asked.

He glanced over his shoulder. Rather than staying by the door, she had followed him into the living room. There was more light here than in the hall, but still, the place was too dim to see more than dark shapes and outlines.

Her outline was worth seeing. Compact, feminine and rounded in all the right places. She must have been fresh from the shower when she'd answered the door. He'd caught a whiff of fruit-scented soap—apple or cranberry, he'd guess. Her hair was wet, plastered flat to her head until just below her ears, where it coiled into heavy curls. She probably hadn't realized that the drips from her wet hair had been turning her white blouse transparent.

Flynn kept his flashlight aimed at the floor. "Like I said, I traced the short to your apartment, but that's about as specific as the gauge gets. I need to test each one of your electrical outlets until I find the source of the problem."

"But wouldn't each apartment be on a separate circuit? I still don't understand how a problem here could black out the entire building."

"Seems the wiring in this building wasn't done to the standards specified in the electrical code," he improvised. He had to distract her before she realized how flimsy his story was. "Wow, I still can't believe we share a birthday."

"Me, neither."

"And that we'll both be spending it with our parents."

"Mmm. Yes."

"Are you close to your folks, then?"

"Yes, you could say that."

He heard the caution in her voice go down another notch. He decided to play up on the family angle. "So am I. A lot of people would call it old-fashioned, but there's nothing like family."

"Especially on birthdays."

"You got that right." He paused, trying to think of the most likely spot for her to have dropped that backpack.

"Kids make it the most fun, though. I've got two nephews who can't wait to blow out my candles."

"Do you like children?"

"Love them," he said, figuring that would be what a schoolteacher would want to hear.

A sigh whispered through the darkness. "So do I."

He used the flashlight to scratch his elbow as he moved toward the outline of the living room window.

"Oh, watch out for the—"

Something stiff and dry hit his face. He automatically brought his forearm up to block the next blow and jumped backward.

"—avocado plant," she finished.

Flynn directed his flashlight upward. A branch thick with long, wavy leaves hung at head level. He traced the branch to an enormous plant that grew from a pot beside one wall. "What the…"

"It's an avocado plant," she repeated. "I started it from a pit. I know it's in the way but it does best in that spot. Are you all right?"

"Sure. I managed to fight it off."

"Don't worry, it's not carnivorous."

Flynn heard a smile in her voice. It reminded him of the private smile that had so intrigued him before. He swept his flashlight around the room, this time aiming the beam higher. A pair of monster plants hulked under the window. No, it was a glass door, not a window. Probably led to a balcony, but he hadn't been able to see it before because of the plants. More pots of foliage clustered on the top of a low bookshelf. "I see you're good at growing things."

"It's my hobby."

"I'm a civil war buff myself," he said, remembering what Sarah had said about Abigail's library books. Maybe he was piling it on a bit too thick, but he'd do whatever it took to keep her off guard.

"I enjoy studying history, too," she said. "I believe there are worthwhile lessons to be learned from the past. As long as a person is smart enough to remember them," she added under her breath.

Not a good topic, he decided, hearing the note of thoughtfulness in her voice. He didn't want her thoughtful. He wanted her off balance. He chuckled. "Let's not mention history on our birthday, okay? After the day I've had, I feel ancient enough already."

"I know what you mean." She sighed and moved toward him. "You'll never find what you're looking for in this jungle. Better let me help you."

The flashlight was still aimed high, so when Abigail walked into the beam, it shone directly on her wet blouse. Flynn tried not to look, but it was impossible not to notice how the patches of wetness from her dripping hair had spread. The fabric wasn't white as he'd first thought, it was the color of ripe melons. Or maybe the fabric's color was due more to the lush curves it was plastered to, particularly since it turned dark where it clung to her nipples.

And Flynn suddenly realized that the innocent, house-plant-loving, visit-her-folks-on-her-birthday Abigail Locke wasn't wearing a bra.

He turned the light aside and scowled. She hadn't provided the peep show deliberately—she must have been in a hurry to get dressed when the lights had gone out.

But he was supposed to be the one distracting her, not the other way around.

Find what you're looking for, she'd said.

Well, he sure wasn't here to look for a pair of breasts, however lush and temptingly displayed they might be. He had to find that backpack, he reminded himself. A green backpack. In a jungle of green houseplants.

She touched his arm. "You might as well start in the kitchen. The outlets are easiest to get to there."

Her touch was soft, hesitant. It was meant impersonally, a practical way of getting his attention in the dark. He felt her warmth through his sleeve, through his skin, right to his bones.

He couldn't afford to feel anything. He had a job to do. A kid's life and the political stability of an entire region was resting on the success of this mission. He had to stay focused.

The outlets, she'd said. Right. He took a screwdriver from his tool belt, turned around and followed her to the kitchen.

The receiver in his ear crackled. "O'Toole."

Flynn was careful to betray no reaction to Redinger's voice. The radio had been silent since he'd made face-to-face contact with Abigail. The major had been monitoring everything, of course, but for him to risk direct contact, it had to be important.

"A car passed one of the roadblocks one minute ago," Redinger said. "They flagged it as suspicious so we ran the plates. It was reported stolen this morning."

Okay. Redinger had to let him know about anything suspicious. This could be coincidence, nothing to do with them.

"Three male occupants."

Three. The LLA operated in cells of three.

"Sarah turned the parabolic mike on the car. It picked up a snatch of foreign language conversation. She identified it as Ladavian."

That clinched it. They were about to have company.

"The stairwell is getting busy with tenants making their way downstairs," the major said. "We'll run interference there when our visitors arrive, but we still can't risk a confrontation. I estimate you've got five minutes tops."

So much for the half hour he'd hoped for.

"Better wrap things up, Flynn."

Sure, find the ransom, get it and Abigail out of this apartment before the terrorists dropped in without compromising the mission by blowing his cover.

Why had he thought he didn't like things easy?

Chapter 3

Abbie pointed out the electric sockets over her postage-stamp-size counter and in the corner above the baseboard, then stepped to the side as Flynn squeezed past her. His sleeve brushed her arm, and she inhaled a scent that reminded her of an April sunrise. Sharp and earthy, restless, filled with the promise of warmth. The fine hairs on her arm tingled.

She pressed her hands to her stomach, trying to calm the butterflies that were dancing around there. No, they were probably moths. With crusty brown singe marks on the edges of their wings.

She wished she could blame the tickle of excitement on hunger—she was growing later by the minute for dinner and her surprise party—but if it was hunger, it was a kind that couldn't be satisfied with food.

This was a superficial physical attraction, that's all, a natural reaction to a physically appealing man. After all, she was a woman in her sexual prime, right? But she'd taken a detour down that road and knew better than to trust it. She didn't want to acknowledge the bump of her pulse each time she looked at him. She should be ignoring his appearance and regarding him with the same polite, professional distance with which she treated the building superintendent or the cable guy or the men who had delivered her new sofa.

Then why couldn't she? Was it the sense of intimacy from the semidarkness? Or was it the way Flynn moved? It wasn't only his appearance that drew her. For a large man, he was light on his feet. He had the total body control of a dancer, making each movement a smoothly coordinated sequence of toned muscles working in harmony. She could easily imagine the way he would be flexing and bulging under that soft flannel shirt and those snug jeans....

But she shouldn't. No, she wasn't going to picture his muscles or anything else. She wasn't going to watch as he hitched up his tool belt and leaned over to look in the corner under the table...even if he did have the firmest, most perfectly formed set of buns Abbie had ever seen.

"No luck in here, ma'am," he said, straightening up. "Where's your bedroom?"

The kitchen seemed to shrink as he moved past her. Considering his height and the breadth of his shoulders, she should have felt uncomfortable to be alone in the dark with him, regardless of her personal prejudice against handsome men. Why wasn't she?

It must have been the way he had mentioned his nephews. Any man who willingly claimed he liked children couldn't be all bad. He was a history buff, too, which meant they had something else in common. He took his job seriously, so he was a hard worker and would be a good provider. He was hurrying because he didn't want to disappoint his parents. Everything he'd said would lead an unbiased, unprejudiced observer to assume he was a nice, stable, family-oriented guy. Exactly the kind of man she'd hoped to marry someday....

Abbie grimaced, chagrined by the direction of her thoughts. Marriage was on her brain because of today's date, but she wasn't pathetic enough to think he really *could* be a karmic birthday gift, was she?

He spent even less time checking the outlets in her bedroom than he had in the kitchen. It couldn't have been two minutes before he moved on to her bathroom. He had to duck his head to get past the spider plant that she'd hung from the ceiling. "Nothing here, either," he said. "Must be in the living room after all."

His pace was increasing—it seemed that he had barely touched those plugs in the bathroom. He must be anxious to finish up here so he could go home, as he'd said. He muttered something under his breath as he ran into the avocado plant again.

"I'll have to move the fig tree if you want to check the outlet beside the balcony door," she said. "The pot would be in the way."

"No, I can get it."

"Better let me. It's a bit finicky. It's been dropping leaves lately, so I have to be careful how I handle it." She went to his side and leaned down to grab the edge of the pot. It had just started to slide across the carpet when she heard him make a sudden exclamation.

"Got it."

She turned her head. He was crouched beside her, his face level with hers, so she had a close-up view of the smile that flickered over his face. It wasn't charming or friendly like the other ones she'd seen. It was...hard.

He caught her gaze, and his smile instantly eased.

It had been a trick of the lighting, she decided. Anyone's face could look hard when it was lit by a flashlight from below, as all kids who had ever told a ghost story around a campfire knew.

"Okay, I'm almost done." He pushed aside her purse and the stray backpack that she'd dropped beside the plant, then slid his screwdriver back into a slot in his tool belt. "I'll need to open up the electric box here, so for your own safety, I'm going to have to ask you to leave the apartment now."

She sat back on her heels. A fig leaf wafted downward and settled on her lap. "What do you mean?"

"It's routine, in case something goes wrong. The power company would be held liable if you got accidentally injured while I was doing repairs."

"I can't see why I need to leave. That seems excessive. I'll just stand out of the way and—"

"I'm sorry, ma'am, but you're going to have to leave."

"If it's that dangerous, shouldn't you be wearing protective clothing or something?"

"Don't worry about me, I'm a trained professional." He placed his hand under her elbow and gently but firmly helped her stand up.

She looked at the place where he held her arm… although, she didn't really need to look because she felt what he was doing with every other one of her senses.

"It will only take a few minutes," he said. "I know you're in as much of a hurry as I am, so I'd appreciate your cooperation."

Before she could form a reply, there was a sudden commotion from the corridor outside her apartment. Men's voices raised in anger.

"Hey, take it easy," someone shouted. "Watch where you're going."

"Get out of my way, idiot," a heavily accented voice said.

"You could have broken my nose, slamming through the doorway like that."

There was a spurt of muttered words that Abbie couldn't make out. They sounded foreign.

Flynn tightened his grip on her elbow and pulled her toward the door. "Please, ma'am. You're going to have to get out," he said. "Right now."

"But I can't just—"

Something heavy slammed into her apartment door.

"Oh, my God," she said. "They're fighting out there. The blackout must be making them panic."

Flynn switched direction, pulling her back toward the balcony door. "They're coming in. We're going to have to use the balcony."

"What?" She tried to tug her arm free, but his fingers couldn't be budged. "Who's coming in? What do you mean we have to use—"

Something hit her door again. There was a sharp, splintering sound.

Flynn shoved the fig tree to one side with his foot and lunged for the balcony door. It slid open only a few inches before it was stopped dead by the broom handle Abbie kept for security in the sliding door's track.

"What are you doing?" she shrieked.

The apartment door burst inward and slammed against the wall. Three men rushed in.

Before Abbie could draw breath to scream, Flynn spun her behind him. "Get down," he ordered.

She hadn't meant to obey him—she hadn't even registered what he had said—but she stumbled over the fig tree pot and lost her footing, going down to her knees, anyway. More leaves rained down around her.

The intruders were silhouetted against the emergency lighting from the corridor. There were two short men and one tall, and the tall one appeared to be holding a...

''Oh, my God, he's got a gun,'' Abbie said.

The words had barely left her mouth when Flynn made a sudden movement. The flashlight he'd been holding hurtled across the room and struck the armed man in the wrist. His gun fell into the avocado plant.

They must be looters, Abbie thought, groping on the floor for her purse. She'd heard of looting in prolonged power failures, but she'd never dreamed it could happen so fast, and in her building.

The two short men babbled something incomprehensible and took out more guns. Abbie saw the metal gleam in the light from the hall and screamed a warning to Flynn.

Instead of retreating, Flynn advanced on the intruders. He unbuckled his tool belt, hung on to one end and whirled it through the air. The heavy, tool-laden, hard leather pouch was suddenly a weapon. It made a clinking thud as it connected with the closest man's head.

The man crumpled and fell to the floor. Flynn swung the tool belt again, dispatching a second man with the same brutal speed.

Abbie clutched her purse to her chest and scooted backward, her shoes sliding through the leaves that now littered the carpet. What had happened to the nice, stable guy who liked children and had dinner with his parents? He was fighting off three armed looters all by himself, as if he did that kind of thing every day.

The tall man, the one Flynn had hit with the flashlight, was clawing at the avocado plant, likely looking for the gun he'd dropped.

In a move that Abbie had only seen in movies, Flynn spun around on one foot, swinging his other foot in an arc that connected with the tall man's jaw. The looter flew sideways into the bookshelf. A geranium that had been on the top shelf wobbled and crashed on his head. He didn't move again.

"Oh, my God." Abbie struggled to draw a breath. Her pulse was pounding so hard, her lungs didn't work. "Oh, my God."

"They're down," Flynn said.

He stated that as if he were making a report, she thought. She ran a hand over her face, her fingers shaking. "Oh, my *God!*" she repeated. "What…who…?"

"Throw the switch. We're getting out now." Flynn rebuckled his tool belt over his hips and strode over to where she was crouching.

Switch? What switch? "But…" She shook her head, still trying to absorb what had happened. "Police. We have to call the police."

"Later." He leaned down and reached past her to pick something up from the floor.

It was the backpack she'd brought home from the class trip, she realized. "What are you doing?" she asked.

He slung the strap of the pack over one shoulder and reached down to grasp her arm. "Damage control," he said.

"What? I don't understand. Why—"

"Later," he interrupted. He pulled her to her feet with a strength that would have surprised her two minutes ago, before she had seen him in action. "Right now we've got to get you out before more of them show up."

"More? Do you mean more looters? But that's why we have to call the police."

He shifted his grip from her arm to her wrist and started for the door. "We'll call them from somewhere safe."

Abbie stumbled after him, stepping over the unconscious men who lay sprawled on her floor. Pot shards crunched under her feet. "All right, maybe we should call the police from somewhere else, but—"

Her words cut off as the lights came on. She squinted

at the sudden brilliance, then gasped at the scene the light revealed.

Her neat, orderly apartment was in shambles. Leaves, potting soil and bright-red geranium petals were scattered everywhere. The men she had stepped over weren't merely unconscious, they were bleeding. She felt her stomach roll as she saw the damage the tool belt and Flynn's foot had done to their battered faces.

Yes, Flynn had done that, she thought, her gaze snapping to the broad back that moved in front of her. He'd done it to defend her, but still, what kind of man was capable of fighting that viciously? He was an electrician, for God's sake.

And why had the power come back on when he hadn't done any repairs?

And why on earth did he want that green backpack?

The caution she should have felt ten minutes ago when he'd first talked his way into her apartment finally asserted itself. She braced her feet and hung on to the broken door frame with her free hand before he could drag her through. "Let go of my wrist," she said.

He turned toward her. This was the first time she had seen his face clearly. She saw details now that she hadn't seen before: laugh lines at the corners of his eyes, the hint of a cleft in the center of his chin, the shadow of a dark beard along the sharp edge of his jaw.

He was as startlingly handsome as before, but something was different. There was no flashlight beam to light his features from below, so there was no way to mistake what she saw. There was more going on behind those sparkling blue eyes than she'd assumed. His expression was more than hard. It was predatory.

"Abigail, please." He released her wrist and placed his hands on her shoulders. "We've got to get away from this apartment."

"No, you go ahead. I'll—"

"I can't risk your safety by leaving you here." He looked toward the stairwell. "There could be more men on their way."

"How do you know that?" She inhaled sharply, realizing what he'd just said. "And how do you know my name?"

Flynn met her gaze squarely. His eyes probed hers for a few tense seconds. "All right. I've got no choice. Keep running the security check, and we'll sort it out later."

He was still looking directly at her, but she had the feeling he was talking to someone else.

"Are you going to come with me, Miss Locke?" he asked.

Her mind was reeling. There was simply too much to take in, to figure out, to try to make sense of. She shook her head.

"I should have known you wouldn't do this the easy way," he muttered. In a move too swift to follow, he leaned forward, wrapped one arm around the back of her knees and straightened up, flinging her over his shoulder.

She tried to scream, but the force of his shoulder hitting her stomach had knocked her breathless. Her head bounced against his back as he jogged to the elevator. She hit him with the purse she was somehow still clutching, but the blows had no effect—beneath his loose shirt, he was built like a brick wall. She clawed at the backpack he carried over his other shoulder in an attempt to lift herself up. "Put me down!" She gasped. "What do you think—"

"I'll explain everything later, Abigail," Flynn said, carrying her into the elevator. "We're using the central car, Gonzales. I'll need a control override so it won't stop on the way down."

"What? Who's Gonzales?"

The doors slid shut, and the car started downward. It

plummeted past the other floors without showing any signs of slowing. Just as Flynn had said, it didn't stop.

Abbie wriggled, trying to kick free from his grasp.

Flynn tightened his grip on her legs. ''Please, don't do that, Abigail. You're only making this more difficult. I promise I'm not going to hurt you.''

Her fingers latched on to the backpack's buckle. She braced her arm against its side and lifted her head just as the buckle snapped. The pack had been crammed so full the top flap sprang open the moment the pressure from the buckle was released.

Abbie went still. She'd wondered briefly about what was in this pack, but she hadn't bothered to look. She'd known children liked to carry an incredible amount of paraphernalia with them, so she hadn't found the weight that unusual. Nor had she been surprised that the owner hadn't claimed it—her classroom was full of items that had been left behind.

But judging by what she could see poking out of the top of the green canvas, she was certain this pack didn't belong to one of her students.

Money. The pack wasn't full of Pokémon cards, it was stuffed with money. Thick, bundled wads of it. So much that she could actually smell it.

It couldn't be real. No, this must be some kind of joke, and the wad of bills next to her nose had to be from a board game with very, very realistic props....

Game? Joke? Those looters who had broken into her apartment had been dead serious. As was the blood on their faces and the vicious way Flynn had fought them.

The looters? Had they been after this money? How had they known she had it, when she hadn't known she had it? And why had Flynn grabbed this pack...unless he, too, had known what it contained?

Something clicked in her brain. *This* is what he'd been

after all along. He was no electrician. He'd lied. He'd used that story to get into her apartment.

And she'd believed every word. She'd looked at that charming smile and those oh-so-sweet dimples and she'd been so sure she'd had his number, but she hadn't, had she? She'd thought she'd learned her lesson about believing handsome men, but she'd been played for a fool. Again.

Dammit, she should have followed her instincts and slammed that door while she'd had the chance.

What was she mixed up in?

The elevator bypassed the ground floor. It didn't stop until it reached the first level of the basement parking garage.

Where was Flynn taking her?

And why in God's name was she letting him?

He shifted his grip, sliding her down the front of his body until she was standing on her feet. The instant the doors opened, he fastened one arm around her waist, drew her against his side and started forward.

Abbie didn't wait for answers to any of her questions. She didn't pause for regrets or self-recriminations. She reached for the screwdriver on Flynn's tool belt, yanked it out of its slot and drove it as hard as she could into Flynn's arm.

He muttered a sharp oath and loosened his grip for a vital second.

Abbie dropped the screwdriver, twisted out of his grasp and ran.

''Miss Locke, stop!''

At the shout from behind her, Abbie moved faster. She darted toward the nearest row of cars, the sound of her footsteps echoing through the cavernous garage. Her parking spot was on the next level down. Should she try to make it to her car, or head for the exit ramp? She glanced over her shoulder.

Flynn was following her. He was pressing his hand against his forearm, and she could see blood on his fingers. Her stomach churned. How badly had she hurt him?

"Abigail!"

She veered to the right, choosing to try to reach the exit instead of her car. The sooner she got outside where she could get help, the better her chances of escaping this… this…whatever she was mixed up in.

"Block the exits," he said. "She's heading for the ramp."

His voice was low and hard. Who was he talking to? Was he crazy? She looped the strap of her purse around her neck and broke into a sprint, her arms pumping as she gulped in air. Her foot hit a patch of oil as she followed the ramp around a pillar. She slid sideways and crashed into the wall.

"Abigail, please stop!" he called. "We're not going to hurt you."

We? *We?* She slapped her hands against the cement wall and pushed off. She didn't see the van that was coming down the ramp until it was directly in front of her.

Tires screeched as the vehicle skidded to a halt. A trim blond woman in a yellow cardigan set stared through the windshield at her, then opened the driver's door and hopped out. "Are you all right?" she asked. "I didn't hit you, did I?"

Abbie heard footsteps pound up the ramp behind her. She glanced over her shoulder and saw that Flynn was steadily closing the distance between them. His jaw was clenched. The sleeve over his forearm glistened dark red. She whipped her gaze back to the woman from the van and made a split-second decision. "Please. You've got to help me," she said, racing around the hood to the passenger door. "That man's crazy. I need to get out of here and call the police."

The woman didn't hesitate. Abbie had barely pulled the door closed behind her when the woman slid behind the wheel, flipped the power locks on the doors and threw the van into reverse.

Abbie braced her hands on the dashboard, trying to catch her breath. She saw that Flynn had stopped running. His lips moved, as if he were talking to himself again.

"No problem, Sergeant," the woman said. "I'll take it from here."

Flynn smiled and lifted his bloody hand to his forehead in a crisp salute.

Abbie whipped her gaze back to her rescuer.

The blond woman palmed the wheel as she changed gears, expertly sending the minivan into a skidding half circle so that it was pointing up the ramp instead of down. She gave Abbie a tight smile. "Relax, Miss Locke. If you had the good sense to run away from Flynn O'Toole, then you won't have any trouble understanding what I'm about to tell you."

Chapter 4

The warehouse looked as if it had been empty for years. The weeds that poked through the cracks in the asphalt loading area were waist high in places. Rust stained the overhead doors and trailed down the brick wall beside the corroded rain gutters. High in the wall beneath the eaves, the rising moon glinted from a row of windows. The darkness behind the broken panes stood out like missing teeth.

Flynn eased back on the throttle and let his bike coast toward the middle door. "It's O'Toole," he said quietly.

The door lifted on well-oiled rollers. Staff Sergeant Lang was on guard duty. He averted his rifle and motioned Flynn to drive inside.

The bike's headlight revealed several parked vehicles beside a canvas tarp that formed a wall directly in front of him. Flynn took off his helmet and waited until the warehouse door rolled shut, then swung his leg off the bike and headed toward the tarp.

In fact, the tarp was one side of a large canvas military

tent that the team had erected inside the warehouse as part
of their security precautions. The ruse was low-tech, fast
to implement and surprisingly effective when it came to
ensuring the outside of the building continued to appear
dark and deserted.

The operational detachments from Delta Force were accustomed to working on their own—after some spectacular
failures decades ago when the force was first formed, they
had learned the hard way not to trust outside intelligence.
They'd also learned the more fingers there were in the pie,
the more likely that matters would spiral out of their control. The best way to keep a secret was not to tell anyone,
so besides the president and the brass at the Pentagon, no
one knew that Eagle Squadron was here.

Flynn lifted aside a flap, stepped over a bundle of electrical cables that snaked along the cement floor and strode
into a blaze of light and activity. The tent was organized
into two areas: one for equipment, the other for personnel.
To his left he saw two soldiers cleaning their guns while
Rafe Marek sorted out the ordnance they'd assembled. On
Flynn's right, the team's communications center had been
set up on a table crammed with radio, telephone and computer equipment. Scale maps of the area and photos of
known members of the LLA had been taped to the poles
that supported the roof. Some folding chairs, a trestle table,
a small refrigerator and a microwave oven marked the
mess hall and beyond that were two rows of cots that
would serve as their barracks for the duration of the mission.

They'd brought only the bare necessities to Washington
when they'd loaded the transport plane at Fort Bragg—
vehicles, equipment and shelter. This self-contained temporary base of operations could be packed up and stacked
in the back of a truck as quickly as it had been assembled.
The living conditions were cramped and far from com-

fortable, but the plumbing in the warehouse bathrooms worked, and Gonzales had coaxed hot water out of the showers. Compared to other places where Eagle Squadron had set up shop, this tent was downright luxurious.

As far as Flynn knew, the mission was still a go. According to the latest news, the damage done by the mix-up at the ransom drop and the scuffle at Abigail's apartment appeared to have been successfully contained. To everyone's relief, the team had moved swiftly enough so that no word had leaked to the media or to the local authorities. How much damage had been done to the Ladavians' negotiations with the LLA was another matter.

Flynn turned right and headed toward the stocky, bald man who was seated in front of the radio. "Is there any word from the Ladavian Embassy yet, Chief?"

Chief Warrant Officer Esposito shook his head as he glanced up at Flynn. His forehead creased like a pit bull's. "The LLA hasn't been in contact since they put the boy on the line."

"How's Vilyas?"

"Not doing well. He had to be sedated."

"That's rough. He didn't look in good shape when I saw him at the ransom drop."

Esposito bared his teeth, exposing a flash of gold. "I can't blame him. If anyone snatched one of my boys, I'd have to be tied down to keep from going after the bastards myself."

"Do you think the Vilyas kid is still alive?"

"At this point, the odds are in his favor. The ransom money isn't all the LLA are after. They want to terrorize Vilyas and the Ladavian government, and as long as their hostage is alive, they can keep turning the screws."

"Yeah, it's a win-win situation for them. If they get the money, they finance more terrorism. And if they execute their hostage, they demoralize the royal family and gain worldwide publicity.''

"Hanging would be too easy for bastards like that." Esposito gestured toward the pack that Flynn carried on his back. "Is that the money?"

Flynn slipped the straps of the pack off his shoulders and held it out to Esposito. "Yeah. It's all there. What do you want me to do with it?"

"The box I used for my equipment is under the table. You could put the money in there to keep it out of the way until we're ready for the next round."

Flynn peered under the table and spotted a battered steel trunk. He bent down to slide it toward him, stuffed the pack inside and closed the lid. By the time he had straightened up, Esposito had already turned back to the radio as if he were totally disinterested in the twenty million dollars in cash that rested inches away from his feet.

Neither man considered the situation to be strange. People in their line of work were motivated by loyalty, honor and duty—if they'd been interested in money, they would have been accountants.

"Hey, O'Toole. Let me take a look at that arm."

Flynn glanced at the lanky man who was walking toward him. Sergeant Jack Norton had the easy gait and whipcord leanness of a marathon runner. His specialty was field medicine, but no one made the mistake of believing that made him soft. Norton could pop dislocated joints back into place or fish through a guy's guts for shrapnel in the morning, then proceed to take advantage of their grogginess to rob them blind at poker in the afternoon.

"Forget it, Norton," Flynn said, moving toward the mess area. He grabbed a can of soda from one of the cases on the floor, opened the top and took a long swig. "It's just a flesh wound."

"Yeah, I've heard that before," Jack said as he followed

him. His soft Louisiana drawl echoed in his loose-limbed strides. "Humor me, anyway. It's the major's orders."

Flynn looked around. "Where is the major, anyway?"

Jack tipped his head toward the far corner where some extra canvas tarps had been strung to partition off a small room. "Back there, doing his best to keep any more, ah, surprises from hitting the fan. He told me to send you in when I'm done."

"Fine," Flynn muttered. He pulled one of the chairs close to the trestle table, sat down and extended his arm. "Knock yourself out."

Jack sat across from him and opened up the red tackle box where he kept his medical supplies. He let out a low whistle as he peeled back the blood-encrusted sleeve of Flynn's shirt.

Flynn gritted his teeth. Not from the pain—he was trained to ignore far worse than this—but from embarrassment. He was a Delta Force commando. He was an expert marksman. He could use his feet and his hands as lethal weapons. He'd disabled three LLA terrorists less than an hour ago without breaking a sweat.

But he hadn't been able to stop a five-foot, four-inch schoolteacher from stabbing him with a screwdriver.

Why? Sure, the grip he'd used to restrain her hadn't been all that solid because he hadn't wanted to give her bruises, but he should have been able to catch her before she'd bolted into the parking garage. The truth was, she'd distracted him with all that wriggling in the elevator.

What normal man wouldn't have been distracted? Flynn asked himself. His hand had been clamped over the backs of her thighs, his face had been level with the curve of her buttocks and her unbound breasts had been jiggling against his shoulder blades. He'd been engulfed by the warm scent of fresh-washed female. Even with the voices of his team giving curt reports through his earpiece, he'd been aware of every panting breath she'd drawn.

Yet the lapse in his concentration could have been more than embarrassing. It could have been dangerous. If Sarah hadn't shown up with her van when she had, the outcome might have been entirely different. The mission could have been compromised because, instead of focusing on his job, Flynn had been thinking about how good Abigail Locke had felt against his body.

He scowled. Hell, she wasn't even his type.

"Hold on there, son. I'll be done in a minute."

Flynn returned his attention to Jack. "Did Captain Fox get in yet?"

"Uh-huh. She and your little friend are in with the major."

Flynn's gaze strayed to the partition that defined the major's "office." He should be wondering how the security background check had panned out, or how Abigail was handling the situation. Yet instead he wondered whether her blouse had dried.

"This looks ugly," Jack added, his voice suspiciously sympathetic as he cleaned the dried blood from the area around the wound. He swabbed on a generous amount of disinfectant. "I have to give the schoolteacher credit. She got some good penetration after she pierced your sleeve."

"It wasn't that deep. The bleeding stopped after a few minutes."

"I can't tell the caliber or the make of the screwdriver she used." Jack took a pair of tweezers and picked out some shirt fibers that clung to the sides of the hole. "Was it a Robertson?"

"It was a Phillips," Flynn said.

"Ah, yes. Now that you mention it, I can see the four points of the star." He gave the wound a final cleaning, laid a piece of gauze over the top and taped it in place. "Next time, make sure your tool belt isn't loaded."

Flynn folded the bloodstained sleeve above his elbow and flexed his arm, watching the white bandage ride up on a ridge of muscle. He wasn't going to respond to Jack's ragging. If the men knew how much this bothered him, they'd never let him hear the end of it. "I'll ask Rafe to install safeties on all the screwdrivers, okay?"

Jack packed up his supplies. "Good idea."

Flynn finished his soda and got to his feet. "Thanks for the Band-Aid, Jack. Got any lollipops to go with your usual, sweet bedside manners?"

"I'm fresh out of both." He lowered his voice. "If you're going to see the major now, you might not want to go in there unarmed."

"He's not still pissed about the mix-up at the ransom drop, is he?"

"Not him. I'm talking about his guest." He raised an eyebrow. "I heard she might be armed with a pencil."

Unbelievable. That's all that came to Abbie's mind. The whole situation was simply beyond her comprehension. Things like this didn't happen to people like her. She glanced around the canvas cubicle. It didn't look like a rabbit hole, and her name wasn't Alice, but any minute now she half expected to see a white hare in a waistcoat and top hat—

The bubble of hysteria that rose in her throat frightened her almost as much as the events of the past hour. Had it only been an hour? She rubbed the empty spot on her wrist where her watch should have been. She felt naked without it, but she hadn't been able to find it when she'd been scrambling in the dark for her clothes, and then she'd gone to answer the door, and Flynn had talked his way inside, and her life had turned upside down....

Oh, God. She had to get a hold of herself. She took a deep breath, and her head reeled at the strong aromas of canvas and dusty cement. This cubicle was the only private area of the hidden tent Sarah had brought her to. It was tiny, with barely enough space for a small table and a handful of folding metal chairs. A bare lightbulb hung on a cord from one of the poles that propped up the roof, adding a stark glare to the already-grim surroundings.

"These are standard government nondisclosure forms, Miss Locke. You're welcome to read them over before you sign."

Abbie jerked as a sheaf of papers was pushed across the table in front of her. She looked at the man who sat on the other side.

Major Mitchell Redinger wasn't wearing a uniform—in his knit golf shirt and pleated khakis he should have looked more like a lawyer on his day off than an army officer— yet he radiated an air of authority. Maybe it was from the distinguished-looking silver that threaded the dark hair at his temples or the ramrod stiffness of his posture. Or maybe it was the unwavering gray steel in his gaze. Whatever the cause, the overall effect made her grateful she was facing him across a table and not a battlefield.

She took the papers from his hand, but when she tried to focus on the words, her shaking fingers made the print blur.

"We're sorry for the inconvenience," the major continued. "We'll take you home as soon as it's safe to do so."

Inconvenience? she thought wildly. Was that how they described having her door broken down by three armed men and being kidnapped by a bunch of soldiers?

Abbie moved her gaze to the third person in the room. Sarah Fox stood by the canvas flap that formed the door, her arms folded over her chest. Like the major, she didn't need a uniform to assume an air of command. Even in her lemon-yellow sleeveless sweater and her short skirt, there was something intimidating about her. She was only a few inches taller than Abbie, but she was one of those people who had the kind of presence that made her appear larger than she actually was.

She had seemed so nice at first, Abbie thought. Before they'd left the garage, Sarah had identified herself as a member of the United States Army and had done her best to stem Abbie's budding panic. She'd explained that Abbie had accidentally put herself in the middle of a ransom exchange, then she'd calmly taken off the cardigan that matched her yellow sweater and loaned it to Abbie to cover up her wet blouse.

It had been a kind gesture—Abbie hadn't realized how indecent she had looked with that soaked cotton plastered to her breasts. Had Flynn noticed?

What a stupid thing to worry about. How could she be concerned about herself at all? She wasn't the only one who had been kidnapped. A child's life was at stake here, and she had unwittingly made things worse. The papers crumpled in her grasp. "What's going to happen now?" she asked.

"As Major Redinger said, you'll be taken home as soon as possible," Sarah replied.

"No, I meant to the child? Is he going to be all right?"

"We're working on it."

"Who is he?"

"I'm sorry, Miss Locke, but in the interests of national security, we can't give you any more details," Sarah said.

"I hadn't meant to interfere. I hadn't realized what was in that pack. I had thought that one of my students had left it."

"Yes, we realize that."

"What happened to those men who broke into my apartment? Were they arrested?"

"No, we couldn't do that at this stage," the major said. "Once they regained consciousness and saw that the ransom was not in your apartment, they left. They're under surveillance, so they won't pose any further danger to you."

"But what about the child they kidnapped? If they didn't get the ransom—"

"Don't be concerned. They'll negotiate again."

"But I still don't understand why the army is involved. Isn't the FBI supposed to deal with kidnappings?"

"Normally, yes, but these are special circumstances. When it comes to hostage rescue, our expertise surpasses that of the FBI."

Something stirred in Abbie's memory. A movie she'd seen, or some news report about a clandestine mission. The army had commandos who were trained in hostage rescue. Their skill and dedication were legendary, but they were so secret, their existence wasn't officially acknowledged. These people weren't ordinary soldiers, they were... "Oh, my God," she said. "Are you from *Delta Force?*"

Sarah and the major exchanged a look.

"That has to be why this is all so secret," Abbie persisted. "You're from Delta Force, right? Like those movies?"

"We're a far cry from the Hollywood version, Miss Locke. We're Special Forces soldiers, not Ninjas." The major held up his palm. "Please, don't press us for more information. We want to keep your involvement to a minimum so that you can return home. You do want to help us, don't you?"

"Of course I want to help."

"Then all you need to do is sign those forms in triplicate and give us your oath that you won't divulge anything that has happened."

She had to suppress another bubble of hysteria. How

could she divulge what had happened? Even if she wanted to, who would believe her? She placed the forms on her lap, smoothed them out and bent over to read them. She had only managed to finish the first paragraph when footsteps sounded outside the cubicle. There was a sudden draft of cool air as the door flap was pushed aside. "You wanted to see me, Major?"

At the deep voice, Abbie's head snapped up. It was Flynn. Or to be more accurate, it was Sergeant First Class Flynn O'Toole.

He was a soldier, just like everyone else here. No, he was more than simply a soldier. He was a Delta Force commando, one of the most elite fighting men in the armed forces. She could see it in the proud tilt of his head, the square set of his shoulders and the rigid straightness of his spine. The rumpled plaid flannel shirt and those worn jeans didn't detract from his air of confidence. Neither did the dark stain that covered his sleeve where he'd rolled it above his elbow or the small white bandage that was taped to his forearm.

Abbie felt sick as she saw the evidence of her attack on him. So far no one here had appeared to blame her. Sarah had seemed to find the incident amusing and had even joked about the way Abbie had been running away from Flynn.

But it hadn't been funny. Abbie had been terrified and had believed she'd been acting in self-defense. She cleared her throat. "Mr. O'Toole...uh, Sergeant?"

Flynn turned his head to look at her. He wasn't smiling. No, Sergeant O'Toole's gorgeous dimples weren't anywhere to be seen. He looked hard, as predatory as the last time she'd seen him. Yet he was still handsome enough to send her stomach into that doomed little dance.

She had to fight the urge to make another run for it. "I'm sorry about stabbing you."

"No problem, ma'am," he said stiffly. "It was a minor injury."

"Still, I want to apologize."

"You did what you had to do. You can't be faulted for that."

"Are the repairs at Miss Locke's apartment completed, Sergeant O'Toole?" the major asked.

"Yes, sir."

"What repairs?" Abbie asked.

"We fixed your door frame and cleaned the blood out of your carpet," Flynn replied. "I'm sorry about those red flowers. They couldn't be saved."

It took her a moment to realize he was talking about the geraniums that had been on the bookshelf. The pot had fallen on the tall man's head. The petals had mingled with the blood....

Blood on her carpet. Guns in her apartment. Soldiers and secret tents and national security. Her life was spinning out of control.

Oh, *God!* The sooner this ended, the better.

The sound of crumpling paper made her glance down. She smoothed out the nondisclosure forms once more. She scanned them as fast as she could, then reached for the pen the major had placed on the table. Without any more delay, she scrawled her signature in triplicate.

Rumor had it that Redinger didn't have a sense of humor, but Flynn wasn't so sure. Why else had the major assigned Flynn to take Abbie home? Sarah had already established a rapport with her, so she would have been a better choice. Was this the major's subtle way of reminding Flynn of his failure to keep the woman contained in the first place?

The major was a fair man. He never chewed anyone out when they made a mistake. Instead, he found a way to work with them to ensure the mistake wouldn't be repeated. But had it really been necessary to use this particular mode of transportation?

Bringing his motorcycle on this mission didn't seem like such a good idea now. Sure, it was maneuverable, but it required body contact with his passenger. Requisitioning a van like Sarah's would have been better. Hell, when it came to that, maybe he should have gone with a Hum-Vee. A vehicle that size would have kept Abbie safely out of his reach.

Riding in a Hummer wouldn't have kept him from smelling her, though. Whenever she moved, he got a whiff of apples and cranberries. The scent wasn't seductive. It was as wholesome as apple pie and Thanksgiving dinners, but it was wrapping around his senses as intimately as Abbie's arms were wrapped around his body. With each bump in the road that the bike hit, the inside of her thighs rubbed his hips. Her hands had started out clasped over his chest, but they'd gradually slid lower until they were now only a stray thought above his belt buckle.

Ignore it, Flynn told himself as he turned into the street that led to Abbie's apartment building. He had to stay alert. Traveling on a bike like this, they were completely exposed to anyone who might be watching....

Understanding finally dawned. Of course. This was the reason the major had insisted that Flynn use the bike. It wasn't only a lesson in keeping his mind on business, it was for the sake of any potential observers. If someone from the LLA was watching for Abbie's return, they would see she didn't have the money with her. They'd also see her wrapped around Flynn's back and assume he had to be her boyfriend, which could explain why he'd been in her apartment and why he'd defended her.

Good. The loose ends were getting tied up in a nice,

neat package. He could consider this awareness of Abbie's body all in the line of duty.

The only people they encountered once they entered the building were other tenants, so they reached her apartment without incident. Flynn locked the door behind them and instructed her to wait there while he turned on the lights and did a thorough check of the rooms. Once he was satisfied that everything was as he'd left it, he returned to where she was standing and held out a set of keys. "Here. The new dead bolt I installed won't pop open as easily."

She hesitated, then reached out and plucked the keys from his fingers. "Thank you."

"We appreciate your cooperation, Miss Locke."

"Would you let me know how everything turns out?"

"I'm sorry. That information would be classified."

"Can't you at least let me know whether or not the child is all right? There wouldn't be any harm in that, would there?"

"Fine," he said. "I'll be in touch."

"Thanks. I'll give you my number."

"That's okay. I've got it."

"Oh. Of course. I should have thought of that." She slipped the strap of her purse off her shoulder and put the keys inside, then stored the purse on a shelf in the closet beside the door. "Captain Fox said she did a background check on me before I signed those papers. You'd have to know something as simple as my phone number."

"Yes."

"This has all happened so fast, I'm still having trouble taking it in." She reached for the buttons of the sweater she was wearing. "Could you give this back to Sarah for me?"

Flynn told himself not to look as she shrugged off the sweater, yet at her whispered exclamation he glanced down. Her blouse was dry, but her hair was caught around one of the buttons. She fumbled to untangle it.

"Here." He gently moved her hands aside. "Let me help."

"No, please. I can manage."

"It's no problem." He eased her hair from the shank of the button and brushed the lock behind her ear. The curl sprang back, wrapping itself around his thumb in a sensual caress. He rubbed it against his forefinger, enjoying the texture for an instant before he realized what he was doing and dropped his hand.

What was it about this woman, anyway? Why did she affect him like this? The more he learned about her, the more he realized how poorly suited they were. He usually gave women like Abigail Locke a wide berth, yet even if he didn't know the facts of her profession and her family background, the details he'd noticed while he'd cleaned up this apartment should have doused any interest before it got started.

In addition to those overgrown, man-eating plants, she had populated the place with snapshots of her family and framed photos of her classes. There were wooden geese with blue bows around their necks in her kitchen and a cross-stitched house with a white picket fence on her bedroom wall. Obviously, she was a serious nester, which confirmed his initial assessment of her. She would want more from a man than a few nights of mutual pleasure.

That was too bad. Considering what he'd seen and felt of her body, a few nights with Abbie definitely would have been pleasurable.

Sweet words and sex. That's what women usually wanted from him, and he was only too happy to oblige. He genuinely liked women. He liked the way their softness fit against a man's strength, he enjoyed the desire that sparked when two people were physically compatible. He respected women's differences, their fondness for romance, their female way of regarding the world through the eyes of primal gatherers rather than hunters.

And Flynn was definitely a hunter. He thrived on the chase, on moving from one mission to the next. He took pride in being able to fit everything he owned into a duffel bag and be good to go before the dust settled.

Flynn took the sweater and moved past her to the door. "As I said, we appreciate your cooperation, Miss Locke."

"And you'll tell me what happens, right?"

"Absolutely." Just as he reached for the doorknob, the phone in the living room began to ring. He looked back at Abbie. "Better let your machine pick up until you know who it is."

The color drained from her face. "Would those men have my number?"

"This is merely a precaution," he said.

There was a beep, then a woman's voice came through the answering machine. "Abbie? If you're there, please pick up. We're getting worried."

She covered her mouth with her hands. "Oh, Lord," she mumbled. "My birthday. I can't believe I completely forgot about it."

Flynn left the door and returned to her side. "Is that your mother?"

"Yes. I was supposed to be there hours ago. I don't know what to tell them."

"You have to make an excuse. You can't tell them the truth."

"I know, I took an oath. I just don't know what to say."

"Say you had car trouble."

"They'll offer to pick me up."

"Say you're sick."

"Someone will want to come and check on me."

"Say you're contagious."

She frowned. "It's easy for you, isn't it?"

"What?"

"Lying."

"I do whatever's necessary for the good of the mission." He caught her shoulders. "You need to tell them something or this could get more complicated."

"*More* complicated?" She made a noise that was a cross between a laugh and a sob. "As if that were possible."

"Abbie, please. It's almost over. This is the last loose end."

She stepped back, jerking away from his touch. She held his gaze for a long moment, then spun around and walked to the phone. "Mom, hi. I'm sorry I—"

There was a frantic burst of conversation from the receiver that was audible across the room. Flynn moved closer and watched Abbie carefully. She seemed reliable, but he was prepared to sever the telephone connection if she showed signs of revealing too much.

"Yes. I mean, not really," she said. "It's a long story. I'm sorry for worrying you." There was a pause. "I was on my way to your place when I started to feel sick and thought I'd better come home."

Flynn caught her gaze and nodded encouragement.

She inhaled deeply through her nose before she continued. "I couldn't call earlier, Mom. I was, uh, indisposed. I must have picked up something nasty on that class trip today.... No, I'll be fine. I don't want to spread this to the rest of the family. Joshua's still recovering from that ear infection, and if Ellie caught this on top of her morning sickness—" There was a longer pause. Abbie's knuckles tightened on the phone. "It's all right, Mom. You knew that I knew about the party, and I'm really sorry for missing it. I'm sure Martha's brood will be happy to eat the cake. Give some hugs to the kids for me and pass on my apologies to everyone, okay? ...Love you, too. 'Bye.''

She hung up the phone and stared at it blankly. She looked lost.

"You did well," Flynn said.

"This is the first time in thirty years that I've missed my party."

"I'm sorry."

"You would have missed yours by now, too...." Her words trailed off. She shook her head. "Today isn't your birthday, is it?"

"No, I'm afraid not. I told you that so you'd let me in."

"How did you know what to say?"

"Captain Fox had already started running your background check. She conveyed the information to me through my ear piece."

"And so you would know exactly the right buttons to push. I should have known it was too much of a coincidence. You're not a history buff, are you?"

"Puts me to sleep."

"And I bet you don't like children, either."

"Never had much to do with them."

"I should have known."

Flynn felt a stirring of guilt. He shouldn't. "I said those things for the good of the mission. It wasn't personal, Abbie."

"No, of course not. None of it was. And with a child's life in danger, it was completely justified." She sighed. "And it's not as if I wanted to celebrate turning thirty. It's just that..."

"Let me guess." He put his finger under her chin. "Getting manhandled by a complete stranger and shanghaied by an operational detachment from Eagle Squadron wasn't how you planned to mark the occasion, right?"

She gave another one of those part laughs, part sobs. "No, that wouldn't have been my first choice."

"Then what would have been?"

She blinked a few times, then lifted her gaze to his. "What do you mean?"

"If you had a wish, what would you have wanted for your birthday?"

She regarded him in silence for a minute before her lips curved into one of those intriguing, private smiles. "I have my wish on a list somewhere, but I already decided I'd have to make a few adjustments."

Why did she have to smile? He'd been doing fine. He'd been almost out the door. Now that she'd explained her absence to her mother, the last loose end had been tied up and he was free to get on with the mission.

But there was no way he could walk away from that alluring tilt of her mouth.

Oh, what the hell. They'd never see each other again, anyway, so what harm would there be if he indulged himself before he left? Besides, after what she'd gone through tonight, she looked like she could use a kiss. He crooked his finger to tip her chin upward and lowered his head.

The contact jolted him. Heat flowed through his veins and stiffened his body. He'd meant to keep this friendly, a casual kiss for an attractive woman, but there was nothing casual about the way he wanted to feel her thighs rub over his hips and her hands reach for his belt buckle and be nowhere near a bike this time.

Her breath mingled with his—she tasted as good as she smelled. She kissed the same way she smiled, as if there were secrets here only waiting to be discovered. Flynn dipped his tongue past her lips in a bold exploration. She responded with a low sound in her throat that was somewhere between a moan...and a protest.

Flynn lifted his head. He searched for something clever

to say, something that would smooth over the situation, but for the first time he could remember, his usual knack with words had deserted him.

Abbie pressed her fingertips to her mouth. She seemed as much at a loss as he was.

He stroked her cheek and tried to smile, but his easy charm had deserted him, too. He didn't want to smile and he didn't want to say anything. He wanted to thrust his fingers into her hair, haul her against him and kiss her again. He wanted to *stay*.

Flynn turned around and walked to the door. He gripped the knob so tightly the tendons ridged across the back of his hand. "Happy birthday, Abbie," he said.

Then he did what he'd done all his life. He left.

Chapter 5

Abbie didn't know how she got through the next day. For a while she'd been tempted to play out her excuse of the stomach flu to her principal and spend the day in bed with the covers drawn over her head.

But hiding wouldn't do any good. Neither would denial. As much as she'd like to, she couldn't pretend that the events of yesterday hadn't occurred. She was as jumpy as a cat in a strange house, startling at every noise or unexpected movement.

It was a good thing that her students were still tired out from the field trip and didn't demand her full attention, because she went through her classes in low gear. Several of her friends on the school staff noticed that something was wrong, but she deflected their curiosity by alluding to her birthday, hoping they would assume she had celebrated too heartily.

The message light on her answering machine was blinking furiously when she arrived home. She dashed across

the room, hoping it was good news about the kidnapped
child, but none of the messages were from Flynn. Her
mother had called twice, offering to bring over ginger ale
and rice water, her two surefire remedies for the stomach
upsets of Abbie's childhood. Both Martha and Ellie had
called, too, wishing her a belated happy birthday and a
speedy recovery. None of them had seemed worried that
she hadn't answered—they'd assumed she had been resting and hadn't wanted to get up.

Abbie slumped down in the chair and covered her eyes.
This lying business was far too easy to continue once it
got started. If she didn't watch out, she would get as good
at it as Flynn.

*If you had a wish, what would you have wanted for your
birthday?*

Flynn's question teased through her mind. She'd known
exactly what she wanted. Children, a home, a nice, stable
husband. She certainly hadn't wanted that…kiss.

She rubbed her face. Now she was even lying to herself.

Of course she'd wanted that kiss. He was an attractive
man, and her emotions had been stirred up because of the
excitement of the evening. It was the natural reaction of a
healthy thirty-year-old woman. It was the same as wanting
a double-chocolate-fudge sundae. Neither one was good
for her, and she would regret both in the long run, but they
tasted so good.…

And he had. Oh, Lord, he'd tasted even better than she
could have imagined. His lips had been warm and firm and
had molded to hers as easily as if they'd been lovers for
years. He hadn't touched her with anything more than his
fingertip and his mouth, but he'd made her feel as if his
entire being was focused on that kiss, as if he saw only
her needs, wanted only her pleasure, and then…

And then he'd left.

Right. She knew all about the way men like that left.

She'd been through this before, eight years ago. Stuart had been there for the good times—their lovemaking had burned up the sheets. She'd believed it was love, she'd thought it was the real thing, but it had all been a lie. She'd been so dazzled by his looks and his passion, she'd given him her heart along with her body. She'd listened to her instincts instead of her brain and hadn't seen beyond her own desire.

But she'd learned from the past. Sexual attraction was no basis for a lasting relationship, and she wouldn't make the same mistake again. No matter how sweetly Flynn kissed.

Everything that had redeemed Flynn in her eyes—his fondness for children, his closeness with his family, his interest in history—all of it had been as phony as that story about the power failure. He'd had an Army intelligence specialist feeding him lines, so he'd been able to say exactly what she'd wanted to hear. The only fact that remained true was his dedication to his job.

And what a job. A Delta Force commando was about as far from the ideal of her nice, stable ordinary man as one could get. He would do anything in the line of duty, even if it meant kissing a woman into silence.

Well, it had worked. She'd been too shaken to say a word when he'd walked out the door. And she'd been too wrapped up in reliving that kiss for the rest of the night to have time to have nightmares about foreign kidnappers and mysterious ransoms and a child held captive.

But it was over, she assured herself, pushing out of the chair. She was wearing her watch and was back in her everyday life once more. She needed her schedules and the order of her days. She hated surprises, and yesterday served as a good reminder of why.

The phone rang. Abbie paused, debating whether or not to let the machine pick it up as Flynn had advised her. No, she was going to get her life back to normal, she decided. Major Redinger had thought it was safe enough for her to come home, so she was going to put this…episode behind her. She returned to the phone and snatched up the receiver.

"Miss Locke? It's Peter Hedgeworth. Bradley's father."

She paused. "Oh, hello, Mr. Hedgeworth."

"I'm sorry to disturb you at home, Miss Locke. I tried to catch you after school but you'd already left. I hope I'm not intruding."

She grimaced to herself. Normally she remained in her classroom to prepare for the next day, but she'd cut out earlier than usual today. She'd just wanted to come home. Run home, to be more accurate. "No, not at all, Mr. Hedgeworth. What can I do for you? Bradley's all right, isn't he?"

"Yes, he's fine. Actually, that's what I wanted to talk to you about. He had a great time on the trip to the museum yesterday. He hasn't stopped chattering about it."

"I'm glad. I'd hoped to get the children interested in our history."

"And you succeeded. You've done wonders for Bradley. We're planning to join a walking tour of historic sites this weekend. I wanted to express my thanks."

"No thanks are necessary, Mr. Hedgeworth. I enjoy my job."

"You're an exceptional teacher."

"Thank you."

"Would you be free for dinner tomorrow?"

That threw her. She must have misunderstood. "Excuse me?"

There was an awkward silence. "Sorry, that was kind of sudden," he said. "It's been a long time since I dated, so I guess I'm out of practice."

Abbie knew that Bradley's parents were recently divorced. They shared joint custody of their child, so she had met both Peter and Beth Hedgeworth when it had been their turn to pick up Bradley from school. They were both likable people. But Abbie had never regarded Peter as a potential *date*.

Actually, she'd never thought much about him. Unlike his lively son, he was on the quiet side. He dressed in tasteful suits and wore shoes that always appeared freshly polished. She couldn't picture the color of his hair or his eyes, but his features were…nice. Not handsome or memorable, just nice. Like vanilla custard made with skim milk.

She realized she'd been silent too long. The problem was, she didn't know what to say. "Mr. Hedgeworth…"

"Please, call me Peter."

"All right. Peter."

"I don't want to make you uncomfortable, Abbie. I'd like to get to know you better, and I thought a quiet dinner with us would be a good way to start."

"With us?"

"Yes, Bradley will be with me for the entire weekend. He'd be thrilled if you agreed."

She was fond of Bradley, just as she was fond of all her students. Still… "I'm really sorry, Peter," she said. "I— I've been fighting off a flu bug. I'd planned to spend the weekend resting, so I wouldn't be good company."

It was a cowardly way to turn down Peter's invitation, but she didn't want to rule out the possibility of accepting an invitation in the future. She needed more time to think about it, that's all.

Yet what was there to think about? He had a home in the suburbs. He already had a child. He was a nice, stable, responsible man. Wasn't this what she wanted?

And would she have needed time to think about it if he'd asked her yesterday, before she'd met Flynn?

* * *

Abbie dreamed about double-fudge sundaes that night.
They were arrayed on a table in front of her, the chocolate
dark and decadent, glistening with heat where it oozed
over rich mounds of melting ice cream. The scent was
bittersweet, a contradiction of hard and soft, hot and cold,
drawing her closer with the promise of sensual delight.

But there was a maze of tall, thick candlesticks between
her and the table, and clouds of moths were singeing their
wings as they fluttered around the flames.

She moistened her lips, stirring restlessly on the bed.
Oh, it had been a long, long time since she'd indulged in
fudge.

She felt someone touch her hand. She knew who it was.
It was the man she'd been waiting for. He was the one
who had lit the candles, so he'd show her how to get past
them without getting burned.

Abbie.

She stretched her arms over her head and rolled to her
back. She couldn't see him, but she sensed his presence in
his scent, his warmth, the tingle of awareness that she felt
whenever he was near. She made a low noise in her throat.
She was hungry. It really had been a long time.

Abbie, wake up.

She felt the dream receding, but she didn't want it to
end yet. She reached for her pillow and pulled it to her
chest. It was oddly heavy. It smelled like an April sunrise.
Like Flynn.

She smiled and rubbed against him. Her nipples tightened at the contact, hardening into firm points. Her palms
skimmed over wide shoulders and trailed down muscles as
solid as brick. She curled her fingers around his arms.
Through the fabric of his sleeves she could feel his tension.
Could he feel hers? Flattening her hands over his back,
she pulled him closer.

"Abbie, please."

Something was wrong. This dream was becoming too real. She fought the lethargy that tugged at her, and strained to open her eyes.

A palm settled over her mouth.

She came awake with her heart pounding. She drew in her breath and tasted a mixture of soap and masculine skin. Someone was lying on top of her, crushing her into the mattress. It wasn't a pillow that she was holding, it was a man.

Before she could panic, she heard a familiar voice. "Abbie, it's me. Flynn." His breath wafted over her cheek as he put his lips close to her ear. "Wake up."

She wrenched her head to the side and gulped for air. "Flynn! What are you doing here?"

Her pillow dipped as he braced his hand beside her head. The weight on her chest eased. "I need to talk to you."

Her arms were still wrapped around his back. She released her hold, and he sat up to reach for the lamp on her bedside table.

The room flooded with light, yet Flynn still appeared to be in shadow. He was dressed all in black. Black jeans, a black windbreaker, even a dark shadow of unshaved beard stubble on his jaw. Against the backdrop of her rose-colored wallpaper and the frame that held her grandmother's embroidery, he appeared large, male and dangerous.

And sexier than any man had a right to be. The last time he'd seen her, he'd kissed her. Even in her sleep Abbie had reached out for him—she could still feel the imprint of his chest on her breasts.

He looked at her as he stroked a lock of hair from her face, his fingertips grazing her cheek. His voice was a low rumble. "What were you dreaming about, Abbie?"

An image flickered through her mind. Sensual chocolate, thick, erect candlesticks, flames of passion... She wouldn't need to be Dr. Freud to interpret that erotic symbolism.

He toyed with one of her curls, coiling it around his finger. "Were you dreaming about me?"

For a mad instant she started to lean into his caress. Did it really matter whether he was the right man or not? He was here, and she wanted to follow his touch and pull him back into her arms. Oh, it was so tempting....

She clutched the sheet to draw it to her chin. It was a prudish gesture—the oversize pink T-shirt she slept in covered her from her neck to her knees—yet she felt exposed. Not just her body, but her thoughts...and the dreams she didn't even want to admit to herself.

Damn the man, she'd thought this was over. "How did you get in here?" she asked, refusing to answer his question.

"I picked your lock."

"Flynn, you got the wrong idea. Just because I let you kiss me yesterday doesn't mean you have the right to show up in my bedroom like this."

"I know. That's not why I'm here."

"No?"

He paused. Her hair slipped from his grasp. "No," he said. "It's something else. I needed to talk to you in person. There's been a development."

As she took in his sober expression, her head finally cleared. How could she have been thinking that Flynn had come back because of that kiss? He was a soldier. That's why he was here. That's why he'd barged into her life in the first place. She pushed herself up on her elbows. "Is this about that kidnapped child?" she asked. "Is he..."

"He's alive," Flynn said. "The kidnappers want to arrange another ransom drop."

Abbie rolled to the other side of the bed and picked up

her robe from the floor. She drew it on as she got to her feet, doing her best to tie the belt securely despite her shaking hands. "That's good news, isn't it?"

"Depends how you look at it."

"I don't understand."

"Last time they wanted the boy's father to deliver the money. This time they want someone else."

"Well, as long as the child is released unharmed—"

"It's not that simple."

"What do you mean?"

He stood up and raked his hands through his hair. "The boy's father told them that a schoolteacher accidentally picked up the ransom at the museum."

"Yes, I know. Sarah said that's why those men were able to find me."

"They thought he had double-crossed them. They say the only way he can prove his good faith now is to have the woman who picked up the ransom the first time deliver it the second time."

She was sorry now that she'd stood up. Her knees felt too weak to hold her. She staggered sideways and flung out her hand, clutching her dresser to retain her balance. "Are you saying that they want *me* to do it?"

He moved around the bed and caught her shoulders. "There is an alternative. Sarah can do this in your place. With a dark wig and some contact lenses, there's a chance she could fool them."

His touch was firm, meant to support, not caress. She felt his strength and it steadied her. "Is that what Major Redinger thinks?"

"What matters is what you think, Abbie."

He'd avoided her question, she realized. "The major doesn't think Sarah can impersonate me, does he? Otherwise, he wouldn't have sent you here."

"You're right. I'm here because I was ordered to ask

for your assistance, but it should be our risk, not yours. This is what we're trained for.''

''What about the child? What will happen to him if the kidnappers find out they were deceived?''

''We'll continue our efforts to find him. When we do, we'll rescue him.''

Abbie studied Flynn's face, trying to read the truth. ''He'll be killed,'' she stated. ''That's what will happen, isn't it?''

A muscle in his jaw twitched. His grip on her shoulders tightened. ''The people we're dealing with are fanatics. Even if you follow their instructions to the letter, there's no guarantee they won't kill their hostage, anyway.''

For one cowardly moment she longed to crawl back into bed and pretend she was still dreaming. This was supposed to be over. Her involvement was a fluke. If only she could wake up and somehow be back in her own life....

''How old—'' She had to swallow hard before she continued. ''How old is the child? I asked before, but no one would give me any details because of security. Can you tell me now?''

''Seven.''

That was the same age as Bradley Hedgeworth, the same age as most of the children in her class. She thought about how excited they had been on their trip yesterday and how noisy they'd been on the ride back. They'd tumbled out of the bus when it had reached the school, and they'd run to their parents' arms. They'd been bubbling over with enthusiasm and the innocence of childhood.

And while she'd been watching her students leave for their homes, somewhere in this city, a child who should have been safe with his parents was living a nightmare.

''I'll do it,'' she said.

Flynn studied her face. ''Are you sure? Because once we bring you into this operation, there's no going back.

You're going to be given classified information that you'll never be able to reveal to another soul.''

''All right.''

''And until the mission's over, we're going to need you with us 100 percent. You'll become part of the team and have to be available to move at a moment's notice. That means you need to stay with us.''

Stay with those soldiers? With *Flynn?* The flash of eagerness she felt at the thought jarred her. This wasn't about him, it was about the child. ''Fine,'' she said. ''I'll do whatever is necessary.''

''You're going to have to make up excuses to explain your absence to your family. If the mission extends past the weekend, you'll have to make up an excuse for your principal, too.''

''Are you trying to talk me out of this?''

He dropped his hands from her shoulders. He stepped back, his eyebrows angling upward. He appeared surprised by her question. ''I shouldn't. It's my duty to bring you in. I just want you to be sure you know what you're getting into.''

''All I care about is helping the child.''

''You don't even know him.''

''I don't have to. I love children, Flynn. That's why I'm a teacher. It makes no difference who the child is. All of them are precious.''

''He's the grandnephew of the king of Ladavia.''

''The king...'' She paused. ''Ladavia?''

''It's a small country in the Balkans.''

''Yes, yes, I know where it is. It was in the news last month because of that terrorist bombing outside the king's palace....'' The memory of a black-and-white photo sprang to her mind: pieces of glass and rubble strewn across a cobblestone street, people with dust on their faces and blood on their clothes. The image was far too common these days. She crossed her arms, suddenly chilled. "Those kidnappers, are they connected to the terrorists?"

"Yes. It's the same group. They want to overthrow the monarchy and seize control of the country before the king can complete the transition to democracy. Do you still want to go through with this?"

No! The logical, reasonable part of her mind screamed at her to refuse. A child connected to European royalty? Terrorists? This had to be why Delta Force was involved, and why everything had been so secret. The kidnapping would have political repercussions. This was completely beyond the realm of her experience.

And yet...the kidnap victim was still just a child, with a child's hopes and fears. This was completely beyond *his* experience, too.

Abbie concentrated on that as she shut out the voice of reason. For once, she was going to listen to her instincts. Gathering her courage, she looked Flynn in the eye and nodded. "When do we start?"

Flynn leaned his elbow on the side of the refrigerator and stretched out his legs, trying to find a more comfortable position on the metal chair, but it was no use. He glanced toward the darkened area at the rear of the tent where the men who were off duty were snoring on their cots. At this point, even a blanket on the floor would feel good to him, but he wouldn't allow himself to rest until Abbie was settled in.

Flynn returned his gaze to the group in the middle of the tent. Redinger was holding his briefing near one of the central support poles beside the communication equipment. He and Sarah had already given Abbie the background information on the mission. Esposito was currently bringing her up to date on the state of the negotiations between the Ladavian monarchy and the American government. It was a lot for her to take in at once. Abbie absorbed it all with an air of determined concentration…interspersed by flashes of panic.

If anyone else noticed the panic, they were ignoring it. Flynn couldn't. Each time she chewed her lip or her gaze darted around, each time she tightened her clasped hands until her knuckles turned white, he felt an odd pang in his chest. Some of it was pity, some was admiration. He wasn't sure about the rest.

Flynn didn't make a habit of analyzing his emotions—when it came to his dealings with women, he tried to keep them as simple as possible. He should be keeping things simple with Abbie, too.

For someone who had been awakened in the middle of the night and had been whisked off in secret to a military briefing, she was holding up well. She appeared to have understood the urgency of the situation and hadn't fussed with her appearance, throwing on a sweater and a pair of pants and pulling her hair back into a ponytail. Yet the effect was more striking than hours of primping by some of the high-maintenance women he had known. Under the glare of the overhead bulb, Abbie looked fresh scrubbed and innocent…and far too appealing.

She didn't belong here any more than he belonged in her world. She was from the realm of family dinners and snapshots of kids, not Army-issue decor and international crises. She was the only person here who wasn't a trained soldier, so she had a different way of looking at the facts she was told. It showed in the questions she had asked.

The first thing she'd asked Redinger was the name of the kidnapped child. It was Matteo. Until now, Flynn had only thought of him as the Vilyas kid, or as the target they had to free. That was the best way to approach a mission. He had to maintain his objectivity. Getting emotionally involved was murder on a man's concentration.

So was getting pulled into bed by a warm, sleep-softened woman. He was getting too damned familiar with the way Abbie felt when she wasn't wearing underwear.

His chair creaked as he shifted his legs again. His discomfort wasn't due to fatigue this time, it was due to the snug fit of his jeans. There was nothing complicated about that aspect of his feelings for Abbie. It was simple, basic sexual attraction. He kept telling himself to ignore it, but he wasn't having much success.

He still couldn't forget that kiss yesterday, so it hadn't been smart to let her pull him on top of her tonight...but he hadn't tried to avoid it. The sight of her in bed, with her hair spread in a soft cloud on the pillow and her body caught in the slow-motion movements of a dream, had hit him almost as powerfully as one of her smiles.

And that was the problem. She might be a wholesome schoolteacher and a serious nester but there was passion in her kiss and passion in her dreams, and he felt a hunter's urge to pursue it. So he'd sat beside her on the mattress, closer than he'd needed to, and he hadn't awakened her as quickly as he could have.

Yeah, well, he'd still managed to do his duty, so the rest of it didn't matter. She'd agreed to join them, hadn't she? Her usefulness to the mission was the priority here, not her effect on his libido.

It had taken her only a few minutes to haul a tapestry-patterned suitcase out of her closet and pack what she would need. She'd taken almost as long to tend to her plants. That had been the only bad moment—she'd been hesitant about leaving them without having someone come in to check on them. They were *plants*. Lucky for him she didn't have pets or children.

I love children, Flynn. That's why I'm a teacher.

He deliberately replayed her words in his head. Oddly

enough, it did nothing to ease the tightness in his jeans. He scowled and thought about a cold shower.

"Did you have any trouble?"

At the low voice he looked over his shoulder. "No problem," he replied quietly.

Rafe Marek pulled up a chair, turned it around and straddled the seat as he sat down. He folded his arms over the back, nodding toward the group near Abbie. "Good thing she agreed to help," he said, keeping his tone low enough not to carry. "Sarah's a good operative, but she wouldn't have fooled anyone for long. The Locke woman's too short and her body type's all wrong."

"Abbie's not that short," Flynn said. "And there's nothing wrong with her body type."

Rafe shot him a look. "That's not what I meant and you know it."

Flynn realized his mistake immediately. Rafe hadn't been assessing Abbie's body, he'd been referring to the next ransom exchange. Rafe wouldn't be looking at another woman like that anyway—ever since he got engaged, he'd been downright puritanical.

That's what commitment did to a man. It tied him down and snipped off his freedom.

Then again, Rafe didn't look as if any parts were missing. Lately he'd been almost cheerful. He'd begun to develop a dimple among the scars on his bad side.

Flynn put on a yawn and decided to change the subject. "Man, I'm beat. This waiting around is starting to get to me."

"Look's like that's not all that got to you." The good side of Rafe's mouth twitched upward. "How come you're still awake? You're not on this watch."

"I brought Abbie into the mission. She's my responsibility."

Rafe grunted. "That sounds familiar. Isn't that what I said about Glenna?"

It was, Flynn realized. Glenna Hastings, Rafe's fiancée, had helped the team from Eagle Squadron plan a mission a few months ago. Flynn had done his best to counsel his buddy on the risks of getting serious, but nothing—not even a vengeful drug lord—had been able to keep Rafe and Glenna apart.

"Don't even think it," Flynn muttered. "This is entirely different."

"You're right." Rafe propped his chin on his folded arms and studied Abbie. "If she's a schoolteacher, she's way too smart for you."

Chair legs gritted across the cement floor. Flynn looked past Rafe and saw Jack Norton pulling up a seat beside them. "What are you doing here?" he asked.

Jack winked. "Same thing as you and Rafe. I wanted to get a look at our new recruit."

Flynn didn't find Jack's interest in Abbie amusing. Normally he enjoyed talking about women. He liked flirting with them and he had no problem when other men did the same. But not with Abbie. He wanted to protect her, shelter her, keep her as safe and innocent as she was before. And he didn't want anyone else to discover the passion she kept behind those private smiles. "Dammit, I just talked her into joining us. You two scarecrows are liable to frighten her away."

Jack chuckled. "Do I need to point out that you were the one she was running from?"

"The woman has taste," Rafe said. "I think Glenna would like her."

"With any luck Abbie won't be staying around long enough to meet her," Flynn said. "The LLA could set up the drop tomorrow."

Rafe's expression sobered immediately. "Any word on that yet?"

"Not yet." Flynn tipped his chin toward Esposito. "The chief said the Vilyas phone line has been silent all night."

"This doesn't feel right," Jack said. Like Rafe, he'd become all business the moment the subject had turned to the mission. "What's the LLA waiting for? The longer they delay, the better the chance we'll learn where they are."

"Makes you wonder whether the money is all they're after," Rafe said.

"Esposito thinks they're doing this to harass the Ladavian government." Flynn paused. "What's the latest on those three men we're sitting on?"

"That LLA cell hasn't moved from their rooming house since they were followed from Miss Locke's apartment," Jack replied. "They would know their security could be compromised, so it's unlikely they'll be used again."

"We could bring them in for interrogation if things go sour," Rafe said. "They'd be a link to the organization."

"Yeah, but the LLA cells operate on a need-to-know basis. Those men might have no idea where the kid is stashed." Jack returned his gaze to Abbie. "I hope she's got the guts to go through with it."

Flynn's chest tightened when he noticed that Abbie's knuckles were white again. The adrenaline that had been pumping through her system since she'd awakened would be wearing off by now. She was going to crash soon. He hoped Redinger was perceptive enough to realize that.

Apparently, he was, since the briefing concluded a few minutes later. Redinger and Esposito headed for the equipment storage area. Flynn was out of his chair and striding to Abbie's side before she had the chance to stand. He cupped her elbow to help her to her feet. "Are you okay?" he asked.

She nodded. "I think so."

"Abbie's going to be bunking in the office with me, Sergeant," Sarah said, waving toward the partitioned-off area at the back of the tent. "So if something comes up, you'll know where to find us."

Flynn let go of Abbie's elbow and picked up her suitcase. "I'll give you a hand getting set up."

"I've got it covered, Flynn," Sarah said, taking the suitcase from his grasp. "Why don't you get some rest? Your watch starts in two hours."

"Yeah, O'Toole," Jack drawled. "You know how you need your beauty sleep."

Flynn saw that Jack and Rafe had approached while he'd been talking. He moved closer to Abbie, unconsciously angling himself protectively between her and his friends.

Jack was undeterred. He stepped to the side and held out his hand. "Hello, Miss Locke. I've been wanting to compliment you on your handiwork."

Abbie looked puzzled. "I'm not sure I understand."

Jack cocked his thumb toward the spot where he'd bandaged Flynn's arm. "I'm Jack Norton, the team's medic. You're a dead shot with a screwdriver."

Two spots of color appeared in her cheeks as she shook his hand. "Oh, no."

Jack grinned. "I've always admired a woman who's good with tools."

"Take a pill, Jack," Flynn muttered.

Rafe nudged Jack aside, then stepped forward as Jack regained his balance—even a gentle nudge from Rafe could flatten a man who was unprepared for it. "I'm glad you agreed to work with us, Miss Locke," he said. "I'm Master Sergeant Rafe Marek."

Abbie hesitated a beat before she took his hand and returned his greeting. "Would Rafe be short for Rafal?"

"Yes, it is."

"I thought so. Your family must be Polish."

"That's right," Rafe replied. "My grandfather was born in Krakow."

She smiled. "One of my brothers-in-law is from the Krakow region. His coloring is identical to yours."

Flynn regarded Abbie more closely, but her smile appeared to be genuine. The men of Eagle Squadron were accustomed to Rafe's disfiguring scars, but not many strangers could look him full in the face without flinching. The flesh on his right cheek was a network of white ridges and gullies from his eye socket to his jaw. Although his pale-blond hair and piercing blue eyes were remarkable, that wasn't what most people noticed first.

Yet Abbie seemed unimpressed by appearances. Flynn was fully aware that most women considered his own features attractive. It wasn't vanity—he couldn't take credit for something that was merely an accident of genetics— but most of the time Abbie didn't seem to want to look at him. Why was that? Was that part of her appeal to him, because she was a challenge?

Still, she wasn't indifferent to him. She hadn't minded kissing him or pulling him into bed with her....

But she was part of the team now. If he kissed her again, he'd better be damned certain he knew what he was doing, because next time there would be nowhere to run.

For either of them.

Chapter 6

Abbie stored her toothbrush in her suitcase and sat on the edge of her cot. It was so low to the floor, her knees came up to her chest. She grasped the edges and swung her legs up carefully, afraid the frame might tip over, but it was sturdier than it looked.

Sarah toed off her shoes and dropped down cross-legged in the center of the other cot. "Think of this as a camping trip," she said.

Abbie glanced at the canvas wall beside her. A few snores and the low murmur of masculine voices came from the other side of the partition. She kept her own voice just above a whisper. "I haven't gone camping since I was ten. I got poison ivy."

"You're perfectly safe here, Abbie," Sarah said. "You're surrounded by a team of the best-trained commandos in the United States Army."

"I'm well aware of that." She pulled up her feet and wrapped her arms around her legs. "They all seem to be—'' she searched for a word ''—in excellent condition.''

Sarah smiled. ''Their size can be a bit intimidating at first.''

When Abbie had been brought here before, she'd been restricted to this room—she hadn't seen much of the rest of the tent or met the other soldiers. She understood it was because of their concern over security. She was only now beginning to grasp the scope of what she had stumbled into. ''It's not just their size,'' she murmured. ''It's the way they move. They're so…''

''Male?'' Sarah suggested.

Oh, yes. They were definitely male. The introductions tonight had begun gradually, when that lanky medic named Norton and the big blond man called Rafe had approached to say hello after the major had left, but within minutes practically every man on the team had drifted over to introduce himself and say a few words to her. Flynn's presence by her side had made her pulse trip anyway, but being surrounded by so much rampant masculinity was…stimulating, to say the least. Not something that would happen during the course of a typical day at Cherry Hill Elementary School. ''It's difficult to ignore.''

''Believe it or not, you get accustomed to all that testosterone after a while.''

Abbie smiled crookedly. ''Is that what it is? I thought it was the smell of canvas.''

''You'll get used to that, too.'' Sarah tugged her sweater over her head and stripped off her pants, leaving her in an olive-colored undershirt and shorts. She grabbed a hairbrush from the duffel bag she'd stored at the foot of her cot and leaned over her ankles, flipping her hair forward so she could brush it from the roots. ''Don't let the men's appearance fool you,'' she continued, her voice muffled by her hair. "They're all extremely bright. Their brains are just as impressive as their brawn."

Abbie watched Sarah's easy movements and marveled at how relaxed she seemed. Sarah appeared to have a comfortable camaraderie with the men. She treated them with a combination of the authority of a ranking officer and the protectiveness of a sister. Her manner toward Abbie had warmed considerably after their brief chat with Rafe—Abbie suspected Sarah's manner would have cooled just as quickly if Abbie had shown any sign of revulsion to his scars.

"Are you the only woman in Eagle Squadron?" Abbie asked.

"That's a tricky question. Officially, the only women in Delta Force serve in the support squadrons, not the assault squadrons, because of the rules restricting us from combat roles. I'm an intelligence specialist, part of what's affectionately known as the Funny Platoon. When Major Redinger was putting together a team from Eagle Squadron for this mission, he needed someone who could speak Ladavian, so I'm on temporary duty." She chuckled. "Actually, I've been 'temporarily' assigned to the Major's teams on and off for over three years now."

"You must be very courageous to have chosen a career in the military."

"I grew up in the military, so it was a natural choice. This is my family." Sarah straightened up, pushing her hair back from her face so she could look at Abbie. "I understand this whole experience must be tough for you, Abbie. We really do appreciate your cooperation. It's a lot to ask."

"I couldn't refuse."

Sarah smiled. "Sergeant O'Toole does have a way with words. He could charm the hairs off a camel if he could speak Arabic."

"Flynn's charm has nothing to do with why I'm here. It's the child. Matteo Vilyas. How could I refuse to help?"

"Yes, it's a sensitive situation. Ladavia is a small nation, but its location makes it crucial to our government. It also has untapped oil reserves that several countries besides us are vying to develop."

Abbie frowned. "I would have agreed to help if he was only an ordinary boy from Baltimore. Am I the only one who realizes he's still just a kid?"

Sarah stored her hairbrush. She was silent as she twisted around to draw back her blanket. "No, you're not the only one, Abbie. It's easier for us to function if we maintain our objectivity, especially in a situation like this. We have to focus on the mission."

"I'll try."

"You're doing fine so far."

"I don't seem to be doing anything."

"That's all you need to do for now. Just like the rest of us, we wait for the LLA to make the next move."

"When do you think that will happen?"

"It should be soon. With any luck we'll have you back home within a day or two. You'll be able to pick up where you left off."

"I hope so."

Sarah punched her small pillow and stretched out with a sigh. "You must be exhausted, Abbie. You should try to get some sleep. It's going to be daylight soon."

"I don't think I'll be able to sleep."

"Sure, you will. I can see your adrenaline high has already worn off. Your hands stopped shaking ten minutes ago."

Abbie held up her fingers and saw that Sarah was right. She twisted her wrist to check her watch. She stared. That couldn't be the correct time, could it? Where had the night gone? It seemed like only minutes ago that she'd awakened with Flynn in her arms.

Her gaze went to the canvas wall. Where was he now? Was he sleeping? Was he thinking about her?

Idiot, she told herself. She was here because of the mission. As he'd said once before, it was nothing personal. She tugged out the scrunchie she'd used for her ponytail and fluffed out her hair. She grasped the lower edge of her sweater and had started to pull it off when Sarah's voice stopped her.

"By the way, you'd better yank the chain on that light bulb before you undress, Abbie. The way your cot's positioned, it would throw your shadow on the wall next to the men." She yawned. "No point yanking their chains, too."

Abbie dropped the hem of her sweater and stood up to reach for the chain that dangled from the lightbulb. The cubicle went dim and she stumbled against the edge of her cot. Somehow she managed to get back on without tipping onto the floor.

The coffee was strong enough to dissolve a spoon, but this was all there was, so Abbie held her breath and took another swallow. She didn't expect special treatment, and she wasn't about to complain. Considering the lack of amenities, she was grateful to have found real coffee in a real mug rather than freeze-dried rations or cans of beans or whatever it was that soldiers in the field usually ate.

Propping her elbows on the mess table, she looked around the tent. Everyone seemed to have a job to do except her. Sarah was working at a computer. The pit-bull-like Chief Warrant Officer Esposito was fiddling with the wires that led from what looked like a small radio. Sounds of metal scraping on metal came from the far side of the tent, where she spotted the pale gleam of Rafe Marek's hair as he bent over some kind of machinery. Other men came and went, saying a few words to her or nodding courteously as they passed by, but no one stopped.

Normally, at this hour on a Saturday morning, Abbie would be reading the paper while she took her time over a second cup of coffee. She'd planned to go to the library today, since her books were due. She'd also planned to work on the crib blanket she was knitting for Ellie's baby shower. This would be her sister's third child. Ellie was only twenty-seven, but she and her husband, Tomasz, hadn't wanted to wait to start their family. Their first had been born nine months after their wedding night.

Abbie's older sister, Martha, had needed Caesareans with both of her sons and had no intention of having any more. She spent most of her weekends shuttling her boys from piano lessons to soccer practice or whatever new activity had caught their attention. She often joked it was the only way she could escape from the chaos of her husband's never-ending renovating projects, but anyone could see that she and Barry were as deeply in love now as they had been ten years ago.

Abbie and her sisters had learned by example what a good marriage was like. Their parents had weathered more than thirty-five years of life as a team. They were both strong, competent individuals on their own, yet together they became more. It wasn't surprising that Abbie had hoped to find the same for herself someday.

Sarah had said that the military was her family. Was it the same for the other soldiers of Eagle Squadron? Only three of the men Abbie had met so far had been wearing wedding rings: Chief Warrant Officer Esposito, the sergeant named Lang and Major Redinger. Were the rest of the men unmarried because of the demands of being a Delta Force commando?

Or was it because the type of man who was drawn to

becoming a Delta Force commando preferred to remain unmarried? With the excitement and danger that filled their lives, settling down to a home in the suburbs would seem tame. Someone like Flynn would have too much testosterone to be a good candidate for domestication.

On the other hand, he'd be an excellent candidate for stud service. Just think of the beautiful babies he would make—

Abbie choked on her coffee. She set the mug down on the table and pushed to her feet.

"Are you okay?"

She started. For a large man, Flynn could move in complete silence when he wanted to. She hadn't heard him approach, even though she'd been watching for him.

Yes, there was no point denying it, she'd been watching for him. He'd been the first person she'd looked for when she'd emerged from the cubicle at the back of the tent, and why shouldn't she? He was the one who had brought her here, he was her link to her normal life.

He was also far more effective than even this dissolve-a-spoon coffee when it came to kick-starting her pulse.

Damn. She knew better than this, didn't she?

"Abbie?" He put his palm between her shoulder blades and rubbed gently. "Do you want some water?"

"No, I'm fine, thanks." She turned to face him. She cleared her throat and kept her gaze on his shirt. He was wearing pale-blue chambray today. A few fine, dark hairs showed at the base of his throat where he'd left the top button open. "Has there been any news?"

He shook his head. "Nothing from the LLA. We did get a call from Ambassador Vilyas."

"The poor man. He must be beside himself with worry by now."

"Yeah, he's strung out. He said he wants to meet you."

"Of course. When?"

"Now."

That was something else that was different between her normal life and Flynn's world, Abbie thought. There was no room for hesitation here. When these Delta Force soldiers decided to do something, they simply did it. It spoke of the confidence they had in themselves, that straight-ahead self-assurance that seemed to color every action.

Like the way Flynn kissed.

Abbie's gaze rose to his chin. He must have just finished shaving. There was no beard stubble to darken the lines beside his mouth. She caught a whiff of lime aftershave and the earthy freshness that was pure Flynn.

"In case anyone asks why you're at the embassy, keep the lies simple," he said. "Say your class is doing a project on Ladavia."

Lies. Right. That's what Flynn was good at. "Wouldn't the embassy staff know about the kidnapping?"

"Someone had to have tipped the LLA to the kid's movements before the snatch," Flynn said. "Vilyas doesn't want to trust anyone except the immediate members of his family. He's afraid there could be terrorist sympathizers at the embassy."

"How awful."

"If he could trust his people, Delta Force wouldn't have become involved in this in the first place," he said. "We'll be taking my bike this time, so you'll need a jacket. Did you pack one?"

"Yes, I did, but why would we take your motorcycle again?" she asked. She wasn't accustomed to traveling by motorcycle. The men of her acquaintance used more sensible, conservative modes of transportation, something that would hold a child safety seat. Like the boxy Volvo station wagon Peter Hedgeworth drove when he picked up Bradley from school. "Why can't we use that van you were driving yesterday?"

"That was so we could carry your suitcase." He started toward the cubicle she and Sarah shared. "We'll be meeting Vilyas at the embassy, so we're being highly visible in case anyone's watching."

She hurried to catch up. "I don't understand."

"This would have been the next logical step if Vilyas had contacted you himself. You'd be expected to meet him in person."

"Then wouldn't I be going there on my own?"

He held aside the canvas door and waited while she retrieved her jacket. "You're not going anywhere without me, Abbie. It's my duty to ensure your safety while you're on this mission. Until it's over, consider me your shadow."

She didn't like the tickle of pleasure she felt at his words. She frowned as she put on her jacket and followed him back across the tent. It was his duty to stay with her, nothing more.

"Do you have a problem with that?" he asked.

Of course she did. But this was about the child, not Flynn, she reminded herself yet again. "I don't have a problem as long as you understand our relationship isn't personal."

He stopped walking and faced her. "And by that you mean…?"

She might as well clear this up now. She should have cleared it up before they'd left her apartment. "I don't want to repeat what happened the other night."

"Check. No kissing or fooling around in bed. Got it."

The blunt comment startled her into meeting his gaze.

He was watching her intently, his eyes gleaming. "Did I misunderstand what you were referring to?"

"No, you understood perfectly."

"Too bad. I enjoyed kissing you and being in your bed. I think you enjoyed it, too."

"That's beside the point."

He smiled. "I disagree. Mutual pleasure would *be* the point. It's what men and women were made for."

"That's a cynical way of looking at it. There should be far more to a relationship than just a physical attraction."

"But think of how boring things would be without one." He stroked the pad of his thumb along her jaw. "You did like it, Abbie, didn't you?"

"Yes, but—"

"Are you involved with someone else?"

"No."

"No? How can a woman with so much passion and such…interesting dreams be alone?"

She tipped her head away from his touch. "Spare me the charm, Flynn. I'm immune."

His smile faded. "What's that supposed to mean?"

"Let's just say you're not my type."

He looked startled.

She felt a stirring of resentment. Both at him and at her persistent reaction to him. "Why does that surprise you? Are you accustomed to having women swoon every time you flash your dimples?"

"I didn't think you'd noticed my dimples."

"Just because I'm not interested doesn't mean I'm blind."

"Then what kind of man is your type?"

Her reply was immediate. "A history buff who likes kids, drives a station wagon and lives in the suburbs."

"Sounds exciting. Have you picked out your china pattern and the names for your firstborn yet?"

"Yes, as a matter of fact, I did that eight years ago, not that who I want or what I want or the details about my love life are any of your business." She paused, finally aware that her voice had risen. She glanced around. Sarah and several of the men had turned toward them and were regarding them with interest. She pressed her lips together. She was abashed. It wasn't like her to lose her temper.

Flynn scowled at the other soldiers and took Abbie's arm to guide her toward the entrance of the tent. He lifted the flap and led her into the warehouse.

A bird chirped and fluttered among the steel rafters that supported the roof. Sunshine poked through the windows under the eaves, making streaks through the dust motes that floated in the air. After the cramped quarters of the tent, the sudden spaciousness was a relief. Abbie took a few quick breaths to clear her head.

Flynn nodded to the man who was standing by the warehouse door, then helped Abbie over the bundle of electric cables on the floor and walked toward the relative privacy of the row of vehicles that were parked along one wall. He stopped beside his bike, let go of her arm and turned to face her. "You're right," he said.

"What?"

"It isn't any of my business. I'm sorry."

She rubbed her forehead. "I'm sorry I snapped at you, Flynn. I shouldn't have."

He shrugged. "No problem. Many of my closest friends regularly tell me to shut up."

"We seem to have gotten off the topic."

"As I recall you were saying our relationship isn't personal."

"It isn't."

He shoved his hands into the pockets of his jeans and regarded her in silence for a while. "Fine, it won't be," he said. "Not as long as I'm on duty."

"What does that mean?"

"I won't pretend that I don't find you attractive, Abbie. I do. I enjoy looking at you and touching you."

What could she say? She'd wanted him to be honest, didn't she? "Flynn..."

"But that's beside the point. Whatever else you might think of me, I'm a soldier first and foremost. My priority is always the mission."

The mission. The innocent, seven-year-old boy named Matteo. Abbie sighed. "That's my priority, too."

"If you truly object to my presence, we can talk to the major and have someone else assigned to escort you." He paused as he continued to look at her. "But I hope you don't. When I'm given an order, I carry it out. I don't like to fail."

He was offering her an out. Yet considering what was at stake here, it would be petty to take it. What could she tell Major Redinger? That Flynn was too handsome and charming to work with? That he found her attractive, and she found him attractive, but ever since her affair with Stuart she'd had a serious hang-up about sex? "I won't object," she said. "I think we've got things straightened out."

"Good." He picked up a helmet from his bike and held it out to her. "Vilyas is expecting us."

She took the helmet and hesitated, looking down at the sweater and slacks she was wearing. "If I'm going to meet an ambassador, I'd like to change into something more formal."

"Vilyas won't be concerned about protocol. And besides, with your body, you'd look good even in a gunny sack."

Her gaze snapped up to his.

He turned away and swung his leg over his bike. "It was just a compliment, Abbie, not a kiss."

The Ladavian Embassy was tucked into a quiet, tree-lined street of restored Georgian houses. It had been constructed twenty years ago, when the small monarchy had first opened diplomatic relations with the United States.

The architect had taken care to preserve the charm of the neighborhood—the red brick looked as if it had been mellowed over centuries rather than merely decades. High casement windows gleamed from the front of the first two stories, and neat gables graced the roof.

Yet while the embassy building might have blended with the Washington neighborhood, the grounds had an unmistakably European air. Cobblestones paved the courtyard, water sparkled from a stone fountain, and the wrought iron gates at the edge of the street were adorned by the crest of the Ladavian royal family, a falcon with its talons clutching a sword and a mace. A Ladavian flag, deep blue with the royal crest outlined in gold, snapped in the breeze. The guards at the entrance wore uniforms of the same deep blue, with polished brass buttons and plenty of ornamental gold braid. The overall effect might have been picturesque, even quaint...if not for the automatic rifles the men carried.

"The security at the embassy was stepped up by Vilyas," Flynn said as they walked toward the gates. "These men are members of the royal guard. They're the traditional protectors of the Ladavian monarchy."

Flynn was in what Abbie was coming to think of as his soldier mode. True to his word, he was all business, no charm or dimples in sight. He'd been that way since they'd left the command center. "Do they know that Matteo is missing?" she asked.

"There was no need for them to know. Vilyas used the recent attack on the palace to justify the reinforcements. He put out the story that his son's in bed with the flu."

"There seems to be a lot of that going around," she murmured.

The guards checked Flynn's and Abbie's identification, then ushered them through a metal detector into a foyer tiled in black and white squares of marble. They were met there by a round gray-haired man with heavy, dark eyebrows that dragged his forehead into a perpetual frown.

"Miss Locke, Mr. O'Toole," he said, his voice as heavy as his brows. An accent tinged his words with extra stress on the consonants. "I'm Radomir Magone, assistant to the ambassador. His excellency is a busy man. He has agreed to see you in his private sitting room. Please follow me."

Abbie felt Flynn's palm settle on the small of her back as they crossed the foyer to a curving staircase. It was an easy gesture, not forceful or possessive. It was the kind of respectful touch that any man might give a woman in public.

Abbie felt like a hypocrite for enjoying it.

Two more men with the blue-and-gold uniforms of the royal guards scrutinized them as they reached the top of the stairs. The second floor of the embassy was divided into suites of rooms for visiting dignitaries and as living quarters for the Ladavian ambassador. Radomir Magone ushered Flynn and Abbie through an ornately carved set of dark wood doors and into a large sitting room.

Sunlight poured through a pair of long windows, spreading squares of gold on an intricately patterned carpet. Several antique chairs and a low sofa were richly upholstered in velvet of Ladavian blue. A sideboard decorated with carving as ornate as the doors held a huge silver samovar and a collection of small china cups. The air was redolent with the aroma of lemon polish and strong tea.

A man not much taller than Abbie stood beside one of the windows, his hands clenched behind his back. He turned to face them. His features were sharp, as harshly honed as the falcon on the embassy gates.

"Your Excellency," Magone announced. "Your visitors have arrived."

The man jerked his head in a quick nod. "Miss Locke, Mr. O'Toole, I am Anton Vilyas."

Abbie was shocked by the bleakness on his face. Before this, she'd only seen an expression like that in news reports of disasters. Her heart contracted with sympathy and she automatically started forward.

Flynn caught her elbow. "We're honored to meet you, Mr. Ambassador," he said smoothly. "We appreciate your interest in the social studies project of Miss Locke's students. It's very kind of you to take time from your busy schedule to speak with us."

Vilyas's gaze flickered briefly. "I believe education is vital to the future of both our countries." He turned to dismiss his assistant. "Thank you, Rad. That will be all."

Magone bowed and left the room. The moment the doors had closed, Vilyas strode forward to catch Abbie's hands. He looked into her eyes without speaking. His jaw was clenched so tightly his cheeks looked sunken.

Abbie felt a twinge of pain from the force of his grip on her hands. It communicated his emotion more clearly than words could have. She met his gaze steadily and gave his fingers an answering squeeze. "We'll bring Matteo home, Ambassador Vilyas."

His dark-brown eyes gleamed. "That is what I pray with every breath I draw."

"I'm sorry I interfered," she said. "If I'd known—"

"Please, Miss Locke, no apologies. I am in your debt for your agreement to help. This is why I wanted to meet you. I wish to express my appreciation in person. You are a very brave woman."

"No, I'm not. But I promise I'll do the best I can."

"That is the definition of bravery, Miss Locke. Continuing to do what you must, when inside your heart is crying to deny the horror." He stopped. His throat worked as he swallowed. He dropped his gaze and released her hands. "What kind of animals would do this to a child?"

"The fanatics of the LLA should know better than to

harm your son, Ambassador Vilyas,'' Flynn said. ''It wouldn't serve their purpose.''

The ambassador spun to face him. ''They claim to be patriots, but they are nothing but thugs. They do not deserve to call themselves Ladavians. If I were not a peaceful man—'' His voice broke. He made a sharp, cutting motion with his hand. ''My rage does no good,'' he said. ''I am committed to peace and the orderly transfer of power.'' He returned his gaze to the window. ''This is why my son suffers.''

Vilyas wasn't looking outside, Abbie realized. He was looking at a framed photograph that rested on a table beneath the window. She moved toward it. ''Is this Matteo?''

''Yes.''

Abbie paused to study it. The picture had been taken in a garden, probably in the early morning or after a rain. Against a backdrop of glistening foliage, a blond, hazel-eyed boy grinned at the camera. His features hadn't begun to develop the sharpness of his father's, but the resemblance was there in his wide-set eyes and the shape of his face. ''He looks like a wonderful child,'' she said softly.

''He wants to be an astronaut.''

''Good for him.''

''His dream would not be possible if our country does not change. But now because I try to change it, he might not have the chance to grow up and pursue his dream.'' He pinched the bridge of his nose. ''Forgive me. As I said, my rage does no good.''

''We're hopeful that another ransom drop will be set up soon, sir,'' Flynn said. ''We're prepared to go into action the second we get word.''

Vilyas nodded, taking a few moments to compose himself. ''Yes. This is why we insisted on Delta Force. We can trust you to fulfill your mission.''

''Yes, sir. We will.''

A door on the far side of the room opened. Abbie turned to look just as a small blond child peeked around the door frame. He appeared to be about three years old, a smaller version of the boy in the photo, but the worry in his hazel eyes seemed far older. "Papa?"

Vilyas's features instantly softened. "Sacha. What is it?"

The child launched himself into the room and ran to the ambassador, wrapping his arms around his knee. He hid his face against his father's pant leg and mumbled something in a language Abbie didn't understand.

"No, I haven't forgotten, Sacha." Vilyas laid his hand on the boy's head and ruffled his hair. "We will read your book, but right now we have guests."

The boy tightened his arms around his father's leg and refused to look up.

"My youngest son," Vilyas said to Abbie and Flynn. "He has become anxious about Matteo's…absence."

"Sacha?" a woman called. Her voice was high-pitched, on the edge of panic. *"Sacha?"*

"He's in here, Neda," Vilyas called.

A woman hurried through the open doorway. It was obvious to Abbie that she was Sacha's mother, not only because her hair was the same fine blond and her eyes the same hazel as the child's, but because of the relief on her face when she spotted him. "Thank God."

Vilyas detached the boy's hold on his pant legs and scooped him into his arms. He closed his eyes and pressed his nose to the top of the child's head for a moment, then settled him on his hip and walked over to the woman. "It's all right, Neda," he said quietly. "He could not have gotten past the doors. More reinforcements from the Royal Guard arrived this morning."

She rubbed the boy's back, then reached out to take him from his father. "I apologize for the interruption. Sacha woke early from his nap and slipped away from his nanny.''

"No, it is fine. You will want to meet my guests." He put his arm around her shoulders. "This is Sergeant O'Toole and Miss Locke, the teacher who has agreed to help us."

Neda Vilyas tightened her hold on her child as she turned her gaze toward Abbie. Her lips trembled briefly before she spoke. "Miss Locke. I am sorry to draw you into our troubles, but I am grateful for your kindness."

Abbie remembered what she'd learned during her briefing yesterday. These were not ordinary people. Neda Vilyas was a princess, the niece of King Kristof IV, the ruler of Ladavia. Her older brother had become the heir to the crown after the king's wife had remained childless. The small blond Sacha who was snuggled in her arms was fifth in line for the throne after his brother, Matteo, and his male cousins. The sharp-featured Anton Vilyas who draped his arm over his wife's shoulders was a diplomat influential enough to wield enormous power during his country's ongoing negotiations with the American president.

Yet whatever else they were, these people were still a family. They stood together, the father holding the mother who was cradling the child. Even though Neda and Anton were caught in the depths of every parent's worst nightmare, they drew their strength from each other and from the love that was glowing around them.

Abbie felt a lump swell in her throat. Maybe this was a reaction to the stress of the situation, too, like her awareness of Flynn, but the wave of longing that hit her was so intense it brought tears to her eyes. *This* was the essence of what she wanted. It's what her birthday wish was all about. Not just the trappings like the house in the suburbs and the sensible car, but this bond of love that transcended circumstance.

She sighed and glanced at Flynn.

He wasn't smiling. He wasn't looking like a soldier, either. It was as if a chink had appeared in his handsome features and what seeped to the surface was pure pain.

Chapter 7

Flynn wasn't often blindsided. When he was in enemy territory, he relied on his teammates to watch his back. He had developed a sixth sense about trip wires. He could isolate the sound of a gun being cocked above the noise of a force-five gale. But he hadn't been ready for this.

It was supposed to have been a straightforward courtesy meeting. Instead, it had turned into a touching tableau that could have been made into a photo with blurred edges and put on the front of a greeting card. Devoted father, loving mother, innocent child, all united in their concern for the missing member of their team.

Flynn felt as out of place as a starving man staring through a window at a banquet table. And for the second time in two days he wanted to *stay*.

It hurt. Damn, it gnawed at the empty place inside him that he did his best not to acknowledge or analyze. Out of habit, he searched for something cynical or witty that would push these feelings away.

Why would he want to stay? Why would he want to be part of this? Family scenes gave him hives.

"Flynn?"

He looked down. Abbie was studying his face. Really scrutinizing him for a change. Why did she have to choose this moment for her sudden interest? He summoned one of his best smiles to distract her. "Do you want to pick up some tourist brochures while we're here? You might want to do a class project on Ladavia for real."

She continued to regard him. "All right."

"We'll get them on our way out. Looks like this meeting is over," he added, tipping his head toward the Vilyas family. The blond kid was sucking his thumb while his mother spoke to him quietly in Ladavian. The ambassador seemed to have temporarily forgotten the presence of his guests.

For a man as steeped in diplomacy as Vilyas, it was unusual. So was the emotional way he'd greeted Abbie. He was in rough shape. Obviously, he was completely focused on the fate of his oldest son.

Yet another point against the family love thing, Flynn told himself. Freedom. No baggage that wouldn't fit in a duffel bag. That's what he wanted.

Abbie put her hand on his arm and leaned closer. "Flynn, are you okay?"

He must be slipping—the smile hadn't worked. He dipped his head toward hers. "No."

Her eyes warmed. "What's wrong?"

"I have an ache." He tapped his finger to his lips. "Right here. Want to kiss it and make it better?"

She frowned and looked away, just as he'd hoped she would.

"You'll be wearing this microphone on your clothing and this receiver in your ear when you do the ransom drop." Flynn held out his hand.

Abbie stared at the pair of tiny gadgets in the center of Flynn's broad palm. They were assembling her gear now so she would be ready to move when they got the word. It was making everything more real…and yet strangely unreal. The microphone was a fraction of the size of a watch battery, and the receiver was no larger than a pea. "They're so small."

"That's the idea. No one will know they're there, but you'll be in constant two-way communication with us the whole time."

"That's reassuring."

Flynn placed the devices into a Ziploc bag, sealed the top and put it in his shirt pocket. He turned to call over his shoulder. "Where's Abbie's GPS transmitter, Chief?"

Esposito looked up from where he was sitting in front of the radio equipment. He tipped his chair on its back legs and stretched his arm behind him to point at a crate near the far corner of the tent.

Abbie followed Flynn around a stack of metal boxes and waited while he sorted through the equipment in the crate. He came up with a slim black box. "You'll conceal this under your clothes," he said. "It uses a satellite signal to keep track of exactly where you are."

"Okay."

"We'll be watching you every step of the way. It's just in case something unexpected happens and you get separated from us, but that's very unlikely."

"I understand."

"There are similar monitoring devices in the backpack. The last time, Vilyas was instructed to drop the money and leave, that's all. We're hoping the next set-up will be similar."

"As long as someone else doesn't step in to mess it up again."

He slipped the transmitter into the same shirt pocket as the bag with the microphone and ear piece, then closed the crate and sat down on the lid. ''I'm not going to let anything happen to you, Abbie.''

She hung on to the deep certainty in Flynn's voice. As he'd told her before, whatever else she might think of him, he was a soldier.

He'd been all business since they'd returned from the embassy. For the remainder of the day, he'd treated her with polite respect. He hadn't given her any more compliments, and he hadn't made any more teasing comments about kissing.

Only, that comment about kissing him hadn't simply been to tease, had it? It had been more complicated than that.

There was more to Flynn O'Toole than met the eye. She might not have realized it if she hadn't glimpsed that flash of genuine emotion this morning…and if he hadn't tried so hard to cover it up. What was going on behind that pretty face? she wondered.

''Do you have any questions?''

She wiped her palms on her pants and sat beside him on the crate. She had been the one to draw the line in their relationship. Yet for all of Flynn's seemingly casual attitude, she had the feeling that he was accustomed to setting limits of his own. ''How will Matteo be released? Will he be at the place where I leave the ransom?''

''That wasn't the deal last time. They said they'd tell Vilyas where the kid was after they had the money.''

''But that means there's no guarantee they'll let him go. What if they change their minds and ask for more?''

''Then we adapt to the situation and go from there.''

''How?''

''We're monitoring the men we followed from your

apartment, we're monitoring the Ladavian Embassy and we're tapping into every law enforcement and intelligence network available. The LLA cells are well organized, but so are we. When the next call comes in, there's a good chance we'll be able to narrow down our search. Best-case scenario, we'll discover where the kid is stashed and get him out before you have to do anything.''

''And the worst-case scenario?''

''Forget it. I wouldn't want to give Murphy any ideas.''

''Who's Murphy?''

''''Anything that can go wrong…'''

''''…will go wrong,''' she finished. ''Murphy's Law.''

''I see you've made his acquaintance.''

''I teach seven-year-olds. I deal with him every day.'' She pulled her feet onto the crate lid and looped her arms around her shins. ''Matteo was taken five days ago. He must be terrified.''

He ran his knuckle along her forearm. ''Don't think about it, Abbie.''

''How can I help it?''

''We all have to maintain some distance to keep our focus on the mission.''

''Sarah mentioned that yesterday.''

''She's a good officer.''

''Yes, she appears to be good at what she does. It's just that—'' Moisture pooled in her eyes. She blinked to clear them. ''I love children, and I want so much to save him.''

''Trust us, Abbie. We're trained professionals.''

She exhaled shakily. ''You said that before, when you were pretending to be an electrician.''

''Yeah, but I'm telling the truth this time.''

She looked across the tent. The activity had fallen off after the evening meal, but there were still soldiers going about their various tasks. ''What are your missions usually like, Flynn?''

"There is no usual," he replied. "We go wherever we're needed. A few months ago we stormed a hijacked passenger plane in the Caribbean. Before that we put together a rescue mission in the Middle East."

"It sounds very exciting."

"It's not like the movies. We spend most of our time planning and training. The technical term for it is 'hurry up and wait.'"

"Where do you live when you're not in a tent?"

He arched an eyebrow. "Believe it or not, I have an apartment just like real people."

"Where?"

"In Fayetteville, North Carolina. Delta Force is based at Fort Bragg."

"Is that where you're from originally?"

"No, I'm from the West Coast."

"You must miss your family."

"You've already met them," he said, nodding toward the other men.

"What about your real family? Your parents, your sisters and brothers?"

"We don't keep in touch."

"I'm sorry."

"Don't be. The arrangement suits everyone just fine. We move around a lot." He laced his fingers together and stretched his arms over his head, his jaw working as if he were suppressing a yawn. "Why all the questions, Abbie?"

She watched the play of muscle beneath his shirt as he moved, although she still felt a twinge of guilt for enjoying it. "You know everything about me because of the background check Sarah did. I thought it would be fair if I learned a bit about you."

"It sounds to me as if you consider us off duty."

She gestured toward the electronic devices he'd stored in his pocket. "Unless there's some more equipment you needed to show me?"

He grinned. "I've got plenty of equipment I'd like to show you, but if you want to appreciate it properly we'll need more privacy."

She felt her cheeks heat. "Very funny."

"Making you laugh isn't what I had in mind."

She focused on his smile. It was attractive and charming with just a hint of good-natured naughtiness. It was the same as the one he'd given her this morning. It might not be genuine, but as a distraction, it was very effective. Was he using it to change the subject? "Why don't you want to talk about yourself, Flynn?"

"There's not much to talk about. Why are you so interested?"

"As I already said, it would be fair if I knew more about you."

He slid off the crate and held out his hand. "Come with me. I have a better idea."

"What?"

"It's getting late. I'll help you take a shower."

"Flynn..."

"Relax, Abbie. I meant I'll stand outside the door to make sure no one intrudes."

It was a practical offer. While the warehouse toilets were private, there was only one communal shower. She hadn't considered the difficulties of using it.

She bypassed his hand and got to her feet. "Thanks," she said. "That's a good idea."

Good idea, my ass, Flynn thought, gritting his teeth. He crossed his arms and leaned his back against the bathroom door frame. He'd mentioned the shower in order to put an end to their conversation, but the interior walls of the warehouse were thin. He could hear every drop of water that hit the tile. Worse, he could hear when the water drops *didn't* hit the tile. That meant they were hitting her skin.

She was using that apple-and-cranberry soap. The scent had wafted under the gap in the door and was curling around him like a shy caress. It was wholesome and sensual at the same time, just like Abbie.

There was a soft thud. The tone of the drops changed briefly, then resumed the muted patter of water on skin. She must have dropped the soap and had leaned over to pick it up....

Flynn let his head fall back against the door frame and tried to think of something else. He concentrated on a patch of starlight he could see through a broken pane in one of the windows on the far side of the roof. Was that bright one Aldebaran? He couldn't see enough to identify the constellation that contained the star, but for this latitude and this time of year, it could be Aldebaran.

Vilyas said that Matteo wanted to be an astronaut. Had he taught him about the stars and the constellations? Or had the kid found a book and taught himself the way Flynn had?

Flynn had been around Matteo's age when he'd learned the map of the heavens. It had started out as something to do when the arguing he could hear through the walls would keep him awake at night. He remembered the first time he'd crawled out of his bedroom window onto the roof. He'd been cold, and the pebbly surface of the shingles had scraped the soles of his bare feet, but he'd stretched out on his back, anyway, and had watched the stars until the dawn had swallowed them.

He had never wanted to be an astronaut when he was a kid. He'd never wanted to reach the stars, because their distance made them safe.

There wouldn't be any starlight in the shower room. The windows there had been blacked over when the team had set up in the warehouse. The ceiling lights would be gleaming from Abbie's wet body. The lather would be sliding over her shoulders and down the groove of her spine and past the curve of her buttocks and between her thighs—

He muttered an oath and squinted at the star. No, Aldebaran would be closer to the horizon. It was probably Capella.

"What are you doing here, Sergeant?"

Flynn straightened up. "I'm guarding the door, Captain."

Sarah tilted her head to the side and studied him. "Why? Are you expecting trouble from that quarter?"

"No, ma'am. I'm just ensuring our civilian guest gets some privacy."

She shifted the towel she was carrying to one arm and pointed to the hand-lettered cardboard sign that hung by a piece of string from the door handle. It said Men's Shower. She flipped it over. The other side read, Women's Shower.

They'd used variations of this arrangement before when Sarah had accompanied them in the field. It had worked well, although no one had made a big deal out of it when it hadn't. Modesty wasn't high on the priority list for any of them. They were usually too focused on the mission to get excited over an accidental glimpse of bare butt.

Not that Sarah wasn't an attractive woman. She was. She had an athlete's body, a husky voice and the kind of delicate beauty that could have been painted by Rembrandt. But it was more than her rank and army policy that put her off-limits. She'd been up-front about the fact that her heart still belonged to the dead Special Forces soldier who had been her fiancé, and the men respected that. Over the course of the past few years, she'd become like a sister to the soldiers of Eagle Squadron.

"Since when has the team forgotten how to read, Flynn?" she asked.

"The lighting isn't good here. Mistakes can happen."

"Uh-huh."

"Abbie's under enough stress. I don't want her to be nervous."

"The only person who seems to be making her nervous is you, Flynn." Sarah crossed her arms and leaned one shoulder against the opposite side of the door frame. "I don't think I've ever seen a woman actually run away from you before. It's refreshing."

"Don't you start, too. I've already heard this from the guys."

"Is that why you volunteered to be her baby-sitter?"

"Someone had to do it."

Her eyes gleamed in the dimness. "She's a nice woman."

"Seems so." The sound of the water shut off. There was the soft splash of bare feet in a shallow puddle and Flynn pictured Abbie walking across the floor to the bench against the wall across from the shower heads. She'd be reaching for her towel now, her skin all rosy and damp. Her hair would be curling over her shoulders, a few locks swaying against the upper curves of her breasts.

A snatch of melody drifted through the door. She was humming quietly to herself, an old Beatles tune. He ran through the words in his mind. It was something about still needing her and still feeding her when she was sixty-four.

"Abbie's not your usual type, Flynn. I thought you preferred tall, leggy blondes, like that model you dated last year who was into yoga."

He turned his attention back to Sarah. "Yeah, and you

probably heard that I'm not Abbie's type, either. It's unanimous all around. Works out well, doesn't it?''

"I don't know about that. You must find it tedious, with so much time to kill while we wait."

"We manage."

"I heard that Jack and Rafe are trying to get a poker game going."

"I can't afford to play cards with Norton. He's a shark."

"Maybe Abbie would like to play. I'll ask her."

"She's tired," he said immediately. "She wouldn't want to."

"I'll ask her, anyway. I'm sure Jack would be pleased to have her join them." She watched Flynn thoughtfully. "They have many interests in common. Did you know that Jack's an expert on the Civil War? His great grandfather on his mother's side fought for the Confederacy." Her right eyebrow arched teasingly. "Maybe Jack can show her his saber."

Yes, Sarah was just like a sister, he thought. He hadn't had much personal experience with any—none of his stepsisters had stuck around long enough to bother to learn how to needle him—but Sarah was doing a good job. "I heard his great-grandfather was a riverboat gambler," Flynn muttered.

"That, too," Sarah said. "Abbie would probably find that fascinating, don't you think?"

"Sergeant O'Toole?"

At the sound of Major Redinger's voice, Flynn twisted to look over his shoulder. "Over here, sir," he replied.

The major strode forward. He nodded to Sarah. "Captain, you'll have to postpone your shower."

Sarah straightened up from the doorframe. "What's going on, Major?"

"The LLA has just contacted Vilyas."

Flynn felt his pulse pick up. "Have they set up another ransom drop?"

Redinger nodded. "Ten tomorrow morning at the Lincoln Memorial. They've upped the ante to thirty million. We're assembling for a briefing in fifteen minutes. Where's Miss Locke?"

Sarah indicated the door to the shower room. "In there."

"Get her. We couldn't get a fix on where the call came from, so this is our best shot at locating the LLA base. We can't afford any mistakes this time."

Flynn had already put his palm against the door to push it open when Sarah's grasp on his arm stopped him. She gave him a quelling look, then used her free hand to rap on the door. "Abbie?"

A minute later the door swung open. Abbie stood on the threshold, a pale-peach jogging suit covering her body and a towel clutched in her hands. Her hair was wet, coiling in heavy curls, making wet patches on her shoulders. Her face was scrubbed clean, her eyes were wide, filled with a mixture of apprehension and eagerness as she tilted her head to look up at Flynn.

It was the same way she'd looked at him two nights ago when she'd first opened the door of her apartment. It was ironic that it was about to end the same way it had started. By ten tomorrow her role in this mission would be over. She would go home. Flynn would go on to the next challenge, the next woman, the next goodbye.

And as always he would make damn sure that he'd be the one to leave first.

Chapter 8

The knapsack hadn't felt this heavy the last time. It hadn't been light, but it hadn't weighed on Abbie's shoulder like this. It wasn't simply because there was more money inside. It was because now she knew what was in it.

Thirty million dollars. It was incredible. It was the stuff of fantasies, the dream of every soul who had purchased a lottery ticket. It was more money than Abbie could possibly use in a lifetime....

It was the price that had been put on a child's life.

Abbie swung the pack from her shoulder to her lap and locked her arms around it. She closed her eyes and inhaled deeply a few times, just as Sarah had shown her. She had to stay calm. She needed to think clearly, and oxygen was supposed to help.

The bus jerked forward. Abbie inhaled the tang of diesel fumes. It was probably only her imagination that made her think she also caught the scent of Flynn, but tension was sharpening her senses. Even if his leg hadn't been pressed firmly against her thigh, she was sure she would have felt his presence.

They were using public transit to get to the Mall so that no one could trace the vehicle she arrived in. Most of the team had been in position since before dawn. The rest were arriving at the target zone gradually to blend in with the civilians.

Target zone. Civilians. After only a few days with Eagle Squadron, she was starting to think the way the major talked.

Flynn laid his palm lightly on her knee. "We get off at the next stop. How are you doing?"

She opened her eyes and turned to look at him. He was sitting beside her on the seat that ran across the back of the bus. She suspected he hadn't gotten any more sleep than she had after Major Redinger had finished his briefing last night. The lines beside his mouth seemed deeper, and there was a hint of shadow beneath his eyes. Yet his gaze was clearer and more focused than she'd seen before.

He thrived on this. She could see it in his body language, in the way he was leaning forward as if he wanted the bus to move faster. He was eager to go into action, to face whatever challenge and danger might arise.

She just wanted this to be over.

Oh, *God,* how could he do it? How could any of them? Abbie felt her stomach contract with panic.

Flynn squeezed her leg. "Deep breaths, Abbie," he said quietly. "You'll be fine."

"Yes," she said. "Of course. It isn't complicated. Up the steps, past the statue, sixth column on the right, drop the pack."

"Good. And then?"

"And then I keep going."

"Where?"

"Around the corner and over to Twenty-Third Street where I hail a cab that Rafe will be driving."

"There. You see? Piece of cake," he said.

"If it's such a piece of cake, then why do I need this bullet-proof vest under my jacket?"

Flynn gave her knee a light pat. "It's just a precaution, Abbie. We're not anticipating trouble, but we want you to be as safe as possible."

She reached for his hand before he could withdraw it. She needed this physical contact with him. She had been prepared for the communication and tracking devices but when Flynn had produced the Kevlar vest, everything had suddenly become far too real.

It was Sunday morning. For her it should have been like a slower version of a Saturday morning. It should have started with a second cup of coffee, a leisurely perusal of the paper, then a trip to church instead of the library and a visit to her parents later or maybe a quick trip to Martha's to take her nephews to a movie or—

"Abbie?"

She nodded quickly.

He curled their joined hands against his chest. "You won't be alone, Abbie. I'm not going to be more than fifty feet away from you from the time we leave this bus. You might not see me, but I'll be there."

"Yes. I know."

"The team is going to be watching everything. At the first hint that you could be at risk, we're aborting the mission."

"No!" She turned her hand over and grasped his wrist. "No, you can't. This is Matteo's last chance. If they don't get the ransom this time, they might not let him go."

Flynn dipped his head closer to hers and looked at her carefully. "We went over this at the briefing, Abbie."

"I remember."

He continued to study her face. "Even Vilyas understands."

She nodded. She hoped he would assume it meant compliance. It didn't. No matter what happened, she was going to deliver the money to the spot the LLA had specified.

Matteo had been held by those terrorists for almost a week now. Children were resilient, but the longer this took, the deeper the emotional scars would be. Not only for Matteo but for the entire Vilyas family.

Someone near the front of the bus pulled the signal cord. It began to slow. Abbie felt her heart thud. She released Flynn's wrist and clutched the straps of the green backpack with both hands.

"We're coming to the stop," Flynn said.

"I can see that...." She bit her lip. He wasn't stating the obvious, he was reporting their progress.

The receiver in her ear clicked. "All right, Abbie. We're patching you in to the team's frequency now." It was Major Redinger's voice. His words were low and clipped. "You're almost done."

She cleared her throat. "Okay. Uh, roger."

"You don't need to acknowledge transmissions."

He'd already told her that when they'd gone over the mission plan yesterday, she realized. She felt her fingers cramp on the backpack and she flexed her hands.

"You've got fifteen minutes to get there, so you're right on schedule."

She glanced at her watch. It was exactly 9:45. She should be able to cover the distance in ten minutes easily. She moved to the edge of the seat, preparing to stand up the moment the bus stopped moving.

"Hang on a minute, Abbie," Flynn said. "There's one more thing."

She looked at him. "What?"

''This.'' He caught her chin in his hand, leaned closer and pressed a soft kiss to her mouth.

For a moment Abbie couldn't breathe. It wasn't anything like the other time he'd kissed her. They weren't alone. There were other passengers near the front of the bus, and there was a team of Delta Force commandos on the other end of the radio equipment.

And yet the sense of…connection with Flynn was the same. She felt as if he was focused completely on her needs. And she needed this. She drank in his strength and his confidence. Even as her pulse soared, she felt her thoughts settle. She could do this.

So she leaned into him and kissed him back. A soft shift of her lips, a quick dip of her tongue, a silent message that was part thanks and part goodbye.

Because more than her duty in the mission was almost over. Once she dropped the pack and walked to the taxi that would be waiting for her, she would probably never see Flynn O'Toole again.

It shouldn't matter. She'd only known him for three days. And she didn't *really* know him—he'd only given her glimpses of the man he was inside. Teasing, fascinating glimpses.

He lifted his head. His eyes were dark. He didn't smile. He looked at her for a breathless instant, then tightened his hold on her chin and kissed her again.

This time it wasn't gentle. It was swift and hard, a bold possession that sent a shock wave all the way to her heart. Then it was over. He dropped his hand and pulled back.

The bus rolled to a stop. The doors slid open. Without another word, Flynn got to his feet and stepped aside so that Abbie could move into the aisle.

Oh, God. What had just happened?

There was no time to think about it. No time for anything but playing out her role. She hitched one strap of the backpack over her shoulder and got off the bus.

"Heads up, people." It was the major's voice again. "Abbie's on her way."

"I've got a visual," Sarah said. "Flynn, hang back. You're following too closely."

The classic lines of the Lincoln Memorial rose on the far side of the Reflecting Pool. Abbie fixed her gaze on the columned building and restrained herself from turning around to look for Flynn. She couldn't do anything to give away the team's presence. Otherwise they wouldn't be able to follow when the LLA retrieved the ransom.

"Any activity around the target zone?" Redinger asked.

"Just a few tourists." Jack Norton's soft drawl was instantly identifiable. "A group of sightseers on a walking tour is heading in this direction. By the way, O'Toole, are you chewing bubble gum?"

"No." Flynn said.

"Oh? I was sure I heard some smacking noises a minute ago."

There were a few snickers.

Abbie realized Jack had to be referring to that kiss. She was too nervous to blush. As always was the case, there were far more important issues going on than her relationship with Flynn.

"Cut the chatter," Redinger ordered. "Abbie, you can slow down. You have plenty of time."

She realized she was almost running. With an effort, she slowed her pace as she neared the bottom of the steps that led up to the monument. She'd been here before countless times. She usually enjoyed the sense of grandeur that emanated from the historic buildings that were situated around the Mall. It gave her a feeling of roots, of being part of something far greater than herself.

In a way that's what was happening now. She was swept

up in something that made her own concerns insignificant. She reached the first step and started to climb.

"There's a male Caucasian standing beside Lincoln's right foot," Flynn said. "Five-eight, 150 pounds, salt-and-pepper hair. Anyone else see him?"

"Wire-rimmed glasses and tweed sport coat," Sarah said. "Is that the one?"

"Affirmative," Flynn said. "He's watching Abbie."

"Who's on him?" Redinger asked. "He could be an LLA lookout."

"Got him," Norton said.

Abbie kept her gaze on the steps and concentrated on breathing. Oh, God. She didn't want to look up. She just had to get to the top of these stairs and then walk to the sixth column on her right—

"Two vans just pulled up at the curb." It was Rafe's voice. "Three occupants visible in the first. At least three in the second."

"Captain Fox, can you get line of sight for the mike?" Redinger asked.

"Adjusting my position now, sir."

"Are the chase vehicles in place?"

More voices responded. Abbie kept climbing. She knew all these soldiers. She knew the plan, too. They'd gone over it yesterday until everyone could repeat it by memory. She would do her part, then they would do theirs. She was supposed to be long gone before the chance of a confrontation arose.

But what if the terrorists didn't want to wait for the money to be dropped this time? What if they were coming for her?

"Two men exited the first van," Rafe said. "One man got out of the second. They're heading toward the memorial."

"Male in the tweed jacket is starting to move," Flynn said. "Coming this way."

"Don't approach unless he threatens Abbie," Redinger ordered.

"I don't want to risk it," Flynn said. "I say we abort."

"Negative. Play this out."

"Major—"

"You have your orders, O'Toole."

Abbie stumbled on the next step. The pack on her shoulder wobbled. She swallowed a sob and tightened her grip.

"Abbie?"

She didn't acknowledge the voice. She waited for whoever it was to state their instruction.

"Abbie?"

It took her a moment to realize the voice wasn't coming through her ear piece. She took a deep breath and looked around.

A man was coming down the steps toward her. He wore glasses and a dull brown sport coat. This had to be the one Flynn and Jack had been watching, the LLA lookout. He seemed oddly familiar.

She staggered to a stop as recognition washed over her. "Peter?"

"Abbie, it *is* you." Peter Hedgeworth came to a stop in front of her, pushed his glasses up his nose and smiled shyly. "What an unexpected pleasure. I'm glad to see you recovered from your bout of the flu."

Oh, God. Her brain scrambled to switch tracks. Peter Hedgeworth. He'd asked her to dinner. She'd told him she was spending the weekend in bed. Now what? Oh, God. "What are you doing here, Peter?"

"Don't you remember? I told you Bradley and I were doing a walking tour this morning, since he was so enthusiastic after your trip to the museum." He glanced around.

"He should be here somewhere…. Oh, good. There he is. Bradley!"

The major's voice came over the radio. It was so low it was close to a growl. "Hold your positions, people. He appears to be a civilian."

"I've got the parabolic mike on the men from the vans, Major," Sarah said. "They're speaking Ladavian. They're talking about the money. I'd say they're not here to sight-see."

"Chase team, do you have your targets?" the major asked.

More voices responded, reporting positions. Abbie felt her head start to spin.

"Miss Locke! Hi, Miss Locke!"

Abbie pivoted to see Bradley Hedgeworth waving as he skipped along a step toward her. She looked at Peter. He was smiling and saying something about lunch.

She wanted to scream. It should have been so simple, but it was all falling apart. How long had she been standing here? How much time was left? She had to get away from them. Or she had to get them away from the money. She had a bullet-proof vest, but Peter only had tweed, and Bradley, dear God, Bradley only had a Capitals sweatshirt and a ball cap. If those Ladavians were anything like the men who had broken into her apartment, they wouldn't care who got in the way. Instead of saving a child, she'd just put another one in danger.

Before she could move forward, Bradley skipped down the steps and stopped in front of her. He grinned. "Miss Locke! Did you know there are thirty-six columns on the memorial? That's the number of states there were in the Union when President Lincoln was killed."

"That's right, Bradley." She put her free hand on his shoulder to hold him in place as she started to step around him. "Excuse me," she said. "I'm sorry but I don't have time to chat."

Peter brushed his fingers over the back of her hand where she touched Bradley. "Can I call you tonight, Abbie?"

The scream was rising in her throat now. She pressed her lips together and made a non-committal sound.

There was a blur of movement at the edge of her vision. She jumped, prepared to run when she heard a familiar deep voice.

"Abbie, sweetheart!" Flynn was suddenly at her side, bending down to give her a kiss on the cheek. "I'm sorry I'm so late. Were you giving up on me?"

She shook her head and exhaled hard. She wasn't sure she could speak.

Flynn flashed a smile at Peter and Bradley as he slipped his arm around Abbie's waist and smoothly propelled her up the stairs. "I hate to steal you away from your friends, darling, but we'd better go."

She took a few steps before she glanced behind her. Bradley's grin had faltered. Peter was staring after her with an expression of hurt disappointment. She wanted to explain, to apologize for her lies and her rudeness, but she couldn't. She realized she'd never be able to. She'd taken an oath of secrecy.

Jack Norton moved down the steps to intercept Peter. He made a show of fumbling with a map. "Excuse me, sir," he said, drawing Peter's attention away from Abbie. "Could you show me how to get to Grant's Tomb from here?"

She hurried to keep up with Flynn. "I'm sorry," she whispered.

"You said you didn't have a boyfriend," he muttered.

"I don't. Peter isn't. I mean—"

"The Ladavians are holding at sixty yards from your

position," Sarah said sharply. "They observed Abbie's meeting with the civilian and they're arguing whether to proceed."

"Norton, keep running interference with Abbie's friends," Redinger ordered. "O'Toole, deliver the pack and get out of there ASAP."

Flynn's fingers dug into her hip below the Kevlar vest. "Let's go, Abbie."

"But I'm supposed to do this alone."

"Not anymore."

She didn't know how they reached the top of the steps. She barely had time to catch her breath before they were passing by the marble statue of the seated Abraham Lincoln and striding down the shadowed colonnade. She focused on the sixth column.

"Now," Flynn said.

She swung the pack from her shoulder and dropped it at the base of the column as they passed by.

"They saw the drop," Sarah said. "They're still debating."

Abbie's steps faltered. She started to twist around to look back but Flynn didn't slacken his pace.

"It's over, Abbie," he said. "Your part's done."

"But I want to make sure they get the money even if I have to put it in their hands," she said. "It's my fault this happened. I should have remembered that Peter might be around here. I should have—"

"Miss Locke!"

At Bradley's loud cry, she jerked away from Flynn and spun around.

"Miss Locke!" The boy was waving and racing up the steps toward her. "Miss Locke, you dropped your pack!"

The scene unfolded with the slow-motion horror of a nightmare. Peter stepped around Jack to follow his son. Bradley's ball cap fell off as he ran around Lincoln's statue. Abbie held up her palms as she told him to stop. Other tourists who were scattered around the monument turned to observe the commotion.

"Bradley, no!" Abbie cried.

The child skidded to a stop beside the sixth column and scooped up the green backpack that held the cost of another child's life. He brought it to Abbie and smiled proudly.

She blinked back a surge of tears and took the pack from his hand. She was beyond screaming, beyond disbelief. She watched helplessly as he picked up his hat and ran back to his father.

"The Ladavians are leaving," Sarah reported.

"All right," Redinger said. "Chase teams, move out."

Time snapped into its headlong rush forward. Abbie hugged the pack to her chest. "No. Please. This can't be happening. Give me another chance."

Flynn put his arm around her shoulders. "Come on, Abbie. Let's go."

Her lungs heaved with a sob. "No. Let me try again. *Please!*"

He pressed a kiss to the top of her head and guided her away from the building. "Rafe, are you in position?"

"I'm at the curb with the meter running, O'Toole."

"We're heading your way," Flynn said. "Major, I think it would be best if you took Abbie off the air now."

"It's done, Sergeant."

The voices in Abbie's earpiece suddenly stopped. She rubbed her forehead and glanced at her watch, but she couldn't see the numbers through her tears.

Flynn had never been good around women who cried. He seldom saw actual tears—he knew how to read the warning signs and usually was long gone before they started. Tears were like anchors. Like chains. Slipping past the defenses he'd spent a lifetime perfecting. They were a weapon that, when deployed, was best answered by retreat.

But retreat wasn't an option here. He would no sooner leave Abbie now than he would leave a wounded man behind on a battlefield. He let the canvas partition fall shut behind him, closing them off from the rest of the tent in the privacy of the cubicle that had been serving as her bedroom. He reached down to rub her shoulder. "It's all right," he said. "You did your best."

She was curled into a ball on her cot, her arms wrapped around her legs. She held herself stiffly, her whole body shaking. She'd been like this since Rafe had dropped them off at the warehouse.

"Did my best?" she repeated. "That's what I tell my nephews when they miss a fly ball. This wasn't a Little League game at the community center. This was a *child's life* for God's sake."

"We'll find him."

"I promised his father we'd bring him home. The ambassador and his wife must be frantic. They've already been going through hell."

Flynn maneuvered between her cot and Sarah's and squatted down in front of her, bringing his face level with hers. "Don't give up yet, Abbie."

"But the terrorists won't let Matteo go now. What happens to him if…if… Oh, *God,* this has to be a nightmare. It's my fault. Again. This is the second time I messed up the ransom exchange."

"It's no one's fault," Flynn said firmly. "It's Murphy at work."

She wiped her eyes on her knees and lifted her face. Her skin was blotchy, her nose red. Her lips were swollen and her chin trembled. She wasn't a dainty weeper. No, there wasn't any ladylike sniffling for a woman like Abbie.

The emotion that was pouring out with these tears was as genuine as everything else about her.

Flynn felt out of his depth. He knew he wouldn't be able to remedy this situation with a smile. No clever words were going to help, either. He stroked back a lock of hair that was stuck to her wet cheek. "Except for the men on guard duty and Esposito, the rest of the team is still out there," he said. "Even the major. They're following those men from the LLA the same as if the ransom exchange had gone through."

"I can't believe this happened. I just can't believe it."

He eased the hair behind her ear, then rested his hand on her arm. "Would you feel better if I took you home?"

"God, no! I can stay, can't I?"

"Sure, you can stay. You're still part of the team, and the mission isn't over yet."

"I need to know when…or if…" She paused, her breath hitching. "I need to know how it turns out."

Flynn had rid both of them of their electronics as soon as they'd entered the tent, so he was no longer able to listen in on the team's progress. He tipped his head toward the canvas wall. "Esposito's monitoring the radio. He'll tell us when there's a development."

"A development? That's what you'd call it if you found Matteo Vilyas's body—" She pressed her lips into a firm line as her eyes brimmed.

He leaned closer and caught the front edges of her jacket. He tugged it off her shoulders. "Abbie, you need to relax. Let it go. It's out of your hands now."

She uncurled from her huddle in order to take off her jacket. She stared at the bullet-proof vest she wore beneath it as if she'd forgotten it was there, then jerked back and stripped it off as if it burned her. With a sob she flung it to one side. "I know there's nothing I can do, but I hate feeling helpless. That's why I make lists and follow schedules. That's why I always wear a watch."

He rose from the floor to sit down beside her. The cot started to tip, so he shifted his weight to the center and moved behind her back. With his knees bent, he propped his feet on the cot's frame on either side of her, looped one arm in front of her shoulders and pulled her back against his chest. "We all hate feeling powerless, Abbie," he said. "That's why we commando types like to compensate by carrying big guns."

"What?"

"It goes along with all that equipment I'd started to tell you about yesterday. The army shrinks have a term for it, I think."

She made a choking sound. "Please, don't try to make me laugh, Flynn. It would only make me feel worse."

"What I'm trying to do is to get you to stop blaming yourself."

"Flynn—"

"Did you get any sleep at all last night?"

She hiccupped, then gradually relaxed into his embrace. "I don't know. I don't think so."

"You're wiped out. That's why this is hitting you so hard. Once you get some rest you'll be able to establish some perspective."

"I can't distance myself, if that's what you mean."

"It would be easier for you."

"Sure, it would be easier. You're used to this because it's your job. Nothing personal, right?"

He folded his arms over hers, then closed his eyes as he inhaled the scent of her hair. "Not always."

"I'm just not cut out for this."

"Don't sell yourself short, Abbie. I wasn't being patronizing when I said you did your best. You handled tweed man as well as anyone could."

"Tweed man… Oh, no." She exhaled and let her head fall back against his shoulder. "Poor Peter. He looked like a kicked puppy. So did Bradley. The worst of it is, I'll never be able to explain to him why I acted that way."

"You were trying to keep him and his kid safe by getting away from them."

"Yes, but he'll think I was just trying to avoid him. I'm sure I hurt his feelings. Bradley's, too."

"Sometimes we have to do things we wouldn't normally do for the sake of a mission."

"I'm starting to see that."

He rubbed his nose against her temple. "So what kind of car does tweed man drive?"

"A Volvo station wagon. Why?"

"He seems to like kids. He sounded as if he could be a history buff, too. But he isn't your boyfriend?"

"No."

"Sounded as if he wanted to be."

"He asked me out, but I wasn't sure I wanted to go so I made an excuse."

"Good."

She hesitated. "Why would you say that?"

Flynn remembered the surge of satisfaction when he'd whisked Abbie away from Peter. It hadn't had anything to do with the mission. Neither was what he was doing now. Since when had he held a woman in his arms simply because she needed to be held?

Yet he couldn't pretend he was holding Abbie like this only out of some noble desire to offer her comfort. He did want to comfort her, but there were other things he wanted to do, too.

"Flynn?"

"He might fit most of your requirements for what you told me you want in a man," he said. "But you wouldn't be happy with him, Abbie."

"What do you mean? Why not?"

He shifted her in his arms so that he could see her face. Her tears had stopped. Her eyes were luminous. His gaze dropped to her lips. He couldn't find the words to answer her question.

But that was nothing new. When it came to his feelings for Abbie, words had failed him before.

Why should he try to analyze this? He was simply going to have to show her.

Chapter 9

It was like the first trembling instant when a roller coaster lingered at the crest of a drop. Abbie felt her heart thud painfully. She could see the danger ahead. She could do nothing to stop it.

Somewhere in the back of her mind she'd known this was going to happen. That moment on the bus when Flynn had seared her with his kiss, she'd understood there would have to be more. There hadn't been time then. This wasn't really the time, either. After her spectacular failure this morning, how could she possibly think of her own pleasure? Had she no shame? Had she no conscience? Had she forgotten what could happen if she followed her instincts instead of her brain?

But her mind was still spinning, her emotions in turmoil, and Flynn's arms felt so solid and right that she couldn't turn away. What else could she do but hang on for the ride?

Flynn kissed her gently at first. With one arm supporting

her shoulders and his long legs angled on either side of her, he held her in a secure embrace. Although his big body surrounded her, she felt no uneasiness. She'd never felt uneasy with his size, even on that first evening when she'd let him into her apartment and hadn't known who he was.

That had been Thursday. This was Sunday. Once again she wondered how it was possible that only three days had passed. It was as if she'd known him longer, as if she'd been waiting for him for years, the man in her dream, the one who would guide her through the sensual maze of candle flames without getting burned.

She twisted, tipping up her face to improve the fit of their mouths. She felt a smile flicker over his lips. She followed the smile with her tongue.

He groaned and brought his hand to her face. His fingers were unsteady where they stroked her cheek, the muscles of his thighs and arms were rigid with tension, yet he kept his strength under control. He tunneled his fingers into her hair to hold her steady as he answered her caress with one of his own.

She could feel his erection against her hip. It exhilarated her, like the rush of air on her face as the roller coaster took her through a swooping turn. Her body remembered how this went. Responses long denied were swelling with a force that was far more powerful than anything she could have dreamed.

He pulled back. His gaze burned into hers. "That's why."

She spread her fingers over his chest. "What?"

"Let me show you again," he murmured.

His kiss was more certain this time. He tasted her with lush sweeps, using his lips and his tongue in a way that made her melt. When he closed his hand over her breast, it felt so inevitable, like an extension of his exploration of her mouth, that she didn't even consider resisting. She arched herself more fully into his palm, exclaiming in delight as he found her nipple through her clothes.

Something creaked. Abbie felt herself falling sideways. Before they could tip onto the floor, Flynn flung himself backward and hauled her on top of him. She landed on his chest, her legs sprawled between his, her nose against the hollow of his throat. The cot slid a few inches upward, wobbled, then steadied.

They were both breathing hard. Abbie braced her hands on his shoulders and lifted her head. She shook the hair from her face so she could look at him.

He was smiling, his lips still moist from their kiss. Dimples creased the grooves beside his mouth. Warm little laugh lines spread from the corners of his heartbreakingly blue eyes. His black hair was tousled into soft curls that fell carelessly back from his forehead. And somehow his palm was still cradling her breast.

Oh, but he was a wickedly handsome man. So sure of himself, so sexy, so appealing. He was stretched out beneath her, watching her with a hunger that sent a shudder of response down her spine. He hooked his legs over hers, pressing their lower bodies together. The intimate contact made her shudder again.

"Does that answer your question?" he asked.

"What question?"

He gave her breast a light squeeze, then moved his hand to her cheek. "Why you wouldn't be happy with Peter."

It took a moment for her brain to register what he'd said. The response that bubbled through her started to ebb. "Is that why you kissed me? Were you trying to prove something?"

"Hell, no. I just wanted to kiss you, that's all." He stroked her jaw. "You're a passionate woman. I thought you'd like it."

"Passion isn't all I want, Flynn."

He moved his thumb over her lower lip. "But you did like it."

She sighed and kissed his thumb. "I think we had this conversation before."

"Uh-huh. Right before you claimed I'm not your type."

"You're not."

He tilted his hips. It was a subtle movement, only a slight shift in the angle. The quiver it sent through her body made her a liar.

Oh, yes. *Yes.* At this moment he was exactly the man she wanted. "Flynn, this shouldn't have happened. We shouldn't do this."

He lifted his head and sucked lightly on her lower lip.

Abbie made a low noise in her throat. She tried to summon the energy to argue. She fought to remember *why* she should argue. She moved her head aside. "I'm not that kind of woman, Flynn. I'm not casual about…"

"Sex?" He kissed the side of her neck. "Desire?" He ran his palms down her back and cupped her buttocks. "Mutual enjoyment?"

She pressed her face to his shirt. For a weak moment she let herself absorb the pleasure of his touch, his familiar scent, the rise and fall of his chest as he breathed. But she knew better than this, didn't she? *Didn't she?*

But it had been so long. And this felt so very, very good….

But it had felt good with Stuart, too.

She blinked and raised her head. "Please, stop. I can't do this."

Flynn's smile faded. He immediately took his hands off her buttocks and released his hold on her legs. "Abbie? What's wrong?"

She pushed off his chest. The cot started to tip with the

shift in her weight. She got to her feet and half fell onto Sarah's cot. "Flynn, I haven't had sex in eight years."

He looked as if he'd been punched. He jackknifed upward and twisted to face her. "What did you say?"

She wiped her eyes with the heel of her hand. "Don't look at me as if I'm some kind of freak. Celibacy might not be fashionable, but—"

"No. That's not what I thought. I'm surprised, that's all. I'm…surprised," he repeated. He moved his hand as if he was about to touch her, then shoved his fingers through his hair. "Why, Abbie?"

She hesitated. Normally, she wouldn't talk about this to anyone, not even her sisters. But there had been nothing normal about her life since she'd met Flynn. She glanced around, belatedly aware of how thin the canvas walls were.

"It's okay," Flynn said, as if recognizing the reason for her discomfort. "The men on watch are too far away to hear us and the chief's wearing a radio headset. There's only you and me." He swung his feet to the floor and sat facing her, his forearms braced on his knees. As he continued to regard her, his expression hardened. "Did somebody abuse you? Is that it?"

"No, not in the way you think. Stuart didn't—" She stopped and took a deep breath. "I was twenty-one when I met Stuart Moran. He swept me off my feet. We lived together for almost a year. He was…very skillful when it came to sex. He always made sure I enjoyed myself and he taught me things about physical pleasure that I hadn't known were possible. I loved him with my entire heart."

Flynn's expression didn't ease. If anything, it grew grimmer. "And you're still in love with him, is that it? Like the way Sarah is still mourning her fiancé?"

"No, Flynn. Stuart didn't die. He only left."

"He what?"

"He cleaned out his closet and emptied our bank ac-

count and he left,'' she stated. ''That's when I finally realized that I loved him for his looks and his body. I loved
him for the good times he showed me, all that mutual
pleasure that you said men and women were made for. I
was so completely wrapped up in a sexual infatuation that
I didn't see how empty it all was.''

Flynn regarded her in silence. Apart from a muscle that
twitched in his cheek, he was completely motionless. He
looked as if he'd been punched again.

''And it *was* empty, Flynn. It was hollow, just a shell
of what a real relationship should be. I thought Stuart was
my Mr. Right and that we would build a life together, but
as soon as he learned there might have been consequences
to all the sex, he packed up and ran.''

''Consequences?''

''I thought I was pregnant. I wasn't, but I was eager to
have a child. I love kids. I'd assumed Stuart and I would
get married.''

He rubbed his face, then squeezed his cheeks between
his fingers and his thumb and continued to study her. ''I'm
sorry, Abbie.''

''No, it was just as well I learned what he was like
before I actually did become pregnant.''

''Yes, it was, but I'm sorry for that crack I made yesterday about picking out your china pattern and the names
of your firstborn.''

''You didn't know.''

''That's right, I didn't.'' He took her hands and held
them loosely between his. ''But eight years is a long time
to deny yourself. Plenty of people have bad experiences
and try again.''

''What makes you think I'm not trying?''

''You said you've been celibate.''

''That's because I learned from my mistake. I know

exactly what I want now, and it isn't a few stolen kisses or some shallow affair.''

"Then what do you want, Abbie?"

She knew the answer to this question—she'd thought about it for eight years. "I want the kind of love that doesn't depend solely on how you look or how cleverly you perform a sex act. I want the real thing. I want what my parents have, what my sisters and their husbands have. What we saw when Anton and Neda Vilyas hugged their youngest child." Her throat felt thick. She swallowed and went on. "I want commitment in the truest sense of the word, Flynn. I want a marriage that grows stronger with each baby that's born and every gray hair. Every wrinkle. Every argument, every holiday and every twist in the road of life."

He dropped his gaze to their joined hands. "Most marriages aren't like that, Abbie."

"I know that. That's why it's so important to find the right person to fall in love with."

"You're an idealist."

"You say that as if there's something wrong with it."

"It's not wrong. It's rare."

"Why? Because I have dreams and I won't settle for less?"

"Because you don't hold back. Everything you do, you do a hundred percent. Like the way you've let yourself feel about this mission. The way you cry. The way you believe in love."

"Well, what about you, Flynn? Don't you have dreams? Isn't there anything you want?"

He moved his thumbs over the backs of her knuckles, trailing them down the faint lines of her tendons. "Yes, Abbie. There are things that I want."

She waited for him to continue. Another silence fell, this one longer than the last.

When he finally spoke, his voice was low and rough. "Each time I have to fire a round at an enemy's heart so he doesn't kill my teammate, or I see a wild-eyed teenager with explosives strapped to his chest, I want world peace. Every time the team is bivouacked near some village and I give my rations away to the hungry kids who beg on the edge of camp, or I see farmers with no legs because their fields were full of land mines, I want the scientists who develop our weapons to turn their energies into finding a way to feed the planet's starving people."

She might have been all right if he'd smiled or if he'd followed his comment with some witty quip. Instead he lifted his gaze and looked at her.

His barriers were down. He was dead serious. He was letting her see the pain she'd merely glimpsed before, and the depth of his emotion stunned her.

She felt the memory of her own troubles pale beneath the force of Flynn's sadness. What had happened to him? It had to have been far worse than an unhappy love affair. Had it been a mission? Or was it something to do with the family he didn't want to talk about? "It sounds as if you're as much of an idealist at heart as I am, Flynn."

"No, Abbie, I'm not. I learned a long time ago there's a big difference between what we want and what we can have. This is the only world we've got. All we can do is make the best of it." He tightened his grip and brought her knuckles to his lips. "So go ahead and call me shallow and empty because I believe in living in the moment and grabbing the good times."

"I didn't say that."

"You thought it. And that's fine. Right now, this moment, is the only sure thing in life." He leaned closer. "And right now, I want to kiss you."

Abbie didn't pull away. Somehow she couldn't.

"I'm warning you this has nothing to do with wrinkles

and holidays,'' he said. ''All I'm going to do is kiss you, okay?''

It didn't seem to matter to her anymore that he was handsome enough to steal her breath. The vulnerability he hid behind his perfect face was his most compelling feature of all.

She felt a tear trickle into the corner of her mouth. She licked it off and nodded, then closed what was left of the distance between them and pressed her lips to his.

How could his kisses keep changing? Each time it seemed different, as if he were showing her another level, another layer of himself. His mouth was warm and giving, a silent caress with no demands, no promises, like a roller-coaster car slowing down and coasting to a stop at the end of the ride.

He got to his feet, slipped his arms beneath her and picked her up, then turned and placed her on her own cot. Without pausing, he took off her shoes, spread a blanket over her and tucked it under her chin. ''Go to sleep, Abbie,'' he murmured, leaning down to brush a kiss over her forehead. ''There's nothing more you can do now.''

She squeezed her eyes closed. Nothing she could do. About Matteo Vilyas? Or about her tangled feelings for Flynn?

Although every available man was at this briefing, there were empty chairs—a portion of the team was already deployed, spread out through the D.C. area to keep track of the men who had been followed after the botched exchange yesterday. Flynn focused on the map that was taped to the support pole.

''One LLA cell is in each of these locations. Two are roach motels, one is a rooming house.'' Major Redinger used a pen to point at three of the four circles that had been marked on the map in red. ''According to our information, the rent has been paid in cash through to this coming Friday. I believe that gives us an outside time frame for the LLA's intentions.''

Friday, Flynn thought. That was only four days away. The mission would probably be over by then. He glanced at Abbie. She was standing at the edge of the group, her arms folded tightly over her sweater, her face pale. This morning he'd offered once more to take her home, but she had refused, just as he'd expected. The major had backed her up, saying she should stick around in case the LLA wanted to use her for another ransom drop.

Flynn didn't like it. He didn't want her taking that risk. Besides, she was already too emotionally involved. She was going to be devastated if this didn't turn out well and Matteo was killed. Flynn had tried to warn her about maintaining her distance, but she didn't know how to do anything halfway.

That guy Stuart had been a fool. How could he have tossed aside a woman as compassionate and wholeheartedly honest as Abbie?

How? The same way Flynn had perfected the art of leaving women behind for most of his adult life.

But that was different, he told himself. He'd never hooked up with a woman like Abbie before. That's why he avoided nesters. He made sure there was a clear understanding of mutual expectations up front, and he chose partners who wanted nothing more than he was prepared to give them. Sweet words. Sex. Good memories and an easy goodbye.

Easy and painless. Shallow and empty.

Flynn rubbed his face and turned his attention back to the major.

''This fourth location is the one that shows the most promise,'' Redinger continued, moving his pen to a point across the river in Baltimore. ''It's the only aberration in the pattern. It isn't a rooming house or motel, it's a two-story brick building with a storefront on the street level and an apartment above it. Any progress on the records search, Captain Fox?''

Sarah stood. ''The building was leased two months ago by a corporation based in Atlantic City with a branch office in Slovenia. I've just learned that the principal investors are Ladavian.''

''All right, we're going to do a detailed reconnaissance of a two-block area around that building,'' Redinger said. ''I want all routes in and out accounted for. Blueprints of the building would be helpful. Types of locks, roof access, pertinent data on the neighboring structures. What kind of business is in the storefront?''

''It was formerly a butcher shop,'' Rafe said. ''It's closed, and the windows are soaped over. I observed a sign that says it's under renovation.''

''The city has no record of granting a permit,'' Sarah said. ''There hasn't been any application for a business license, either. Utilities are still turned on, though, so there's no doubt that it's occupied.''

Redinger nodded. ''I'll notify air support to do an infra-red sweep. Captain Fox, your friends in Intelligence can help you analyze the body heat patterns.''

''I'll get right on it, Major,'' she said. ''We'll direct the nearest recon satellite toward those coordinates to give us regular updates.''

''Good. Meanwhile, I want the traffic patterns noted. Sniper teams, scout out the adjoining rooftops for vantage points with clear lines of sight. Set up the parabolic mikes. Trace the power grid for the area. I want all possible information gathered ASAP. Any questions?''

The briefing broke up with a minimum of conversation. A sense of anticipation pervaded the air as the men moved off to their various duties. The major hadn't needed to spell it out. That store in Baltimore could very well be the LLA's base. Whether they were holding the kid there or not was another matter, but setting up the plans for a raid sure beat waiting around.

"Hey, O'Toole!"

At Jack's voice, Flynn looked over his shoulder. "What's up, Norton?"

"I'm all out of chewing gum. You got any?"

"Nope. Sorry."

"You sure?" Jack winked. "It sounded as if you had a good supply yesterday."

"I hope you change your dressings more often than you change your jokes. That one's stale." He crossed his arms. "Don't you have anything else to do, like dull a scalpel or mark a deck of playing cards?"

"No, I did that yesterday." Jack glanced at Abbie. "Want to trade baby-sitting detail for surveillance duty? You've been on it long enough."

"No deal. These are the major's orders. I buddy the civilian."

"Sure, but we all thought she'd be home by now."

"Murphy had other ideas."

"She called in sick to work this morning. If the principal at her school doesn't believe her, she might need a medical certificate to back up her absence." Jack paused. "I should offer her my services. I'd enjoy giving her a thorough physical."

"Back off, Norton."

"Down, son. What are you so cranky about? Has she been running away from you again?"

"Leave her alone."

"Are you?"

"That's none of your business."

"You haven't made a secret out of it. We can all see what's going on."

"Nothing's going on. Abbie's a decent woman."

"Uh-huh. Like I thought, she's not your type."

Flynn said nothing. He couldn't argue with that.

Jack moved off to the area where the equipment was stored. Flynn could tell by Jack's stride that he was as eager as the other men to go into action. He hadn't been serious about trading duties. He'd just said that to needle him.

Normally Flynn would have jumped at the opportunity to change assignments. He thrived on action, and the raid on the base would be a chance to kick some serious butt. Now that he knew where Abbie stood about sex, being around her was only going to lead to more frustration. She wanted love. Marriage. He wasn't exactly the poster boy for either.

"Flynn?"

Abbie had approached while he'd been stewing about Norton. Flynn took a moment to study her up close.

Although Sarah had told him that Abbie had slept practically the whole time since he'd left her on her cot yesterday, she still looked stressed. The tension of the mission and her emotional outburst of the day before were taking their toll. Her lips appeared pinched. Dark smudges shadowed the skin beneath her eyes. Yet her gaze was clear and determined as she met his.

She wasn't shrinking back from the confidences she'd disclosed yesterday. He respected her for that. In an odd way he even respected her for her celibacy—for a woman as passionate as Abbie to abstain from sex would take an impressive amount of inner strength.

That could be part of the reason why she threw herself into her other relationships so completely and why she was so close to her family. It could be why she loved kids so much and had chosen a profession like teaching. She had to have some outlet for her natural warmth and generosity.

But if she ever decided to channel her passion into sex… Oh, man, she would be something. She kissed without holding back. She'd responded so readily to his touch, how would she have reacted if they'd gone further? What would it be like to have her naked on a bed, looking up at him with her gaze hot and her mouth curved into one of those intriguing private smiles?

No man had touched her in eight years. Despite all the reasons against it, the thought wouldn't go away. It roused something primitive and possessive deep inside Flynn.

"I'd like to go to the Ladavian Embassy today," she said.

He clamped a lid on his libido and shook his head. "That's not a good idea."

"I want to see the Vilyases."

"Abbie, there's no reason to put yourself through that. I know you feel bad about what happened but—"

"This isn't about me, Flynn," she said. "All along, this hasn't been about anything other than Matteo. His parents haven't told anyone what happened. They're going through this on their own."

"It's tough for them, but it's their choice. They know what's at stake. With the high-level diplomacy that's happening between King Kristof and our government, the need for secrecy is vital. The LLA want the movement toward democracy to fail and the monarchy demoralized so that they can take over."

"Yes, I realize all that. And if word got back to Ladavia that the king's grandnephew was kidnapped in America, public opinion could be manipulated against closer ties with the West, but it's not the global implications that concern me."

"No? Why am I not surprised?" he muttered.

"Think about it, Flynn. The Vilyases haven't even told the rest of the embassy staff about the kidnapping. They're in a strange country, thousands of miles from their home, separated from their family and their friends with no one they can trust. I want to go there to offer my support.''

Once more Flynn noted the signs of fatigue on Abbie's face and the determination in her eyes. She had been frightened yesterday, but she'd still been willing to risk her safety by delivering the ransom. Now she was willing to open her heart to strangers.

She was a hell of a woman. Stuart really had been a fool for running away.

''I don't expect you to come with me,'' she said. ''I saw that you were uncomfortable the last time, so I can get there on my own.''

Flynn didn't want to acknowledge the feeling that stirred to life inside him. Because in all the years that he'd been a soldier, he'd never considered himself a coward.

Chapter 10

"Where was this one taken?" Abbie asked as she pointed to the next photograph on the page.

"We were on holiday in Greece last spring. We stayed at my aunt's villa on the Aegean." Neda Vilyas stroked a fingertip along the line of surf in the foreground of the picture. "She and my uncle never had children of their own so they spoil all their grandnephews and nieces outrageously."

Neda's aunt and uncle? Abbie thought. That would be the queen and king of Ladavia. She paused for a moment to soak that in, then focused on the two blond boys by the water's edge. "What were Matteo and Sacha looking at? They seem very interested."

"It was a small starfish that had been stranded by the tide. Sacha wanted to play with it, but Matti insisted on putting it back in the sea."

"What a compassionate child. You must be very proud of him."

"Yes, he already shows signs of developing his father's sense of justice." Neda pulled back her hand and clenched it into a fist. "He wouldn't even hold a starfish against its will."

Abbie noticed a tremor in Neda's hands. Matteo's mother was barely holding on—she didn't appear to have slept at all since Abbie had met her two days ago. The blond hair she shared with her sons was dull and lifeless, pulled back into a tight braid, and the lines of strain around her mouth had deepened.

Yet as soon as Abbie had asked to see pictures of Matteo, Neda's gaze had sparked with animation. She had needed to talk about her son. It was a comfortably normal activity, and it was helping her to balance her worry with hope.

Once Sacha had been tucked into his bedroom for his afternoon nap, Abbie and Neda had made themselves comfortable on the blue-velvet upholstered sofa in the sitting room of the ambassador's quarters. They drank black tea made with steaming water from the silver samovar. She and Neda found so much to talk about, it was hard to believe they were from such different backgrounds. It was also hard to believe they'd only just met.

Then again, Abbie had known Flynn only a short while. A crisis tended to forge relationships that wouldn't have been possible under the restraints that were present in normal life. It engendered a special kind of intimacy.

She glanced across the room where Flynn and the ambassador were conversing quietly about politics. She had been glad that Flynn had insisted on escorting her. It had been difficult at first to face the Vilyases after yesterday's fiasco at the ransom drop, so she'd been grateful for his solid presence at her side.

That had been happening a lot lately. Only, it was more than gratitude she felt for Flynn. She was getting far too accustomed to having him at her side. Was that just because of the situation? Maybe. But he'd be the same person once the mission was over.

And that was the problem, wasn't it? No matter how fascinating she found him, and how…necessary he was becoming to her, he was still a man who lived for the moment and who thrived on the excitement of a dangerous profession. He wasn't the kind of stable, sensible man she would want to plan a future with—

She reined in her thoughts with a jerk. Plan a future? From what the major had said this morning, the LLA were intending to finish this standoff by Friday…if the raid on their Baltimore base didn't end it sooner. Four days at the most and this mission would be over. Flynn and the team from Eagle Squadron would pack up their tent and melt back into the shadows to await the next crisis.

And little Matteo's fate would be decided. One way or another.

Abbie put the photo album on the low table in front of them and covered Neda's hands with hers. "You all love him very much."

"He is a part of us."

"Children know when they're loved. It gives them strength."

"That is what I must believe," she whispered.

"Most of my students are the same age as Matteo. Does he like school?"

"He is enrolled at a private school with children of other diplomats, and he adores it. His mind is like a sponge. Until we came to America, he had a succession of tutors and he missed the stimulation of being around other children his age. The educational system in my country is poor. The division between the privileged class and the common citizen is too great. It breeds unrest."

"You hope to change that with democracy."

"Yes, it is the only chance for the future. There must be an orderly transition from the monarchy to the modern world. All Ladavian children deserve the opportunity to pursue their dreams."

"After Matteo comes home, would you consider asking someone from the embassy to visit my classroom? I'd like my students to learn more about your country. Even though I used it as an excuse for coming here, I've decided to have them really do a project on Ladavia. I think it's important for them to learn that no matter what language we speak, we all want the same things."

Neda turned to face her. For the first time that afternoon, she smiled. "Thank you, Abbie. I will speak to my husband about this. We would be pleased to honor your request."

Abbie released her hands and got to her feet. "Thank you for the tea," she said.

Before she could move away, Neda stood up and gave her a quick hug, then stepped back and straightened her spine regally, a touching echo of the nobility from which she was descended. "No, it is I who should thank you, Abigail Locke. I will never forget your kindness."

She started to reply, then caught sight of Flynn's face. He was worried. It took her a moment to realize it was about her.

How many times had he cautioned her about not getting too personally involved? She didn't care. Caution didn't seem to have much effect on her feelings lately.

There was a brisk knock on the door. Flynn's expression shuttered. He became all business, holding up his palm to the ambassador as he crossed the room. "I thought you told your assistant you didn't wish to be disturbed," he said.

Anton pursed his lips. "That is what I told him, but Rad often takes it upon himself to amend my orders."

Yet again, Abbie was surprised at how swiftly and silently Flynn could move, for a large man. He was at the door before the ambassador reached it. He positioned himself to the left, his weight on the balls of his feet, his arms relaxed at his sides. The way he stood reminded Abbie of the stance he'd adopted the night he'd fought off the terrorists in her apartment. He gestured for Anton to open the door.

The round, heavy-eyebrowed Radomir Magone stood on the threshold. He held a padded envelope. ''Your excellency, this just arrived for you.''

''I appreciate your efforts, Rad, but you can leave the mail in my office.''

''Yes, Mr. Ambassador, I have already delivered the day's mail to your desk. This came by special messenger.''

At a nod from Flynn, Anton took the envelope, dismissed his assistant and closed the door.

''Better let me take a look at that first, sir,'' Flynn said, holding out his hand.

''It is probably the documents I had requested from your government's State Department.''

''There's no official seal.''

Anton started. He looked at the envelope more closely. ''Rad should have noticed that.''

Flynn took the envelope from him by one corner and carried it to the window. He held it up to the light and studied it carefully, then set it down on a table and bent over to inspect the glued flap. ''Does your embassy security staff normally screen your correspondence?''

''Yes, of course. Since the bombing at the royal palace they have been trained to intercept anything suspicious.''

Neda moved forward, then stopped. ''What is it? Do you think that's a bomb? We should evacuate Sacha.''

''I'll call the guards,'' the ambassador said.

''Hang on.'' Flynn continued to study it, then slipped

his index finger carefully beneath the flap. He ran it under the edge slowly and peeled it back, then straightened up and left it where it was. "It's seems clear. I didn't mean to alarm you."

"Sergeant O'Toole, we have been living in a state of alarm for what seems like forever," Anton said, walking over to pick up the envelope. "You could not make it worse."

"My husband is right." Neda's smile returned. "Seeing both of you has made it better. Thank you for visiting."

"Yes, it was good to speak freely." Anton opened the envelope and glanced inside. His expression froze. He looked at Flynn, then addressed his wife. "Neda, I think I heard Sacha call. Why don't you take Miss Locke with you to check on him?"

"Anton, what is it?"

"Please, Neda." His voice grew hoarse. "Just do as I say."

Neda's face went blank. She didn't move. "Anton? You must tell me. Not knowing is worse."

He reached into the envelope and withdrew his hand. On his palm lay a lock of blond hair tied together with a piece of dirty string.

Abbie felt her stomach roll. At the same instant, from the corner of her eye she saw Neda's legs give out. She lunged for her but Flynn was there before Neda could fall. He caught her by the waist to hold her upright.

"It's Matteo's," Neda cried. "Isn't it, Anton? It's Matti's hair."

"Yes. I think so."

She clawed at Flynn's arms to free herself and stumbled to her husband. "The beasts. My God. What did they do to him?"

"It's only hair, my heart." He stroked the lock with his

fingertip, his hand trembling. "It was cut. It would not have hurt. He is a brave boy. It will grow back."

As the Vilyases spoke, Flynn took a cell phone from his pocket, flipped it open and punched a number. "It's O'Toole," he said, his voice low and hard. "The LLA has made contact. They didn't use the phone this time."

Abbie listened as Flynn did what had to be done, reporting the development to his team and setting the people who were covering the embassy into motion to track down the person who had delivered the envelope. Although he kept his gaze on the Vilyases while he spoke, he put his free arm around Abbie's shoulders and pulled her to his side. "Is there anything else inside, Mr. Ambassador?" he asked. "Some kind of written message?"

"One moment." Anton placed the hair in his wife's hands, careful not to lose a single strand. He reached into the envelope once more.

The words on the piece of white paper that he pulled out were written in black marker. Abbie squinted but couldn't decipher the scrawl. She realized it had to be Ladavian.

Neda looked at the words and whimpered, cradling the lock of Matteo's hair to her chest.

Anton clenched his teeth so tightly the tendons stood out in his neck. His eyes blazed as he looked at Flynn.

"Sir?" Flynn prodded. "I need to alert the team."

The ambassador shifted his gaze to Abbie. "It says you are to deliver forty million dollars next time or they will continue to return Matteo in pieces."

She felt Flynn's arm tighten on her shoulders. Her part in this wasn't over. The major had guessed correctly. She had to carry the ransom again. And she had to do it right, or the rest of Matteo would be… Oh, *God!* What had they used to cut his hair? How had they held him still to do it? And what would they cut off next?

Flynn's voice was hard as he relayed the information and closed the phone. "We'll obtain the additional funds and keep you informed of our progress, sir. I'll need to take that note and the envelope to be analyzed."

"Whatever you have to do," he said. His voice caught. "Do it. Anything. Whatever means you need, use them."

"We will." Flynn gave Abbie a firm squeeze, then stepped forward to take the items from Anton.

"Perhaps you don't understand me." The ambassador held himself so tightly, he was shaking. "As King Kristof's representative in your country, I am authorizing you to take any measures necessary against the citizens of Ladavia who are perpetrating this crime. There will be no diplomatic incident if these animals do not live to be extradited."

Flynn met his gaze squarely. "Believe me, I do understand, sir. We are soldiers, not policemen. We don't give Miranda warnings during a battle."

"Good." He thrust the envelope at Flynn.

Before Flynn could take it, something small and white rolled out and bounced to the carpet at his feet.

Neda screamed.

Abbie looked down.

It was a tooth.

Abbie walked the length of the warehouse, her footsteps dropping like pebbles into the cavernous silence. Her eyes were well adjusted to the darkness now. In the starlight that streamed through the windows near the roof she could see glints from the row of parked vehicles to her left. To her right, the tent's canvas walls glowed faintly, the thick fabric trapping most of the light inside. A shadow loomed near the door. That would be Specialist Gonzales who was taking his turn on watch. She reached the wall, pivoted and started back the way she had come.

So far she had done at least half a dozen circuits of the warehouse. She wasn't a jogger. She didn't belong to a health club. The exercise she got during the course of a normally hectic day at Cherry Hill School had always been enough to work off her energy.

But nothing seemed to help now. Her pulse was throbbing in her ears, yet she hadn't made a dent in the restlessness that gnawed at her.

How could Flynn and the rest of the team deal with this? How could they choose to do this kind of thing for a living? She'd been warned more than once about getting personally involved. Now she understood why.

She should have been prepared. She'd read reports in the news almost daily of the cruelty that was done around the world in the name of some cause or other. She'd also read about the soldiers and peacekeepers who were sent to the trouble spots to restore order. She'd never actually grasped the kind of inhumanity they faced.

She understood Anton Vilyas's rage. She also understood the matter-of-fact way that Flynn handled it. She had new respect for the strength it took to be a soldier. Flynn, Sarah, Rafe, the major and all the men she'd come to know never lost sight of their objective. Their priority was always the mission.

And she was right back in the middle of it.

The tone of her footsteps changed, as if they had developed a double echo. She realized she was no longer alone. She glanced over her shoulder and wasn't surprised to see Flynn approaching.

He always seemed to be there when she needed him, even before she realized she needed him.

He matched his stride to hers. "What are you doing, Abbie? I thought you were going for a shower."

"I changed my mind. I decided I need exercise more."

He walked a few steps in silence. "When I get the

chance, I usually go a few rounds with a punching bag in the gym.''

''What?''

''When we're out in the field and that isn't possible, I do calisthenics. Sometimes I spread out my bedroll and do pushups. Rafe cleans guns. Sarah does Tai Chi.''

''Why?''

''To work off the stress.''

''That's not going to solve anything. It won't bring Matteo home safely.''

''I'm not talking about solving, I'm talking about surviving. The only thing within your control is yourself. That's where you have to start.''

She reflected on his words as they maneuvered around some broken wooden skids that lay in a heap on the warehouse floor. ''I know you're right. That's one of my faults, trying to control things that I can't. I make all these lists and follow all these schedules, but I'm fooling myself. Nothing's really in my control.''

''It's not a fault, Abbie. The way you refuse to compromise your principles is one of your strengths. It was a courageous thing you did by going to see the Vilyases today.''

''I wish I could have done more. And at the same time, I wish I'd followed your advice and hadn't been there.'' She brushed her hair back from her forehead. She was surprised to notice that her skin was damp with sweat. She had felt chilled since they had returned from the embassy. ''And I wish I hadn't been mentioned in that note. That's not very courageous.''

''Do you remember what the ambassador said about bravery the first time we saw him?''

''I'm not sure.''

''He said that bravery is continuing to do what you must when your heart is crying to deny the horror.''

Yes, that was precisely what Anton Vilyas had said, she thought. Flynn had recalled his exact words. That didn't surprise her any more than his showing up here in the darkness had surprised her. She'd already figured out that his easygoing manner was a sham.

"Now that we've found the LLA base, there's a good chance we'll get this wrapped up before the next ransom drop is set," he said. "You won't need to do anything."

"That's not why I had to come out for a walk, Flynn."

"I know." He walked a few paces in silence, then spoke gently, going straight to the heart of her distress. "Jack studied the tooth, Abbie. He's positive it was only a baby tooth."

Her breath hitched. She wasn't wearing running shoes. She was still dressed in the sweater and slacks that she'd worn to the embassy. She didn't care. She began to jog.

He lengthened his strides. "The root was small and there was very little blood."

She increased her pace.

He matched her effortlessly. "Those marks from the pliers that you saw on it weren't deep. It's possible the tooth could have been loose to start with."

She broke into an all-out run.

He caught up to her. He wasn't even breathing hard. "Jack does marathons. For stress. Never saw the appeal of it myself, but if you want to give it a try, I'm game."

She could barely hear him over the rush of her pulse and the strain of her breathing.

"Watch out for the cables," he said.

She saw the dark mass of the electric cords that snaked across the floor in her path. She hopped over them and kept going.

"Broken crate to your right. Back wall coming up fast."

She changed direction. Her shoes slipped. She thrust out her hands to break her fall.

Flynn grabbed her from behind before she could hit the floor. With his arms locked around her waist, he braced his feet and skidded several yards across the cement. Their momentum carried them to the warehouse wall. He twisted around before they crashed into it, cushioning her with his body and taking the brunt of the impact on his shoulder.

A flashlight winked on near the opposite side of the building. Hurried footsteps approached as the beam sliced through the gloom toward them.

"It's all right, Gonzales," Flynn called.

The steps halted. "O'Toole? Is Abbie with you?"

"Yeah. Everything's fine. I tripped, that's all."

The beam played over them briefly, then flicked out. Gonzales returned to his post by the door.

Flynn set Abbie on her feet and turned her to face him. "Are you okay?"

Her lungs heaved. She put her hands on her thighs and leaned over, struggling to catch her breath.

He rubbed her back. "That's it. Slow and easy."

"I can't do this."

"Sure, you can. Do you need to sit down?"

"No, I mean I can't do *this*." She straightened up. "Flynn, I want to go home."

He looked at her carefully. "I don't think you mean that, Abbie."

"Yes, I do! This isn't my life. In my world, when a child loses a tooth he puts it under his pillow and dreams about the money the tooth fairy will leave for him in the morning. I was at my sister's house last month when Joshua lost his first baby tooth. He's Martha and Barry's youngest. Josh was so proud. I have pictures of his grin. He said he had a window in his mouth."

Flynn didn't say anything, he let her talk. He seemed to know that's what she needed.

"Martha has saved all of Barry Jr.'s baby teeth. He's

their oldest. She has a lock of his hair, too, from his very first haircut. It's dark brown like mine and like our mom's. She tied it with a blue satin ribbon—'' She clenched her jaw. She felt her eyes heat but she refused to cry. She suspected she was getting beyond tears. "It isn't right, Flynn. It isn't fair.''

"No, it isn't.''

"Seeing Matteo's hair tied up with that piece of filthy string, seeing his tooth on the floor… I keep picturing what those men did. And what they might do… Damn it, I can't handle this.''

"You can. You are.''

"No, I thought I could, but I'm a fraud. I went to see the Vilyases to offer them my friendship. I thought emotional support was what they needed, because that's what I know how to give, but what good is that against monsters who would pull a seven-year-old boy's tooth?''

"You *were* good for them. You held yourself together like a veteran.''

"It was horrible. It was obscene.''

"Yes, and you were brave. As the ambassador would say, you did what you had to do. You kept the horror inside. Now it has to come out.'' He opened his arms. "Come here, Abbie.''

She stepped into his embrace without a second thought. She felt his strength surround her, and she turned her face to his chest. She probably should have been worried over how much she needed his embrace…but she needed it too much to be worried.

"You know I'll take you home if you ask,'' he said. "You don't have to go through with this. You're a civilian who's here voluntarily. The major can't make you participate in the next ransom drop against your will.''

"I know,'' she mumbled.

"And like I said, chances are good it won't go that far.

We don't want to put you in danger." He laid his cheek against her head, his breath stirring her hair. "But you don't really want to go home yet, do you?"

She shut her eyes and drew in his scent. "No."

"I didn't think so. You're not a quitter. Once you commit to something, you don't back out. I admire that."

How could someone who was so wrong for her know how to say the right thing? Friends she'd had for years didn't know her as well as Flynn seemed to.

Of course she didn't want to go home. Not really. However difficult this was, it would be harder to walk away. She would see this through to the end no matter what. "Do you think Matteo is still alive?"

He stroked her back. "Yes."

"This latest…message from the LLA. It's the first time they haven't used the phone. What does that mean?"

"They're upping the ante. They're making it clear this will be their last gambit."

"Do you think your team will save Matti?"

His hand stilled. "We'll do our damnedest."

"Thank you."

"For what?"

"For not lying."

"You're welcome."

She splayed her fingers over his chest and lifted her head. "Flynn, could you promise me something?"

He hesitated. "What?"

"You started out with so many lies. Promise you'll always tell me the truth."

"You may not like what you hear."

"I know."

He slid his hand upward beneath her hair and cupped the back of her head. "The truth about the mission, or about everything, Abbie?"

Her pulse hadn't slowed down from her run. Blood

throbbed heavily through her veins. She was no longer cold. Warmth flowed from Flynn's body to hers. The restlessness that had brought her out here shifted to a different level. She moistened her lips. "Everything."

His fingers tangled in her curls. He moved his legs apart and drew her more tightly to the front of his body. He lowered his head to bring his lips next to her ear. "I know another activity that's good for relieving stress, Abbie."

His tone made her thighs tingle. There had to be something wrong with her. How could she feel…aroused at a time like this?

He answered her question with his next words. "It's got something to do with the effects of adrenaline." His teeth grazed her ear lobe. "The fight or flight response. When your heart is pumping hard and your muscles are primed for action, it's only a small step to switch all that energy toward sex."

She moved her hand over his heart. The racing beat matched hers. She ran her fingers downward. Through his shirt she traced the washboard ridges of his abdomen. She felt his muscles tense, and she explored the hardened contours.

"It's about survival, too," he murmured. He drew a slow line down the side of her neck with the tip of his tongue. "Lust is a primitive emotion. It's right up there with anger and fear."

She tipped her head back, exposing her throat to his mouth.

"Lust can let you shut down your brain." He bent down to press his lips to the sensitive skin at the base of her throat. "It's the ultimate way of living in the moment and forgetting everything that's happening around you."

He was right, she thought. The images that had tormented her since Anton had opened that envelope were fading beneath a warm haze of sensation. She wanted to seize this moment and make it last. She didn't want to think, she wanted to feel. She found the buttons on the front of his shirt, wrenched them open and slid her hands inside.

His skin was hot and smooth where it stretched over his ribs. She ran her hands up his chest, feeling the crisp tickle of hair on her palms. She spread her fingers, wanting to absorb as much sensation as fast as she could.

He caught her wrists to hold her hands still. "Damn, that feels good."

"Then why are you stopping me?"

He spun around, backing her against the warehouse wall. His voice was a low whisper. "Do you still want me to be honest?"

Shadows hid his face. He was a dark silhouette looming over her. Tall. Male. Insistent. He thrilled her on a level she hadn't known she possessed. "Yes," she said.

"A quick fumble in the corner isn't going to be enough for either of us, Abbie." He pressed her wrists to the wall above her head. "After going without for eight years, you deserve more than that. I want to be alone with you so we can do this right. I want to be someplace where I can peel off every last stitch of your clothes and see you naked."

Her legs shook. She swayed, but his grip on her wrists held her upright. He wasn't touching her anywhere else, yet the mere thought of him doing what he said made her breasts ache.

He dipped his head and inhaled deeply. "I want to smell the apple and cranberry scent of your skin when it gets slick with the sweat of my body sliding over yours."

She was having trouble breathing. "Flynn…"

"Like that. I want to hear you call my name." He stepped closer. There was a mere brush of fabric on fabric. It seared her from her neck to her knees. "On a bed. On the floor. Against the wall. I want to fill you up and feel you tremble around me.''

Moist heat blossomed between her legs. She arched toward him.

A tremor shook his frame. His breathing was harsh and rapid. Yet he didn't take the final step that would bring him into contact with her. ''It would be lust, Abbie. Sex. That's all. Two people enjoying a physical attraction.''

She wanted to weep. ''No, don't say that.''

''I won't lie.'' He dropped his forehead against hers. ''I respect you too much to lie about this, Abbie. You've drawn me to you since the first moment I saw you at the museum. It's the way you smile as if you know a secret, the quick way you walk, the way your hair curls around my fingers. Hell, I even like your freckles. I can't explain it. I want you.''

Why was everything so confusing? She was so sure she knew what she wanted. She'd been positive it wasn't this. She had vowed to hold out for love.

In eight years she'd had no trouble keeping her vow. She had the normal urges of a healthy woman, but she hadn't met any man who drew her strongly enough to tempt her. Until now.

Why was that?

She immersed herself in her schedules, her family and the safe little world of Cherry Hill School, so she seldom ran into handsome, exciting men like Stuart. And she certainly never encountered virile, testosterone-charged men like Flynn and the soldiers of Eagle Squadron. Flynn had said that she wouldn't have been happy with someone like sensible Peter Hedgeworth. Could he be right? Was it possible that she had subconsciously structured her life so she could avoid meeting men who might touch her heart?

Flynn lowered her arms to her sides and released her

wrists. "I shouldn't have started something we couldn't finish. I'm sorry, Abbie."

She wasn't sure why she didn't step around him and run for the safety of the tent. Instead, she moved closer, slid her arms around his waist and hugged him. "Don't be sorry, Flynn. It worked."

"It did?"

"It was better than running." She leaned back to look at him. She still couldn't see his face. But then, his looks had already ceased to matter. "You make me feel as if I can do practically anything."

"You can, Abbie. You're stronger than you think."

"I won't ask to go home again until I've seen this through."

He pressed a kiss to her forehead and folded her into his arms. He didn't ask whether she'd been talking about the mission or about what was happening between them. It was just as well. Abbie wasn't ready for that much honesty.

Chapter 11

"The satellite infrared images aren't as clear as I'd like." Sarah stepped through the group of men who were gathered around the mess table and hit a few keys on her laptop computer. The screen cleared. The hard drive crackled as a new image began to form. "There's an area in the northwest corner of the ground floor that we couldn't penetrate at all. The place was a butcher shop, so I assumed it was the meat locker. The blueprints confirmed this."

"Are there any identifiable heat patterns in the rest of the building?" Major Redinger asked.

"Yes. This scan was done at 1630 hours. There appears to be a group of people in a room on the second floor." She tapped another key. "I'll augment the resolution.... Here. I count eleven individuals."

"Then it's definitely more than one cell. This has to be the LLA's base."

Abbie moved to the edge of the group and rose up on her toes so she could get a better view of the computer screen. No one was using the chairs—this gathering was more of a discussion than a briefing. And if the men felt a fraction as tense as she did, they would prefer to stand, anyway.

The computer screen showed a pattern of ghostly red and orange blobs on a background of foggy-gray cubes. The picture had been taken through solid walls from several miles above the earth. Under other circumstances, the classified military reconnaissance technology in evidence here might have awed her—she was sure that regular law enforcement agencies like the FBI didn't have access to resources like this—but what was one more secret added to the rest she now kept? All she cared about were the results.

"By 2240 hours they had left this room," Sarah said. "Because the sun had gone down, we had less interference and could determine areas of interest on the ground floor. Several heat sources that fit the human profile are here and here." She moved the cursor's white arrow over the screen. "The scans done between midnight and 0500 show little change."

"We could be looking at where they sleep," Redinger said.

"Yes. That was my conclusion."

"Can you determine the relative sizes of the people?"

Sarah paused. "Judging by the mass, they have to be adults."

"No sign of the hostage?"

"No. My best guess is that he's being kept in the meat locker," she said. "It would be the logical place."

Images of Matteo flashed into Abbie's mind, the hazel-eyed blond boy who smiled from a photograph taken in a rain-washed garden and who could look so intent over a stranded starfish. Gradually, another image arose. A cold, frightened child, chunks of hair missing from his scalp, a tooth missing from his mouth. Locked in, alone, terrified.

For God's sake, hurry up! she wanted to cry. Why were these people taking so long? It had been a full day since that envelope with its obscene message had been delivered to the embassy. Didn't anyone think of what Matteo was going through?

Flynn moved behind her and squeezed her shoulder.

She exhaled hard and put her hand over his. She had to trust them. These soldiers would know better than anyone what the child was going through. They were more experienced at handling this side of life than she was. She shouldn't mistake their caution and clear thinking for indifference.

"You're only speculating about his location," Redinger said. "The hostage might not be there at all."

"That's a possibility, too," Sarah said.

Redinger moved to the rolled blueprints that were stacked on the opposite side of the table. He chose one and flattened it out. "The top story gives us our best options for entry. The door to the roof leads to a narrow stairwell that opens into the upper hallway. The two windows on either end of the hall don't have bars. We can call up a chopper to put us on the roof. If we hit them at night when they're sleeping we can neutralize them before they have a chance to harm the hostage."

"And if he isn't in the meat locker?" Sarah asked.

"Then our raid on the base would send the other LLA cells underground," Redinger replied. "And the hostage would be executed."

There was a rustle of movement from the men. Abbie could feel Flynn's hand tighten under hers.

"The outside time frame is Friday, so we need to move in before then," Redinger said. "But unless we can confirm the location of the hostage, it would be best to wait until the next drop is scheduled. With Miss Locke serving as a diversion, our chances of taking the LLA base by surprise are better. Their attention and manpower will be divided. We can do a sweep by moving on the three rooming houses at the same time and jamming their communications from the base to ensure they don't get off a warning—''

''No,'' Flynn said.

Redinger lifted an eyebrow at the interruption. ''Do you have something constructive to add, Sergeant O'Toole?''

''What you suggest would put Miss Locke at too much risk, sir. Timing a raid to coincide with the ransom drop would expose her to greater danger than doing a straight drop.''

''We will take measures to protect her.''

''They won't be enough. If it goes sour, Miss Locke will be in as much jeopardy as the hostage.''

''Your protest is noted, Sergeant.''

''Major—''

''O'Toole, do I need to remind you why Miss Locke is our guest?'' The major looked pointedly at their joined hands. ''She is not here for your private amusement.''

Abbie could sense Major Redinger's irritation and Flynn's growing anger. She let go of his hand and stepped forward. ''Excuse me?''

The men's gazes shifted toward her.

Abbie had never been more conscious of her size. She was surrounded by hard-muscled, grim-faced soldiers who towered at least a head above her. As always, they were wearing ordinary clothes rather than uniforms, but that made no difference. She couldn't forget they were trained fighters, waiting for the chance to go into action. What made her think she had anything to contribute?

Sarah caught her eye and nodded once, a silent gesture of encouragement.

Abbie drew herself up to her full five foot four, crossed her arms and tipped her chin to look at the major. "I'm here to return Matteo Vllyas safely to his family," she said. "And if I can do that by being a diversion, I will."

"Thank you, Miss Locke."

"Abbie," Flynn said. "You don't understand what this means."

She kept her gaze on the major. "I'll be wearing the same communication equipment and bullet-proof vest as the last time, right?"

"Yes, of course. We will have sharpshooters around the drop point, as well."

"Then I can do it," she said.

Flynn swore under his breath and caught her elbow. "It won't be the same as the last time, Abbie. The situation could deteriorate too fast. I won't let you do this."

"O'Toole, you're out of line." The major's voice was low, as ominous as a roll of thunder.

Flynn seemed to take no notice of the reprimand from his superior officer or the glances from the other men. He continued to stare at Abbie. "Use your head. You're too involved. You're not thinking objectively."

"Are you?" she asked.

Her question made him pause. A muscle in his jaw jumped. Before he could reply, there was the scrape of footsteps behind them. Rafe and Jack stepped forward from the group to move on either side of Flynn. Rafe gave him a solid nudge in the ribs. Jack caught him as he staggered and neatly moved between Flynn and the major.

"Major Redinger," Rafe said. "There is an alley that runs behind the north wall of the butcher shop. The meat locker is in the northwest corner of the building, correct?"

Redinger gave a crisp nod.

"If we could devise some form of cover that would allow us to be in the alley," Rafe said, "we could drill a small hole through the wall of the building into the locker and insert a cable cam.''

Sarah spoke up quickly. ''That's an excellent idea, Major. If we can get a visual confirmation of the Vilyas boy's location with the camera, we would be able to move on the base well before the next ransom drop.''

''Good. Do it.'' Redinger stepped back from the table and skewered Flynn with a look. ''Sergeant O'Toole, I'll see you outside. Now.''

Flynn finished cleaning the last piece of the submachine gun and set it on the cloth he'd spread over the wooden pallet in front of him. The black lacquer that coated the parts had been developed for durability. The pistol grip was ambidextrous, so the gun could be fired with either hand. The suppressor that fitted over the end of the barrel reduced the noise of a shot to the decibel level of a light tap. It was a versatile weapon, perfect for close-quarters combat, both silent and deadly.

With movements that had the choreographed grace of an action repeated countless times, Flynn assembled the gun. When he was finished, he held it loosely, feeling the familiar weight settle reassuringly into his hands.

Every man in Eagle Squadron had been drilled in the use of deadly force. They knew the stakes and they accepted the risks. This was what Flynn was trained for and what he was good at. It was the life he'd chosen. He didn't know what he'd do without it.

Rafe squatted beside him to reach the ammunition case on the floor. ''You okay?'' he asked.

Flynn put the weapon down. ''Fine.''

''The major looked pissed. I thought you'd be pulling guard duty at Bragg for the next year.''

''Redinger's fair. Guard duty would be too easy. He

figured the worst thing he could do to me is leave me where I am.''

Rafe chuckled. ''Yeah, that sounds like the major.''

''Is the camera in place?''

''Norton and Lang are still working on it. First they've got to reposition a dumpster from farther down the alley so it butts against the wall where the meat locker is located.''

''Are they going to drill from inside the dumpster? Is that the plan?''

''Uh-huh. Jack wasn't too crazy about that part.''

''As long as it works. It was a good idea, Rafe.''

''You probably would have thought of it yourself if you hadn't been so wrapped up with Abbie.''

Flynn leaned a hip against the corner of a packing crate and raked his fingers through his hair. ''Thanks for the save back there. I owe you and Jack.''

''You were digging yourself a pretty deep hole with the major. We couldn't stand by and watch you fall in.'' Rafe paused as he counted out thirty shells and lined them up in neat rows on top of the crate. ''And you don't owe me. I was returning the favor.''

''What favor?''

Rafe stood up from his crouch and slanted him a look. ''I seem to remember one briefing about a few months ago when I couldn't keep my mind on the mission. You didn't pull any punches when you reminded me about my priorities.''

Flynn frowned. He knew what Rafe was referring to. They had been planning a raid on the Caribbean island stronghold of the notorious drug lord, Leonardo Juarez. Flynn had been blunt when he'd pointed out Rafe's attention hadn't been with them 100 percent. ''That was different.''

''Uh-huh. How?''

"You weren't listening to the major's briefing because you were thinking about Glenna."

Rafe picked up the first shell in the closest row, wiped it carefully and inserted it into an empty magazine that would fit the submachine gun Flynn had just assembled. "And how is that different?"

"You were serious about the woman. You ended up proposing to her. I was concerned with Abbie's safety, that's all."

"Yes, so you said."

"It's not the same."

Rafe picked up a second shell, cleaned it and put it in the magazine. "Yeah, she's not your type."

"Damn right."

"You told me tall women fit you better."

Flynn thought about how Abbie had curled up in his arms on the cot, and how she had swayed into him as he'd held her against the wall last night. He hadn't thought about fit. Size had been irrelevant. Their bodies had flowed together as naturally as if they'd been designed for each other.

"She looks like a nester," Rafe continued. "I hope she realizes you're not the man for her."

"She knows. We're straight about that."

"Once you get serious about a woman, you lose your edge, isn't that what you told me?"

"I might have."

Rafe cleaned several more shells. He didn't speak again until he'd finished filling the magazine and had handed it to Flynn. "The rest of the guys figure they know why you're hanging all over Abbie. They think it's the challenge that's got you hooked."

"They've got too much time on their hands."

"Is it?"

"What?"

"The challenge." Rafe fixed him with a steady gaze. "Do you consider Abbie sport? Any bets on how much longer it'll take before you get into her pants?"

Anger stiffened Flynn's spine. He remained where he was with an effort. "You're lucky you're already so ugly, Marek," he said quietly. "Otherwise, I might have to rearrange your face for that comment about Abbie."

"Funny, I seem to remember rearranging your uniform when you made a comment like that about Glenna." A dimple folded into the scars on Rafe's bad side. "But go ahead and try, O'Toole. I've always thought you're too pretty for your own good, anyway."

Flynn focused on Rafe's half smile and felt his anger deflate as quickly as it had arisen. Rafe was a good friend, the best man to have at his back in any fight. His crude remark about Abbie had been an attempt to jar Flynn into revealing how he felt.

Problem was, he wasn't sure himself.

You're too involved. You're not thinking objectively. That's what he'd told Abbie. He should have listened to his own advice. "It's my duty to keep Abbie safe," he said. "I don't want her to get hurt."

"I can see that. But are you sure you're not serious about her?"

"I have other plans for my life. I like my freedom."

"That's what I thought until I met Glenna. Loving her opened a whole world of possibilities, made me look at life from a new perspective."

"Geez, can we change the subject? This touchy-feely stuff is giving me hives. Next thing you know you're going to take up knitting."

Rafe continued to look at him, his smile dimming. "Changing the subject won't change what's happening, Flynn. There's something special between you and Abbie.

Just think about it, okay? I didn't until it was almost too late. I could have lost Glenna.''

''This is different. Nothing's going to happen to Abbie. I'm going to make sure of it.''

''Uh-huh. And what happens when the mission's over?'' Rafe clapped his hand on Flynn's shoulder and gave him a shake. ''Better think about that, too.''

A ragged bush grew beside the loading bay. Its branches scraped against the cement platform in the breeze, a light scrabbling noise. A cricket chirped among the weeds that grew through a crack in the pavement. Answering chirps sounded faintly from the corner of the warehouse. To one side the rusted hulks of derelict cars were heaped behind the fence of a junkyard. On the other, the dark outline of an abandoned factory was silhouetted against the glow of the city. Overhead, the blinking lights of a plane mingled with the stars, its engines a faint rumble in the distance.

Abbie pulled her jacket more tightly around her shoulders as she turned her face to the breeze.

''Abbie?''

''Over here, Flynn,'' she replied softly.

He walked past the loading bay to the edge of the lane where she was standing. ''I thought you'd want to know the camera's working. They penetrated the meat locker.''

Chief Esposito had shown her the device they were going to use. It was a glass lens that had been fitted into the end of a flexible metal-sheathed cable no thicker than her little finger. She'd thought it looked like a toy, but he'd assured her the camera was fully operational. Her grip on her jacket tightened. ''What did it show?''

''Nothing.''

''I thought you said it was working.''

''It is. It showed an empty room.''

''Matteo isn't there?''

"No."

A small and cowardly part of her was relieved—she didn't want to see the image of Matteo that haunted her made real—but the relief was quickly submerged by worry. They still didn't know where he was. "Does this mean the raid on the base is off?"

"Not entirely. It's an option of last resort if we don't locate Matteo by Friday. There might be documents or other evidence there that could lead us to him."

"What do we do now?"

"We wait."

"For the next ransom drop to be set up," she said. "I'll be a diversion, just as we discussed this afternoon."

He was silent.

"I'm going to do it, Flynn. I trust Major Redinger. He doesn't strike me as a careless man."

"He isn't. He's the best commanding officer I've served under. He hasn't lost anyone on his watch yet."

"He seemed angry. I hope you didn't get into trouble because of me."

"Redinger believes in doling out lessons more than punishment. He didn't relieve me of duty, he clarified my orders."

"What orders?"

"He told me he's trusting me to put my personal feelings aside and keep you safe within the mission parameters." His arm brushed hers as he shoved his hands into his pockets. "It would have been easier if he'd just reassigned me."

"If that's what you'd like, I could talk to him myself."

"You know what I'd like, Abbie." His voice was rough as it cut through hers. "You know and Redinger knows. Hell, everyone on the team can see that I can't keep my hands off you."

He wasn't touching her. He was merely standing beside

her in the darkness of an October evening while crickets chirped in the weeds and the starlight gleamed from the cracked windshields of the wrecks beyond the junkyard fence. There was nothing romantic about the situation.

Yet every nerve in her body was attuned to him. His warmth, his scent. She didn't *want* him to keep his hands off her.

She shouldn't be relying on Flynn's touch. She was growing too accustomed to him as it was. What was going to happen when he left?

The same thing that had happened the last time she had fallen in love with the wrong man. Her heart would break, but she would go on. Older, wiser, more cautious than before…

Oh, God. In love? She couldn't be in love with Flynn. These feelings had developed too fast. He was completely wrong for her. It was the stress, that's all. A combination of adrenaline and proximity resulting in lust.

"You were right before, Abbie," he said. "I wasn't thinking objectively this afternoon. I have a problem doing that when it comes to you."

"What does…" She hesitated. "What did you mean by the mission parameters?"

"It's my responsibility to get you through the mission unharmed and return you home as soon as it's over."

"And then?"

"We let the diplomats handle the fallout from the kidnapping. Delta's part in this will be finished, so we'll go back to Fort Bragg."

Right. She would go back to her life, and he would go back to his. Well, she'd wanted him to be honest.

Another silence fell between them, this one much longer than the last. She tipped her head to follow the progress of another plane, trying to remind herself of the real world, *her* world, that lay only a few miles away.

"That's Perseus."

"The type of plane?"

"The constellation. I thought that was what you were looking at."

She focused on the stars, grateful to have something else to think about. "I don't recognize much more than the Big Dipper and the Little Dipper. Where's Perseus?"

He took his hands from his pockets and lifted one arm to point overhead. "It's roughly in the shape of a K. That curved line of stars forms the left leg."

"Oh."

He pointed higher. "That star is Algol. It represents the head of Medusa that Perseus is holding."

"It's bright, even through the city haze."

"It's a binary. The smaller star eclipses the larger one every three days so the brightness varies. It's…" He paused. "Are you getting cold? Do you want to go in?"

"No, I'm fine. Show me something else."

He moved behind her and took her shoulders in his hands to reposition her. She closed her eyes, drinking in the brief contact and the sensation of his body behind hers.

"Andromeda is the double line of stars north of Perseus."

She blinked and looked up. "You surprise me, Flynn. I wouldn't have guessed that you'd be an amateur astronomer."

"Why not?"

"It seems a bit…tame for your taste."

"It's something I picked up when I was a kid. Comes in useful when I don't have a compass."

"Matteo wants to be an astronaut."

"Yeah. I remember."

"Why did you decide to join the Army?"

"Because I get seasick and so I couldn't join the Navy."

She turned to face him. "No flip answers anymore, okay, Flynn? You said you'd tell me the truth."

There was a pause. "All right, Abbie. You don't deserve less. The truth is except for the sports teams, I never liked school much. I went to college on a basketball scholarship, but being stuck in a classroom put me to sleep. The morning of my graduation I saw an army recruiting video at a mall and decided that was a challenge I'd enjoy, so I packed my bag and didn't look back."

"Just like that? So fast?"

"What's the use of waiting around once you've made your choice?"

Of course. That's the way Flynn was. Straight-ahead, decisive and to the point. "Weren't your parents concerned about the risks you'd face in the military?"

"My father didn't know I had enlisted until I was half-way through my first tour. He was in the Philippines on some drilling project when my letter caught up to him. He's an exploration geologist so he's never in one place for long."

"What about your mother? Wasn't she at your graduation?"

"I was six the last time I saw her." He kept his gaze on the stars and continued to speak with no trace of self-pity in his voice. "There were a couple of stepmothers with kids of their own over the years, but my father was between wives at the time I signed up."

Oh, how she wanted to hold him. She looked at the tall, proud soldier he'd become and saw the vulnerable child with no roots and no family. She felt her perspective shift. He'd had a father who traveled, a mother who'd left him and a succession of broken homes. It fit. This was why he avoided commitment. This was why he'd once said Eagle Squadron was his family. This was probably why the sight of the Vilyas family's love for each other had hit him so hard.

There's a big difference between what we want and what we can have. That's what he'd told her. He'd said he'd learned that lesson a long time ago.

Would she wish for real love and a family of her own if she hadn't grown up surrounded by examples of it? How different would her dreams have been if she'd had a childhood like Flynn's? She might have armored herself with wit, the way he did. She might have buried her idealism and vowed to seize the pleasure of the moment.

Abbie realized Flynn's interest in astronomy wasn't so surprising after all. She lifted her hand to his cheek. "You like the stars because they don't change," she said. "Your father kept leaving, you had different mothers, but you could count on the stars."

He nodded and brushed his mouth over her palm. "Yeah. Stars don't leave. They're always right where you left them."

Her pulse thudded at his caress. She rubbed her thumb over his lower lip. "Show me more, Flynn."

He nipped the tip of her thumb lightly with his teeth. His eyes gleamed as he moved his gaze from the stars to her face. "Do you see the pentagon shape over my shoulder?"

She glanced past him, trying to spot the pattern in the points of light. "Yes. I think so."

"That's Auriga, The Charioteer." He grasped her hips and eased her against him. His words became a whisper, blending with the breeze on her cheek. "The bright star at the bottom corner is Capella. I could see that from inside the warehouse the night I stood watch while you showered."

The breadth of his shoulders blocked her view of the constellation. She gave up the pretense of looking and put her hands on his arms. "You didn't have to stand watch. Sarah had a sign for the door."

"I know. I wanted to be sure no one else got to see your nipples."

Her fingers tightened over his biceps.

"Your blouse was wet when you first let me into your apartment," he murmured. "It must have been the cold that was making your nipples pucker that way, but I couldn't forget. I still can't forget."

"Flynn…"

"I concentrated on identifying stars while I listened to you shower so I wouldn't keep picturing you naked. It didn't work then. It's not working now." He moved his hands to her waist and lifted her off her feet so that her face was level with his. He held her there for a long, trembling minute. "Maybe you should talk to Redinger after all. Ask him to assign someone else to you, Abbie."

"Why, Flynn?"

"Because every time I see you, every time I hear the caring in your voice, I want you more. But you've told me what you want, Abbie, and I can't give it to you."

She parted her lips. She wasn't sure how to reply.

Before she could make a sound, the warehouse door opened. Esposito's bald head gleamed in the starlight as he strode across the pavement toward them.

Flynn set Abbie down and angled his body in front of hers. "What is it, Chief?"

"We need Miss Locke inside, O'Toole. We've got trouble."

Chapter 12

"Abbie, if you're there, please pick up."

Abbie gripped the edge of the table where Esposito monitored the communication equipment and listened as her mother's voice came over the speaker. The team had been checking the messages on her answering machine regularly in case the LLA decided to contact her directly. This message had been left less than ten minutes ago.

"I'm sorry to be such a worrywart, dear. You're probably safely tucked in bed sound asleep, but I heard you weren't at work today. I'm going to pop over there and bring you some soup, okay? I'll let myself in so you don't have to get up. Bye."

The message ended. Abbie felt her stomach drop. She looked around.

"Your mother can't let herself in," Flynn said. "I changed your lock. Unless you gave her a spare key on Friday?"

"No. I never thought of it." Abbie chewed her lip.

"When she finds out her key doesn't work, she'll bang on the door. If I don't answer, she'll get worried. She might get the building superintendent to break the lock."

Chief Esposito scowled and muttered something about Murphy's Law. "What will she do if she gets into your apartment and sees you're not there?" he asked.

"She'd be even more concerned," Abbie replied. "She believes I'm sick. If I'm not there, she might think I went to a doctor or a hospital."

"And then?"

"She'd call the rest of the family. They'd go into full panic mode. If they don't hear from me they'll probably call the police."

"This has to be contained now or the security of the mission will be compromised." Flynn handed her his phone. "Does your mother have a phone in her car?"

"My dad gave her a cell phone last Mother's Day for emergencies. She keeps it in the glove compartment but I don't know the number by heart. I've never used it. I've got it in my address book, but that's at my apartment."

"Is it registered under her name or your father's?" Esposito asked, swiveling toward his computer.

"Uh, my father's."

"Okay. No problem. The captain showed me this trick a few weeks ago." He hit a sequence of keys. Seconds later the screen filled with lines of names, addresses and phone numbers. "Here it is."

Abbie dialed the number Esposito read to her and put the phone to her ear. It rang eight times. "She's not answering," Abbie said. "Maybe she hasn't left yet."

"If she's anything like you, she would be on her way," Flynn said. "Better try again."

Abbie dialed the number and let it ring twelve times. On the thirteenth ring, the phone was picked up. As soon as she heard her mother's voice, she exhaled in relief. "Mom, I'm glad I caught you. I got your message and—"

"Abbie? Are you all right?"

"I'm...I've felt better."

"Hang on, I've got to pull over." There was a pause. "There. I can't stand those people who talk on cell phones while they're driving. Now, what is it that couldn't wait until I got there?"

"Mom, I hate to have you come all this way for nothing. It's really sweet of you to offer to bring me soup, but—"

"Abigail, how sick are you?"

"It's just the flu."

"You haven't been answering your phone."

"I turned off the ringer so I could rest."

"You don't sound like yourself. Your voice is shaking. Is someone there with you? I can hear noises."

She glanced around the crowded tent. "Must be a bad connection. And I've got the television on."

"You said you were resting."

She rubbed her forehead with her free hand. "Yes. Mom, I don't want to hurt your feelings, but I was about to go to bed and I'm not up to company right now."

"Nonsense. I'm not company. I'm your mother. I'll be there in thirty minutes."

"Mom—"

"Someone's honking at me, I have to go. See you soon."

The connection was broken. Abbie gave the phone back to Flynn. "She's worried about me. I couldn't stop her."

"We could have her intercepted," Esposito suggested. "Call in a complaint to the D.C. police and give her licence number."

"No," Abbie said. "Please don't do that. She has a perfect record."

"Wouldn't do any good, Chief," Flynn said. "If Abbie's family is worried about her, they'd just send someone else to check up on her. We can't afford a security breach at this stage. Our only choice is to let her play out the cover she's established.''

Esposito looked at Abbie. ''How fast a driver is your mother?''

''She taught me everything I know.''

''Oh, hell,'' Flynn muttered.

Abbie locked her arms around Flynn's waist and pressed more closely to his back as the bike tore around a corner. She'd asked to go home yesterday, but she hadn't really meant it. And she hadn't imagined going home like this. The trip from the warehouse to her apartment building should have taken at least forty minutes. Flynn had covered it in twenty-five.

They hit the low curb at the driveway of her building and they were momentarily airborne. Abbie tightened her thighs over Flynn's hips, her teeth clacking together hard with the impact of their landing. The tires screeched as Flynn squeezed the brakes. The back wheel swung out as the bike skidded in a ninety-degree turn and nosed into a narrow gap between two cars in the lot designated for visitors parking.

Flynn shut off the engine, kicked down the stand and jumped off the bike. ''Do you see your mother's car?''

Abbie pulled off her helmet and scanned the parked vehicles. ''No, she isn't here yet.''

''All right, let's go.'' He didn't wait for her to swing her leg over the seat. He caught by the waist and lifted her off, vaulted over the low hedge that separated the parking lot from the sidewalk, then set her on her feet. Holding their helmets in one hand, he headed for the building's rear door. ''Do you have your keys ready?''

She jogged to keep up with him as she shoved her hand

into her jacket pocket and pulled out her key ring. "Got them."

Her apartment was exactly as she'd left it. She didn't know why that surprised her. She had been gone less than a week. The avocado plant looked a bit droopy, and there were a few more leaves on the carpet around the fig tree, but otherwise, nothing had changed.

Yet it looked smaller. It had once seemed so cozy. Now it seemed…confined.

"We don't have much time." Flynn tossed their helmets into the closet beside the door. "Take off your clothes."

"What? Flynn, we—"

"You told your mother you were getting ready for bed." He strode straight to her bedroom and switched on the lamp. "Where's that pink T-shirt you were wearing on Friday night?"

She followed. "Under my pillow."

"Okay." Flynn pulled back the pillow and tossed her the T-shirt, then rumpled the bedding so the bed would look used. "You change, I'll disappear."

She caught the garment and toed off her shoes. "Where?"

"Balcony. Your plants block the view of the patio door. I'll stay out of sight in the shadows."

She reached for the zipper on the front of her pants. "Won't you be cold?"

His jaw tightened as he watched her movements. "No. I won't be cold."

Her hand stilled. Her heart pounded. It wasn't only from the hair-raising motorcycle ride.

"Do you want some help with that zipper?"

She shook her head.

He swore and left the room.

Abbie blew out her breath and finished undressing. She had just pulled on her T-shirt when she heard the faint sound of jingling keys. She kicked her clothes out of sight under her bed, dropped her watch on the bedside table, grabbed her robe and hurried toward the front door.

Before she could reach the door, she heard the scrape of a key. There was a muffled exclamation, followed by a light knock. "Abbie?"

She glanced around. Flynn was gone. Nothing stirred except the branch of the fig tree that was closest to the balcony. She fastened the knot in the belt of her robe and unlocked the door.

Clara Locke stood on the threshold. Her silver-streaked brown hair was pulled into her usual neat bun. The blouse that showed beneath her thick gray sweater had tiny flowers like the wallpaper in her kitchen. A hint of the almond-scented hand lotion she always used floated in with the draft from the corridor, along with the aroma of chicken soup from the round plastic container she held.

She was so blessedly ordinary and familiar that Abbie wanted to cry.

Clara shifted her handbag and the plastic container to the crook of one arm and gave Abbie a lopsided hug. "I'm sorry to get you up, dear, but my key wouldn't work."

Abbie returned the hug. She held on a little longer than usual before she drew her mother inside and closed the door. "I'll give you another key."

"Would you like me to warm up some of this soup for you?" Clara asked, heading for the kitchen. "It's chicken and rice, your favorite."

"No, please, don't go to any more trouble, Mom. I ate a little while ago."

"All right." Clara put the container in the fridge and picked up the electric kettle. "I'll fix you a cup of tea with honey. You always liked that when you had a cold."

"Thanks, but I don't have a cold."

"Yes, I can see that." She filled the kettle and plugged

it in, then came back and studied her carefully. She tested the temperature of Abbie's forehead with the back of her hand. "You look flushed, but you're not feverish. I don't think you have the flu. Actually, you look as if you're brimming with health."

"It, uh, comes and goes."

"Abigail." Clara hesitated. She took her hands. "Darling, is there anything you want to talk about?"

"No, Mom. Why should there be?"

"I came over here because I'm worried."

"Yes, I'm sorry about not answering the phone, but—"

"Oh, Abbie, you never were any good at lying. I suspected as much last week and now I can see the truth written all over your face."

Her mother couldn't possibly have guessed, she told herself. Flynn wasn't visible. Clara couldn't know anything unless she had seen them arrive on the motorcycle, but even then she wouldn't have any idea what was happening.

"It started on your birthday, didn't it?" she asked.

"Yes, that's when I started to feel ill."

"Please, Abbie. You don't need to pretend any longer. I understand."

"Mom—"

"I realize thirty was a milestone for you. We're all aware of how you love to make plans. I was concerned that you might be putting too much importance on the date, and when you didn't come to your party, I feared I was right."

Abbie struggled to grasp what her mother was saying. She lapsed into confused silence.

Clara drew her to the couch and sat down beside her. "Ellie and Martha have been worried, too. They said you sounded distant when you returned their calls. When Joshua heard from some of the other children at his Little

League practice that you weren't at school this week, he told his mom and so Martha phoned to check. She knows as well as I do that you love your job. Only something very serious could keep you away.''

''Mom—''

''I've respected your privacy because I know how determined you can be when you set your mind to something, but you don't have to go through this alone. It's nothing to be embarrassed about, Abbie. Everyone has the blues now and then.'' She patted her hand. ''You can always talk to us, darling. We all love you, and we want to help you in whatever way we can.''

Understanding finally dawned. Tears threatened once more, but this time for a different reason. Her family didn't believe she was sick. They thought she was holed up in her apartment because she was going through some kind of still-single-and-turning-thirty crisis. A biological clock issue triggered by her birthday. Her mother hadn't come over to give her chicken soup, she'd come to give her a heart-to-heart talk and a sympathetic shoulder to cry on.

As if she didn't already feel guilty enough for deceiving her family, now she discovered they were not only willing to forgive her, they were meeting her lies with kindness.

If only she could tell them the truth. She was in the midst of a terrorist kidnapping. She didn't have time for an emotional crisis...or time to fall in love...or time to have her heart broken....

But wasn't that exactly what was happening? Oh, God. *Was* it the truth?

''Don't give up, Abbie.'' Clara smiled, her face settling into a network of lines that were as sweetly familiar as her streaks of gray and her scent of almond lotion. ''Life seldom goes exactly as we planned.''

A lump formed in her throat. ''Yes, I'm starting to realize that.''

''I hope so. Because sometimes we get so focused on what we're searching for over the horizon, we can walk right past the treasure that's under our feet.''

It must be an effect of the stress, Abbie thought, feeling the first tear inch down her cheek. She had cried more in the past five days than in the eight years since Stuart had left her. She did know what she wanted, didn't she? She knew what she was searching for. She did.

''Let's forget about the tea, dear.'' Clara handed her a tissue and returned to the kitchen to unplug the kettle. ''You look as if you could use something stronger.''

Flynn checked the luminous dial of his watch. Almost an hour. How long did it take to placate a worried relative and show her out? He shifted his weight from one foot to the other, tensing and relaxing his muscles in sequence to keep up his circulation.

A siren sounded in the distance. He tuned it out and concentrated on the murmur of voices that came through the glass door. Abbie and her mother were speaking too quietly for him to distinguish any words. He could distinguish the tone, though. It was the same tone he'd heard when Abbie had spoken with Neda Vilyas. Full of sympathy and compassion. Supportive. Loving.

He shoved his hands into his pockets. He could feel the hard case of his cell phone under his right knuckles. He'd switched the ringer to vibrate silently—the team would call him if the LLA scheduled the next ransom drop. Flynn had already warned Abbie she might be needed at any moment. Could she have forgotten why they were here?

No. Not Abbie. She was as serious as the rest of the team when it came to the mission. He knew she was scared. She was determined to go through with it, anyway.

He admired her courage. It was hard to face one's fear. *Show me more, Flynn.*

He dropped his head back against the building's wall and looked at the sky. He'd shown Abbie the constellations because he hadn't wanted to show what he felt. There weren't many stars visible from here. The balcony of the apartment on the floor above shielded his view overhead. The buildings across the street and the light from the city concealed practically everything else. Didn't make any difference. He knew they were there.

Stars don't leave. They're always right where you left them.

Abbie had understood without being told. No one else had made the connection before. It had taken him years to figure it out himself. Yes, stars didn't leave. Unlike parents and sisters and lovers, they were safe. They were constant. They would live forever.

Her insight didn't surprise him. Right from the start she'd had a way of looking past the surface into the depths he'd successfully guarded from the rest of the world.

He turned his head to glance into the apartment. Abbie and her mother were still on the couch in the living room. They were on their second glasses of wine—odd they were having wine when Abbie was supposed to be sick. They wouldn't be able to see him past the leaves of Abbie's plants and the glare of the lamp on the glass door, but he was careful to keep in the shadows.

He was good at that. Standing on the outside, looking in. Passing through without stopping. Did Abbie understand that, too?

Abbie nodded at something her mother said. Clara patted her knee and stood.

Finally, Flynn thought. He edged closer to the glass and watched as they walked toward the apartment door. Abbie gave her mother a hug, locked the door behind her, then turned around and slumped back against the panels. Her shoulders heaved with a sigh as she rubbed her face.

Flynn counted off ten seconds before he slid the balcony door open and stepped inside. He crossed the room, keeping his voice low. "How did it go?"

She started and dropped her hands. "Did anyone ever tell you that you move too quietly for a man your size?

"Not in my profession. Your mother was here longer than I expected."

"I'm sorry to keep you waiting."

"No problem. There hasn't been any word from the LLA. Looks like you convinced your mother of your cover story."

Abbie shook her head and walked over to pick up the empty wineglasses from the coffee table. "She didn't buy it. She never believed I was sick."

"Then what did you tell her?"

"Don't worry, I didn't divulge any classified information. I didn't have to tell her anything." She gave a short laugh and carried the glasses to the kitchen. "My mother assumed I was avoiding everyone because I was upset about turning thirty."

He followed her. The laugh hadn't been from humor. "And are you upset?"

"That would be stupid, wouldn't it? There are more important things to worry about."

"Not for me." He caught her shoulders. "What else did she say?"

"She said I'm too...rigid."

"You're not rigid. You're strong. And you're the most compassionate person I've known."

"She didn't mean it badly. She said it out of love, because she's worried that I'm so focused on my goals I might miss seeing the obvious right under my nose." She shrugged off his grip. "Don't, Flynn."

"What?"

"Don't touch me right now."

He held up his palms and stepped back.

She put the glasses in the dishwasher and brushed past him. "We should get back to the command center."

"We've stayed away this long. Another few minutes won't hurt."

"You're wrong. They will hurt. I'm going to get dressed."

He followed her to the bedroom. "What does that mean?"

"I'm going to put on my clothes so we can leave." She dropped to her knees beside the bed and reached beneath it. She pulled out her jacket.

"What did you mean about hurting? Talk to me, Abbie. Tell me what's wrong."

She thrust her hand beneath the bed again. This time she retrieved a shoe. She tossed it over her shoulder and got down on all fours so she could extend her arm farther. "I pushed everything too far. I can't reach it."

Flynn solved her problem by shoving the bed aside. He knelt beside her and gathered the rest of her clothes.

"I should have thought of simply moving the bed," she muttered, sitting back on her heels. "I guess my mother was right. I miss the obvious."

"You've had a tough few days. Once this is over and your life gets back to normal—"

"Normal. Of course. Once this is over you'll leave and I'll pick up my life where I left off. I'll go back to work. I'll finish the baby blanket I'm knitting for Ellie, I'll take my nephews to a movie on the weekend and return my library books. Those books are overdue. The fine must be stacking up and I wouldn't want to get into trouble."

"Abbie—"

"Oh, yes. There's no lack of things to do. My car needs an oil change soon. I can schedule that for the weekend after next. And I really should shop for some plants to replace the ones that fell on that terrorist's head. The book-shelf looks so empty without those geraniums. Then maybe I'll call Peter and see if he still wants to go out with me. There. You see? I'll be fine. Give me my clothes, Flynn.''

Flynn looked at the garments he held. Her sweater and pants were crumpled into a loose ball. He started to hand them over when a flash of black lace caught his eye. He hooked his finger under it and pulled it free.

It was a bra. Low-cut, underwire black lace that was sheer enough to see through.

She held out her hand.

Flynn let the bra dangle from his fingers. He imagined what it would look like on Abbie. His blood started to pound. The undergarment didn't match the rest of her sensible clothes. It was sexy, meant for seduction, not comfort. Someone else might have been surprised by her choice, but not Flynn. This suited Abbie perfectly. She might not display her sensuality, but it was there beneath the schoolteacher who worried about overdue library books. It was an intrinsic part of the woman who loved her family and could weep over a stranger's son.

He folded the scrap of lace into his fist. "You took this off. Why?''

"I had to. The lines from the lace would have shown through my T-shirt.''

His gaze dropped to her chest. Her robe had fallen open while she'd been reaching under the bed. Her pink cotton T-shirt stretched smoothly over the curves of her breasts. She was right. The bra would have shown through the shirt because the fabric was soft enough to outline exactly what it covered…and supple enough to reveal the way her body responded as he watched.

He lowered his gaze to her thighs. "Did you leave anything on under that shirt?''

"Flynn…"

"Is it black lace too, Abbie?"

"Give me my clothes, Flynn."

He looked her in the eye and pitched her clothes across the bed. They hit the far wall with a whispered thud and tumbled to the floor.

She shuddered.

He leaned toward her. "Peter wouldn't understand the black lace the way I do, Abbie."

"I don't wear it for you or for him. I wear it for myself."

"I know."

"We should leave."

"I know."

"Now, Flynn. We don't have time—"

"We have the moment."

"Yes, that's right. All we have is the moment. That's why we shouldn't do this."

He slipped off his watch, reached into his pocket for his cell phone, then put both on the floor behind him. He lifted his hand to Abbie's face, holding it a breath away from her cheek, close enough to feel the heat of her skin on his palm but far enough to leave the choice up to her. "You're wrong, Abbie. The call that could end the mission might come through at any time. That's why we *should* do this. Because all we can be sure of is the moment."

Her gaze steadied on his. She circled his wrist with her fingers.

Flynn had never begged for anything in his life. He'd learned not to. But the longing that washed over him as he looked into her eyes was so powerful, it would have sent him to his knees if he hadn't already been on them.

Just this once, he didn't want to be on the outside looking in. He wanted to taste the love Abbie surrounded herself with before she, too, would walk out of his life. "Abbie, please."

Her fingers tightened. She didn't push him away. She lowered his hand and brought it to her breast.

Chapter 13

It wasn't adrenaline. It wasn't the wine her mother had given her. Abbie was afraid she knew what was making her heart race and her hands shake, but she wasn't going to think about that now. If she and Flynn would only get this moment, then she didn't want to waste it.

He spread his fingers over her breast.

Abbie moaned and swayed closer.

He moved the heel of his hand in a firm circle, sending bursts of delight pulsing over her flesh. He nudged her robe off her shoulder, dipped his head and replaced his hand with his mouth.

Oh, yes. It was more than adrenaline or wine. Whenever he touched her, wherever he touched her, she felt herself come alive. She braced her hands on his thighs. His muscles tensed into hard ridges. She traced the ridges to his knees and back to his groin, then slid her fingers over his hips and grasped his buttocks.

Less than a week ago she'd tried not to notice how his

jeans had molded what she was now caressing. He'd drawn her then. She hadn't known why. She'd dreamed of him, but she hadn't wanted to admit it. He wasn't what she'd been looking for...but here he was, and this wasn't the time for doubts and it wasn't the time to think. How could she think when he was moistening the front of her T-shirt and sliding the wet fabric over her nipple with his tongue?

She moaned and rose to her knees, her back arching as she followed the pleasure he was giving her. The question was no longer why was she letting him do this. It was why had she waited so long.

She pulled his shirt over his head and splayed her hands on his chest, reveling in the textures and contours she discovered. When she'd touched him like this yesterday, he'd stopped her. Was it only yesterday? Time no longer seemed relevant. How could she measure her feelings in days? Or moments?

Flynn looped his arm around her waist to bend her backward and ease her to the floor. He rid her of her robe and her T-shirt, then hooked his thumbs into the waistband of her panties. "Black lace," he murmured. "I knew it."

She lifted her hips to help him ease the garment off. "I lied, Flynn."

He pressed a kiss to her stomach. "What?"

"I did wear it for you. Only I hadn't known it would be you."

He lifted his head, his eyes dark. The expression on his face was...predatory. He scooped her off the floor and tossed her on the bed.

She raised herself on her elbows to shake the hair back from her eyes. She felt her mouth go dry as she watched him take a condom from the back pocket of his jeans and strip off the rest of his clothes. Each movement sent muscles rippling under taut skin. He was all male, his body lean, powerful and magnificently aroused.

The mattress dipped as he stretched out beside her. He hooked one foot behind her knees and rolled her against him, then slipped his hand boldly between her thighs and made her quiver. And he knew the instant her body needed more.

It was fast, as reckless and exciting as the motorcycle ride over here. Their skin grew slick. The scent of her soap mixed with the earthy scents of Flynn and of sex. She trembled around him as he filled her. She called his name as she climaxed. Everything he'd said the night before while he'd held her panting against the warehouse wall was coming true.

Except for one thing. It wasn't lust. It was love.

Abbie pressed her face to Flynn's neck and whimpered as she climaxed again. He was the wrong man. The worst man. He would be gone by the end of the week.

He slid his hands under her buttocks and tilted her to meet his thrusts.

Damn him. She loved him, anyway. She clasped her legs behind his waist and bit his shoulder.

He wrapped her hair around his fist to tug her head back. Without breaking the rhythm of his hips, he absorbed her burst of anger with his kiss. He made love to her mouth and her body as if there were no watches to check or schedules to keep. He turned the moment into something precious, taking her with him as he shuddered and whispered her name.

Abbie hung on as the tremors faded. The room gradually came back into focus, but her thoughts still spun. What had she done? What on earth would she do now?

Flynn eased his weight onto his knees and elbows, kissed the tip of her nose and looked at her. He didn't say anything. No lover's endearment. No clever phrase to make light of the moment. No lies. Instead he smiled.

If Abbie hadn't already fallen in love, that smile would

have sent her tumbling over the edge. It was more than a curving of his perfect mouth and a glimpse of his dimples. It was a smile that came from within the lonely boy who had been left behind by everyone but the mythical figures in the constellations. He claimed he didn't want love and yet he was always there when she needed him, giving her the strength to get through the twists in the road of life....

Her thoughts steadied. Yes, he was there for her. The bond between them was far more than one of duty. It all seemed so obvious. He wasn't the wrong man, her list had been wrong. Love couldn't be scheduled or planned. It simply happened. And she couldn't imagine loving any other man but Flynn. She smiled back.

"That's the one," he murmured, tracing her lips with his finger.

"Mmm?"

"That smile. It always gets to me. What are you thinking?"

"Do you want me to be honest?"

He rubbed his knee along her thigh. "I don't believe you know how to be anything but honest."

"You may not like what you hear," she said, echoing the words he'd said to her the day before.

"I'll take my chances."

"I think I'm in love with you, Flynn."

He went completely still. Fierce joy danced across his face. His eyes gleamed for an instant. Then it was as if a door slammed somewhere deep inside. The joy disappeared. He rolled to his back. "Abbie...no."

She got to her knees and put her hand on his chest. Her gaze was caught by the red mark on his shoulder, evidence of the passion of moments ago. This might not be the best time to talk, but if she didn't say this now, when would she get the chance again? She ran her fingers over the imprint her teeth had left in his skin. "I don't like it any more than you do, Flynn, but it isn't something I can control."

"I thought you understood what's between us."

"It's you who doesn't understand. You claim you don't want love, but you know how to give it. You've been showing what's inside you with everything you do." She pressed her hand over his heart. "I grew up surrounded by love, but all it took was one bad experience and I did my best to protect myself against being hurt again. You've had so many bad experiences, I'm amazed that you're as good a man as you are."

"I told you before, Abbie. You're an idealist. The world doesn't work the way you want it to."

"It can with the right person. After Stuart left me, I sheltered my feelings behind my rigid ideas of what I thought I wanted. It took meeting you and being swept up in the reality of this mission to jar me out of the walls I'd built."

"Abbie…"

"I know why you say you don't want love. You've been left behind so many times, you're afraid to reach out again."

He sat up and swung his feet to the floor. "You don't know me."

"Yes, I do. My family is my rock. You never had that. Your mother left, and your father was seldom there. From the sound of it, your stepmothers didn't try to be close—"

"Abbie, my mother didn't leave."

"You told me you hadn't seen her since you were six."

He looked at her over his shoulder. "That's right. She didn't leave. She died."

Abbie had thought she understood, but it was worse than she'd imagined. "Oh, Flynn. I'm sorry." She fitted herself to his back. "I'm so sorry. You were so young. Was it an accident?"

"No. It was her choice."

"What do you mean."

"She killed herself, Abbie."

Her heart squeezed hard. She couldn't have heard him right. He'd said it so matter-of-factly. "She…"

"She got depressed when my father was away. They had screaming matches when he was home. She was taking medication for her mood swings and one day she decided to take the whole bottle."

"Oh, Flynn. She couldn't have meant—"

"She meant to, all right. Her note made her intentions perfectly clear. She left the note beside the cookie jar to make sure I'd find it when I got home from school. The doctor said she must have swallowed the pills as soon as I'd left the house that morning so she'd been dead for hours when I called the ambulance."

"You…" This was horrible. Unthinkable. A six-year-old child, coming home, calling for his mother and instead finding… "*You* had to call the ambulance?"

"My father was in Bolivia that time. She planned it that way. No one else was there."

"My God. You were only six."

"Like I said, I learned my lesson early."

"Oh, Flynn."

He reached behind him and hauled her from the mattress onto his lap. "Don't pity me, Abbie. I didn't tell you this to get your sympathy. I told you so that you'd understand."

"Pity isn't what I feel, Flynn."

"You dream of a home and a family and a kind of forever love. Some people aren't meant for that. I've already seen what happens when a man who wants his freedom meets a woman who wants a home. It won't work." He looked at her, his gaze as naked as his body. "I need my freedom, Abbie. It's how I survive. The pleasure of the moment is safe. It's the dreams that will kill you.''

What could she say? Like everything else about the past week, this was beyond her experience. To lose a parent was tragic, but to lose one to suicide… Oh, God. Was it any wonder that Flynn would build barriers around his heart? ''We've had different lives, but we still want the same things. I can see it in your eyes, Flynn. I feel it in the way you hold me.''

''This is what you feel,'' he said, shifting her to bring her hip against his groin. ''Two people enjoying a physical attraction.''

''I'm not denying that, but it's more.''

''Sure, it's more.'' He cupped her breast in his palm as he rubbed his thumb over the tip. ''It's an exceptionally strong physical attraction.''

How could she want to hug him and bite him at the same time? She straddled his lap. ''And why do you think the attraction is so strong?''

''Chemistry.''

''No, it's love.''

He ran his hands along the inside of her thighs. ''Sex.''

She licked his ear. ''Love.''

He groaned and spread his fingers. ''Mutual enjoyment.''

She trailed her palm down his chest. There was no point arguing. She was simply going to have to show him.

A dull, gray dawn was gathering in the sky to the east as Flynn guided the bike along the lane to the warehouse. Abbie tasted moisture in the air and glanced at the low-hanging clouds. A storm front was moving in. It would rain soon, but there was nothing she could do about the weather. There weren't many things in life one could truly control.

Flynn coasted to a stop near the junkyard fence and let the engine idle. He pulled off his helmet and twisted partway around on the seat to look at her. Morning stubble darkened his jaw. His hair was a tousled mass of black curls. He looked tough and adorable at the same time.

Abbie took off her helmet and reached out to smooth his hair. "Thanks for keeping it under sixty on the ride back."

"There was no point hurrying." He caught her hand and placed a kiss in her palm. "They're going to know why we took so long, Abbie."

She glanced at the closed doors of the warehouse. She knew their arrival was being monitored by the soldier on guard duty. "Yes, I realize that."

"They're a decent bunch of guys so I'm not expecting any trouble, but if they treat you with anything other than respect—"

"Flynn, it doesn't matter."

"It does to me."

She put her hand on his thigh. "They have more important things to concern themselves with than our love life. They're probably planning the raid on the LLA's base."

The edge of his jaw sharpened as he clenched his teeth. "I don't want you to carry the ransom, Abbie."

"We've been through this already. I'll do whatever I can."

"Not after last night."

A drop of rain fell on the back of her hand. More sprinkled the pavement around them. "Why? Because we made love? That didn't seem to change anything as far as you're concerned."

He didn't reply.

"Well, did it?"

"I don't want to see you get hurt, Abbie."

Too late, she thought. She'd been destined to get hurt from the moment she'd seen him on her doorstep. She had new sympathy for moths. "It's a risk I'm willing to take. I've learned a lot about courage in the past few days."

He flinched. He had to know they were talking about more than just the mission. "Abbie…"

"It's raining. We should go inside."

He turned up his collar. "I should apologize, but I can't. I'm not sorry about spending the night in your bed. What happened between us was special, Abbie. I'll never forget it."

Oh, God. Why did this sound like a goodbye? "Yes, it was special, Flynn. Because it was love."

The rain grew heavier. He didn't argue. They'd been through this already, and she hadn't been able to change his mind. He grasped her chin. In full view of whoever was guarding the warehouse door, he tilted her face to his and held her steady as he sealed his mouth over hers.

The kiss didn't feel like a goodbye. It was as sweet as a promise. And as fragile as hope. Abbie didn't hold back. She poured out everything she felt, using her lips the way she had used her body the night before.

Yes, she had learned about courage in the past few days. But she'd also learned about fear. What if her love wasn't enough to draw Flynn out from the barriers around his heart? What if he was right, if they were too different to have a future together? The mission would be over by Friday. Did she really think she could change his mind by then?

She was grateful for the rain. She wouldn't need to explain why her cheeks were wet when Flynn put the bike back in gear and drove inside the warehouse.

Abbie sensed the tension in the air the moment they entered the tent. At first she thought it was directed at her and Flynn, but then she saw Major Redinger standing by the communications table with a telephone pressed to his ear. Sarah stood beside him, her expression somber, while several men halted what they were doing in order to listen.

Abbie followed Flynn across the floor until they could hear the major's words.

"Yes, sir," he said. "We are working on contingency plans in any case."

Who was he talking to? Had the latest demand from the LLA already come in? Abbie wondered, peeling off her wet jacket. Someone would have called them, wouldn't they? She glanced at Flynn, but she could tell nothing from his expression. He was back in his soldier mode.

Well, what had she expected? These people were his family, the army was the only real home he'd ever known. He'd carved a life for himself with them. She was the outsider here.

"I understand, Mr. President. Thank you for your confidence. Please be assured we will do our best."

Abbie's hands tightened on her jacket. Water squeezed between her fingers to drip on the floor. She jerked her gaze back to the major. *Mr. President?*

Redinger caught sight of Flynn and Abbie as he ended the call. He motioned to Sarah to accompany him and walked over to intercept them. "I have just learned that King Kristof wishes to postpone the signing of the pact between Ladavia and the United States until his niece's son is found." His gaze moved to Abbie. "The stakes are going up. I hope we can still count on your cooperation, Miss Locke."

She brushed her wet hair from her face. "Of course."

"You were gone a considerable amount of time. Did you have any problems reassuring your family about your continued absence?"

"No."

"Good. The next twenty-four hours will be crucial. We

can't afford any leaks." He turned to Flynn. "You're relieved of your current duty, Sergeant. Captain Fox will see to Miss Locke's welfare from this point onward. Get yourself cleaned up and report to Chief Warrant Officer Esposito. He'll be leading the raid on the base."

"Sir?"

Redinger's gaze firmed to steel. "Dismissed."

Flynn hesitated. He looked at Abbie.

"You were warned once, O'Toole," the major said.

He saluted stiffly and moved off.

Abbie watched him go. He hadn't looked surprised by the major's orders. Had he expected this? She wanted to call him back. It was happening too fast.

But this wasn't about her or about him. It was about a terrorist kidnapping that was escalating into an international crisis. While she had been outside in the rain kissing Flynn, the major had been talking to the *president*. What were one woman's feelings compared to that? The last lingering traces of warmth from her night with Flynn dissolved. She shivered.

Sarah took Abbie's arm and steered her toward the cubicle they shared. "You need to warm up and change into something dry. You're dripping all over the floor."

"No, I'm fine," she said, watching Flynn over her shoulder.

"Let him go, Abbie. I thought you were smarter than that."

She looked at Sarah. "I don't know what you mean."

Sarah ducked through the canvas flap to their cubicle. She returned with a towel and Abbie's peach-colored jogging suit, then led her to the warehouse shower room and rapped on the door. When there was no reply, she flipped the sign on the doorknob and ushered Abbie inside. As soon as the door closed behind them, she turned to face her. "You slept with him, didn't you?"

There was no point pretending innocence. As Flynn had said, everyone knew why they were so late. He'd been concerned that the men might say something. Instead it was the team's lone woman. Abbie hung her wet jacket from a hook on the wall and met Sarah's gaze. "Yes, I did."

"Well, at least you held out longer than most. You can take credit for that much." She handed Abbie the towel and placed her clothes on the bench beside the wall. "You're not his usual type, you know."

"I'm aware of that."

"And it doesn't bother you?"

"No. I think Flynn has done exactly what I've been doing."

"And what's that?"

"We both tried to stick to the type of people who had no chance of reaching our hearts."

Sarah sighed. "Flynn isn't interested in your heart, Abbie. I can understand how he'd wear you down, though. As far as eye candy goes, he's in a class by himself, but—"

"Is that all you think he is? Eye candy?" Abbie yanked off her wet sweater, draped it over the bench and used the towel to dry her hair. "That's not how I see him. He uses his looks as a shield. He doesn't want anyone to get close to him."

"Not to hear him tell it. He's not exactly a monk."

Abbie pulled off her pants, shook the water from them and draped them over the bench with her sweater. "I'm not talking about sex." She sat down to dry her legs. "I'm talking about real closeness."

"And why would he be afraid of that?"

Abbie finished wiping the moisture from her skin and pulled on her jogging suit. "We all have our own reasons.

Considering his childhood, Flynn's are more valid than most.''

Sarah sat on the other end of the bench. "He told you his reasons?''

At the note of disbelief in Sarah's voice, Abbie looked up. "Yes.''

"I can't believe it. Flynn's a clam when it comes to talking about himself. What did he tell you?''

"Why are you asking me all these questions?''

"I'm an intelligence officer. That's what I do.''

"No offense, Sarah, but I don't think this is any of your business.''

"No offense taken, Abbie, but I have to disagree. The men of Eagle Squadron are my business. They're my brothers. I look out for every one of them.''

Abbie could understand that Sarah's inquisitiveness stemmed from concern not idle curiosity, but she wasn't going to discuss the confidences Flynn had shared. "He considers all of you his family.''

"We are.''

"And do you think that's enough?''

"What do you mean?''

"You're all so good at keeping your objectivity and maintaining your distance while you're on a mission, don't you worry that you won't know how to stop?''

"Don't misinterpret our objectivity, Abbie. We need our distance to survive.''

I need my freedom, Abbie. It's how I survive. That's what Flynn had told her. It kept coming back to that. She was going in circles. Frustrated, she returned the towel to her hair and rubbed more briskly than she needed to. "Maybe I'm just not grasping this. You're human. We all want the same things. Is there something about being a commando that rules out normal relationships?''

"Our profession makes a steady relationship challenging,'' Sarah said slowly. ''But yes, I think most of us do want the same things. We're as human as anyone else.''

''Then why are so few of you married?''

''I can't speak for everyone. In my case, my fiancé died five weeks before our wedding.''

Abbie lowered the towel and looked at Sarah. Too late she remembered that Flynn had mentioned Sarah was still mourning her fiancé. ''I'm sorry. That was insensitive of me.''

''No, it's okay. I've been butting into your love life, it's only fair if you know about mine. Captain Kyle Jackson was the best. I'll never find a man like him again.''

''You must have loved him deeply,'' Abbie said.

''Yes, I did.'' A glimmer of sadness softened her green gaze. ''Love is precious. When it happens, you have to cherish every minute you get.''

Abbie thought about something else Flynn had said. ''All we can be sure of is the moment.''

Sarah nodded and regarded her carefully. ''I might have come down too hard on you, Abbie. It's because I care about Flynn. He's a fine soldier, and I don't want to see him neglect his duty because of you. Major Redinger doesn't often give second chances.''

''Flynn never forgot his duty. We kept his phone within reach all night, even when we, uh, used the shower.''

Sarah's lips twitched. ''Although I'm an intelligence officer, Abbie, that might have been more information than I really needed to know.''

''The Washington Monument at midnight?'' Jack shook his head as he poked through the equipment that was arrayed on the table. ''It's as if the LLA are choosing their ransom drops from a tour book.''

''It doesn't make sense,'' Rafe muttered. He picked up his radio headset and adjusted the angle of the microphone.

"After the way the other two drops went wrong, you'd think the LLA would change their pattern. Sure, there will be fewer bystanders around at night, but it's still a high-profile location. It's as if the LLA *want* to have this go public."

"Maybe they do," Jack said. "They wouldn't have expected Vilyas to contact us. They might have been counting on the story getting out to the media. Using our national monuments as their backdrop is their way of thumbing their noses at the diplomats."

Esposito rotated the parabolic microphone on the table in front of him. "You might be right. Terrorism only works if it's given a platform. Without publicity, terrorists are nothing but common criminals. I always thought the money wasn't the only thing the LLA were after. O'Toole, do you have the 2mm Allen key?"

Flynn searched through the tray at his elbow and selected the tool the chief had requested. They had spent the afternoon checking and rechecking every piece of hardware. It was tedious work, but it was vital. When they moved in tonight, they couldn't afford any mistakes. Too much was at stake.

Including Abbie's life.

His hand shook as he passed the tiny Allen key to Esposito. He had to focus. But ever since the details of the third ransom drop had come through at noon, his mind had been seething with worry over Abbie.

There was no point trying to talk her out of it. She was as adamant as ever that she'd play her role. In his head he knew they could protect her—the operation would take place in friendly territory, and police and military backup was only minutes away if it was needed. Whether the choice of location made sense or not, the fact that it was so exposed was in their favor. They could form an airtight perimeter around Abbie. They would be able to see the LLA coming half a mile away.

In the dark? In the rain? Abbie would be up against a group of fanatics who cared nothing for their own lives. His head might accept it, but his heart couldn't.

Damn. This was why it was safer on the outside looking in. He didn't want to be testing microphones and transmitters while the team finalized their plans for tonight's assault. He wanted to scoop Abbie into his arms and take her as far away from this place as he could run. He wanted to hold her and keep her safe until this was over....

And then what?

It kept coming back to that question. He had no answer.

People left. One way or another. Having tasted Abbie's love was going to make it harder, but he knew better than to wish for more, didn't he? He picked up the transmitter he'd just finished checking and got to his feet.

Esposito didn't look up. "Where are you going, O'Toole?"

"I'm taking Abbie her electronics."

"Give them to Captain Fox."

Flynn was losing count of the number of orders he wanted to disobey. He gathered the rest of the equipment Abbie would carry and left before he would need to lie.

He found Sarah and Abbie in the warehouse, sitting in the back of the van Sarah would be using when she took Abbie to the drop. They wouldn't need to use public transit to mask her arrival this time—the darkness would be sufficient. Like Esposito, Sarah appeared to be checking out her surveillance equipment. Through the open rear doors, Flynn could see lights glowing green on the console that was fitted beneath the van's tinted side windows.

Sarah looked up as Flynn approached. "How are the preparations going, Sergeant?" she asked.

"No problem, ma'am." He paused at the open rear door and looked at Abbie.

She was sitting on the bench seat in front of the radio, her knees pulled to her chest, her arms wrapped around her legs. The new larger backpack they'd needed to use in order to fit the money in was on the seat beside her. The bullet-proof vest she would be wearing lay on the floor.

The men of Eagle Squadron were the best there were, Flynn reminded himself. They would protect Abbie with their lives. He had to trust them. He gave Sarah the electronics for Abbie, then clasped his hands behind his back so that neither woman could see how his hands shook. "How are you doing, Abbie?"

Abbie looked at Flynn and knew she couldn't tell the truth. She was a mess. She was terrified. This was the last chance. In a matter of hours everything would be over. Everything. The kidnapping, the mission. Her time with Flynn. "I'm fine," she said.

"You can still back out," he said. "No one would blame you."

Sarah swiveled away from the console. "I already offered to take her place. With the rain and the darkness, the LLA might not be able to tell there was a substitution."

"And I already refused," Abbie said, keeping her gaze on Flynn. "I'm going to see this through to the end."

"You know how I feel about that," Flynn said.

"Yes, but I won't be the only one at risk here. You and everyone on the team are going to be in more danger than I am. Not to mention Matteo."

"It's not your fight. This is our job."

She tightened her arms over her legs, hoping he couldn't see her shiver. "This is my choice to make, no one else's. I won't have any regrets."

He continued to study her, his expression stark. "Be careful, okay, Abbie?"

She wanted to scream at him to be careful, too, but she was unsure she could trust her voice. Like the rest of the men who would be assaulting the LLA base, Flynn was dressed in a black jumpsuit and rubber-soled boots. The black balaclava that lay in folds around his neck would be pulled up to conceal his face when he went into action. There was no longer any need for the team to disguise themselves as civilians—when they moved on the LLA this time, they wanted the terrorists to know whom they were dealing with.

The uniforms made everything too real, like the sub-machine guns, the pistols and the magazines of ammunition the men had been gathering. There were other things, too. Sarah had explained them to her. Concussion grenades, rappelling ropes, grappling hooks, gas canisters. All the tools of a lethal trade. Abbie couldn't hide the shiver that shook her this time.

Flynn muttered an oath and grabbed the van door. "Captain, would you mind if I had a few moments alone with Miss Locke before you move out?"

Sarah lifted an eyebrow. "I don't think the major would approve."

"That's why I'm asking you, Sarah."

She looked at Abbie. "Is that what you want?"

Abbie bit her lip and nodded.

"I need to pick up my parabolic mike from the chief, anyway." Sarah walked to the back of the van and hopped to the floor. "I'll be back in five minutes, no more."

Flynn barely waited for Sarah to clear the doors before he stepped inside and closed them. He stared at Abbie, his throat working. Then without a word he pulled her off the seat and into his arms.

She wrapped herself around him as he sank to the floor of the van. With her legs hooked around his hips and her hands splayed on his back, she got as close as their clothes would allow. She kissed his neck, his jaw, the dimple in his chin until he fisted his hands in her hair and slanted his mouth over hers.

His kiss wasn't like any of the others he'd given her. It was the kiss of a warrior on the brink of battle. Bold, possessive and forceful enough to steal her breath. He used his tongue and his teeth, channeling the tension that hardened his muscles into passion.

Abbie drank it in greedily. She loved him, and so she loved this side of him, too. He was trained in the use of deadly force, yet he was a soldier who wished for peace as he aimed his gun.

But time had been their real enemy from the start. There was nothing either of them could do to fight it. All too soon Sarah's footsteps sounded outside the van. Flynn broke off the kiss and leaned his forehead against Abbie's.

Neither of them spoke. There wasn't anything left to say. This time it really did feel like goodbye.

Chapter 14

It was all or nothing. They would get one shot at this, so there was no room for error. Flynn slung his gun over his shoulder and fitted his night-vision goggles in place. The helicopter dipped as the pilot fought a sudden downdraft. Flynn slid to the open doorway, grabbed a support bar and swung his feet to the landing strut. The other men did the same, positioning themselves three on each side of the chopper. Lightning flashed, illuminating the rooftop of the Baltimore butcher shop that was surging upward to meet them.

"Group one in position." It was Esposito's voice, coming through the radio. He was leading the squad that had surrounded the LLA base and would cut off escape on the ground. "Group two, what's your ETA?"

"Ten seconds," Rafe replied.

The helicopter pulled up in a stomach-wrenching turn and hovered a yard above the rooftop. As one, the men leaped from the landing struts to the roof and linked their arms in a circle to fight the backwash from the rotors. The chopper sprang upward, the noise of its engine blending with a rumble of thunder as it disappeared into the rain.

The storm had made for a bumpy ride, but it had hidden their arrival. Few people would be on the street in weather like this. Just in case, Redinger had asked the Pentagon brass to inform the local authorities there would be an army training op in the area. If some concerned citizen did spot them and called the cops, there probably wouldn't be any trouble.

Probably. That wasn't good enough. Damn, that just wasn't good enough.

Rafe thumped his shoulder and made a quick hand signal to indicate he should move into position.

Flynn took the rope from his belt and jogged to the edge of the roof. All around him the other men were shadows against shadows etched in night-vision green. Less than half a minute later the team was in place and ready to move. Flynn checked his watch. Two minutes to midnight.

"What's happening at the drop, Major?" Esposito asked.

Redinger's voice was tight. "Miss Locke is closing in on the monument. Just starting up the rise."

Flynn secured one end of the rope to the base of a ventilation shaft and pulled on his gloves. He shouldn't be here. He should be with Abbie. And he would have been, if he'd done what Redinger had trusted him to do and kept his distance.

From a strategic standpoint, the major had made the right decision by assigning Flynn to the assault group. If Flynn had been anywhere near Abbie right now, he would have gotten her out of there even if it meant he would have to throw her over his shoulder kicking and screaming, just as he'd done a week ago. But that would have jeopardized the mission and his teammates' lives. Success depended on secrecy and split-second timing.

"Watch her, sir," Flynn said.

"She is in full view of my position," the major replied.

"She feels very strongly about doing the drop right," Flynn said. "She may disobey instructions and put herself at risk."

"I'll be picking her up as soon as the pack drops, Sergeant." It was Sarah's voice. "I'll give the signal the instant she's in the van."

Flynn looped the rope behind his back, lay on his belly at the edge of the roof and inched his way over the lip. Lightning flickered over the window he would crash through when the raid commenced. They would hit hard and fast. He readied his gun, but he knew the element of surprise was their best weapon. "Please, Abbie," he breathed. "Keep safe."

Silence hummed in his ear.

"She's not patched in to this frequency, Flynn," Sarah said. "But I'm sure she sends you the same sentiment."

Despite the men from Eagle Squadron who circled the area, Abbie had never felt more alone in her life. Sheets of rain were obscuring the sidewalk under her feet. Trees flickered ghostly white at the base of the rise in each flash of lightning. The floodlit granite column of the Washington Monument soared into the gloom in front of her, wavering like a mirage.

The receiver in her ear clicked. "Almost there, Abbie," Sarah said. "You're doing fine."

That was why she felt alone, Abbie thought. The team had divided. She couldn't hear Flynn. For almost a week she hadn't been apart from him for more than a few minutes. She needed him. She loved him. She couldn't imagine a future without him. And in two minutes her place in his life would be over.

"Abbie?"

She held the umbrella handle to her chest, fighting to keep it pointed against the wind. "Okay."

"You're in position," Major Redinger said. "Drop the pack."

She shifted the umbrella from one hand to the other as she shrugged the straps of the backpack over her shoulders. It fell to the ground with a splash. She stopped to look at it. "There's a puddle here. The money will get wet."

"It will dry," the major said. "Turn and retrace your steps."

She glanced around. Apart from the swaying trees, nothing was moving. Under other circumstances she might have been nervous about being out here on her own at this hour, but the storm was keeping even the muggers indoors. What about the LLA? Where were they? What if there was some bystander near here, after all, and they picked up this pack before the LLA could reach it?

"Miss Locke!"

The major's voice was more like a bark. Abbie jumped and started walking.

Headlights winked on. "I'm driving along the pedestrian walkway to meet you, Abbie," Sarah said. "You should see my lights on your right."

"Yes, I see you. Are the LLA coming yet?"

"That doesn't concern you, Abbie," the major said. "Just keep moving."

It could have been because she was wet and scared and alone, or it could have been because the major was the one who had sent Flynn away. Whatever the reason, she felt her temper stir. "I don't want to leave it to chance this time. If you don't answer, I'll go back and see for myself that they get the money, *sir*."

There was a brief silence. When Redinger's voice came through her ear piece, it could have cut glass. "A black sedan has crashed through the barriers at the parking area and is cutting across the Mall to your left at approximately thirty miles an hour. The LLA don't appear to be leaving it to chance this time, either. Now I suggest you pick up your pace so we can get on with our job."

She glanced to her left. She hadn't heard anything because of the storm, but she could see headlights tunneling through the rain and the bushes on the far side of the Reflecting Pool. She tossed her umbrella aside and sprinted for Sarah's van.

Sarah flung open the passenger door. The instant Abbie climbed inside, Sarah reached behind her to flip a toggle on her radio equipment. "I have her," she announced. She spun the wheel and headed away from the monument. "Green light. The raid is a go."

Abbie crawled between the seats to sit at the console behind Sarah. "What button do I push?" she asked. "I want to hear everything."

Sarah slowed as she reached the cover of some trees. She engaged the brake and let the engine idle as she turned back to the communication console. "The frequency is already set. All you need to do is switch it to the speaker." She pointed. "That's the square button on the lower right."

Voices flooded the van. Abbie struggled to take in the terse reports. The other teams moved in on their targets. They met no resistance as they hit the three rooming houses. The base was different. Esposito reported gunfire. The team's weapons were fitted with sound suppressors— any gunfire would have to be from the LLA.

"The ransom has been picked up," the major said. "Keep your distance, people, until we can determine the location of the hostage."

Abbie moved to the rear of the van. Through the rain-streaked window in the door she could see twin spots of light at the base of the monument. A black sedan was parked where she'd dropped the backpack.

Rafe's voice suddenly came through the speaker. "Operation successful. Base is secured."

"Any casualties?" the major asked.

"Negative. We found their files. Stand by."

Abbie knelt on the floor and dropped her forehead against the back door, whispering a prayer of thanks. No casualties. Flynn was unhurt. The men were going through the LLA files. They would find Matteo. Thank God, thank God.

"The water must have shorted the electronics in the pack," Sarah said. "We're not getting any audio." She turned the van around. "I need to get the directional mike on that car and hear what's going on. I wouldn't have expected the LLA to remain here once they had the money."

Abbie returned to the front of the van and slid into the passenger seat. She braced her hands on the dashboard, peering through the windshield as Sarah nosed the vehicle forward. The black sedan hadn't moved.

"I found what looks like a press release," Rafe said. "It's in English, spouting off a bunch of anticapitalist rhetoric. Sir, this doesn't make sense."

"Report, Sergeant," Redinger said.

"The LLA are claiming responsibility for the murder of Matteo Vilyas at the Air and Space Museum."

"Say again."

Rafe repeated his statement and added, "It's dated last Thursday."

"Here's another one." It was Flynn's voice this time. "Dated Sunday. Claiming responsibility for the Vilyas boy's death at the Lincoln Memorial."

Abbie was so relieved to hear Flynn's voice, it took her a moment to grasp what he was saying. The LLA had prepared press releases. They had planned to kill Matteo in public at the site of the ransom drops. On Thursday. And again on Sunday.

Why hadn't they done it?

Why? Because she had messed up the drop both times.

"Oh, my God," she whispered, her heart tightening. She focused on the lights from the black car. It still wasn't moving. This time the ransom had been delivered successfully. She hadn't messed it up. That meant this time...

"Oh, my God! Matti has to be here. He's *here!* And they're going to kill him!"

"Call down the chopper!" Flynn said. "We'll meet it on the roof."

"All units, move in!" the major ordered. "Contain the black sedan."

Sarah slammed the van into gear, carving grooves in the grass as she steered back toward the glowing obelisk. She pulled a pistol from her waistband and lowered her window. "Abbie, get down on the floor!"

Abbie stayed where she was, her fingers cramping on the dashboard. The parabolic microphone Sarah had placed beside her was picking up voices. Foreign voices. Men's voices. But in the background, as faint as the whisper of the constellations behind the clouds, she heard a child's sob.

"I can confirm the hostage is in the sedan," Sarah shouted. "Hold your fire!"

"Shoot to disable the vehicle," the major countered. "Do not permit them to escape."

The monument loomed closer. The headlights of the black car glowed through the rain. More headlights appeared, converging on the rise from all directions. The view kept appearing and disappearing as the wipers cleared the windshield. One second the car was there, the next it was gone.

"The LLA are on the move," Redinger said. "They're heading straight for you, Captain."

Approaching lights speared through the van's windshield, turning it to molten white. There was a sharp crack. Sarah cried out and the van swerved. The white became a web of crystal shards.

"Captain Fox?" Redinger called.

"I've been hit, sir."

The scene became another one of those slow-motion nightmares. Abbie looked at the cracked windshield, then at the hole in Sarah's jacket. It was a bullet hole. Sarah had been shot. And if the LLA got past them, they were going to escape with Matteo.

Abbie didn't have time for the terror that screamed inside her. She crawled over Sarah, grabbed the wheel and jammed the accelerator to the floor. She might not know how to fire a gun, but she knew how to drive.

She aimed at the black sedan. The van flew over a bump, hit the ground hard and skidded sideways directly into the path of the oncoming vehicle.

The impact spun the van around and knocked the doors open, propelling Abbie through the air. She curled herself into a ball, skidding across the wet grass as she landed. Pain knifed through her wrist. She lifted her head.

And stared straight into the barrel of a gun.

"What the hell is going on down there?" Flynn yelled. "Goddamn it! Where the hell is she?"

"Miss Locke is in the black sedan with the LLA," Redinger said. He made no mention of Flynn's profanity. He was wise enough to know when a man had been pushed to his limit. "It was disabled by the crash. It can't move."

"She was supposed to be safe. Minimal risk. Easy walk, in and out. How could this happen?"

"There will be plenty of time to sort it out at the debriefing," the major said. "I'd prefer to concentrate on the situation at hand."

Flynn slammed a fresh magazine into his gun and turned to the pilot. "Open the throttle, man. I know a schoolteacher and her mother who can go faster than this."

The pilot ignored him. He needed all his attention in order to keep the helicopter airborne in the raging storm.

Rafe closed his hand over Flynn's arm. "We'll get there, buddy."

"Yeah? When? You saw that last press release. Those bastards plan to kill their hostage and blow up the money. Esposito was right. They'd wanted a public platform. We've got to get there before the media does. Once the LLA have witnesses, they'll follow through with their plan. And Abbie's smack in the middle—" He had to stop. One more word and he knew his voice would break.

He couldn't lose her.

But he'd been ready to walk away.

Damn, he'd done a lousy job of fooling himself. He wouldn't have let her go. After the mission he would have found some way to see her again. He might not put the same labels on what was between them as Abbie did, but whatever it was, he wasn't ready to give it up. He looked at Rafe. "It can't be too late."

"It isn't."

"You warned me. I didn't listen."

Rafe squeezed firmly and released Flynn's arm. "Think about it later. We're coming up on the Mall."

Flynn grabbed a rope and positioned himself near the helicopter door. The other men did the same, three on each side, just like before.

No, damn it. It wasn't like before. This wasn't simply

a mission. There was no distance here. It wasn't only a
hostage rescue. It was *Abbie's life*.

Flynn focused on the huge granite column that glowed
through the rain, then scanned the grounds near the Reflecting Pool. The team's chase vehicles formed a ring on
the lawn, their headlights pointing inward. In the circle of
light Sarah's gray van was lying on its side, its rear side
panels crushed inward. Sarah had radioed from inside the
van that her condition wasn't critical, but she was pinned
down and was unable to help. Several yards away sat a
black sedan. White smoke curled from the edges of its
crumpled hood and was swallowed by the rain.

The helicopter hovered above the sedan. Flynn grasped
the rope in his left hand and his gun in his right. The men
didn't waste time with discussion. This is what they were
trained for. They all knew what to do.

As if materializing from the storm, six black-clad commandos slid down their ropes and descended on the car.
Flynn landed beside the driver's door. With split-second
reflexes that had been honed by years of daily practice, he
sighted his target through the car window and squeezed
off two shots. Double tap. Disable and kill. Glass shattered
as his teammates did the same.

It was over in a heartbeat. As he'd told Vilyas, Delta
Force didn't give any warnings.

And they never missed. There was no movement inside
the vehicle. No sound. Nothing.

The helicopter floodlight switched on. Flynn dropped his
gun and wrenched open the rear door of the car. Abbie
was curled in the middle of the back seat, her head down,
her arms wrapped around her legs. She'd sat like that before when she was upset. But this time she wasn't on a
crate or a cot. She was spattered with blood and wedged
between two dead men.

The cry that came from Flynn's throat was as savage as

the thunder that crashed around him. He flung the first body out of the car and reached to pull Abbie into his arms.

She struggled, lashing out at him with her elbow, refusing to uncurl from her crouch.

The blood wasn't hers, he realized as he ran his hands over her. Thank God. He could breathe again. "Abbie, you're safe," he said. "Abbie, it's okay. Let go."

She lifted her head. Shards of glass winked from her hair. Her eyes were wild. "Flynn?"

He tore off his helmet and his balaclava. "It's over, darling. You're okay."

She focused suddenly. "Flynn! You're here. What—" She whimpered as she watched Rafe and Jack remove the other bodies from the car. "It's over?"

"Yes. Come out of there, Abbie."

"Where's the hostage?" Redinger called, running toward them.

"I'll check the trunk," Rafe said.

Abbie shook her head and straightened up.

A small blond boy was huddled on the car floor between her knees. He was unscathed. No blood, no glass. Abbie had been sheltering him with her own body.

Matteo Vilyas looked thinner than he had in his photograph. His hair stuck up in ragged chunks. A bruise darkened the skin on his cheek. The gaze he turned toward Flynn was too old for his years. It was the gaze of a child who had seen what no child should, a boy who had discovered too soon that the world was full of cruelty and sorrow and death.

Flynn knew that look. He'd seen it in the mirror.

Abbie turned Matteo's face to her chest, put her arms around him and rocked him in an age-old rhythm of healing. Her faith in the power of love shone from her soul.

Flynn knew that look, too.

He'd seen it in his dreams.

Major Redinger drove with the same methodical competence with which he commanded his men. He didn't speed, yet he didn't hesitate. With Rafe riding shotgun in the passenger seat and a helicopter full of armed soldiers providing cover overhead, he steered the armored Tahoe through the rain-slick streets on the most direct route to the Ladavian Embassy.

From the back seat Abbie watched the buildings slide past with a sense of inevitability. "Only a few more minutes," she said, stroking Matteo's hair. She adjusted the gray blanket they'd wrapped him in. "We're almost there."

The boy burrowed his head against her shoulder. He hadn't said a word since Flynn had carried him from the gore-spattered car.

Abbie looked at Flynn. He was sitting on the other side of Matteo. He hadn't left them for an instant. While the rest of the men had cleared away the bodies, the wrecked vehicles and the shell casings, working quickly to remove any trace of their "training op" from the grounds near the monument, he had remained with her and the child.

If she'd had the chance to think, she probably would have fallen apart. But there hadn't been time. The nightmare of terror and bullets had blended into a fast-forward blur as Flynn had removed her blood-soaked jacket and had wrapped her in a blanket like Matteo's. His hands had been as gentle as a whisper as he'd cleaned the blood from her skin and removed the glass from her hair. His voice had pulled her back again and again from the brink of collapse. The tenderness in his gaze was her anchor to reality.

"How's your wrist feeling now?" he asked softly.

She glanced at the elastic bandage Jack had wrapped

from her knuckles to her forearm. She'd been lucky the ground had been softened by the rain where she'd landed. The joint was sprained, not broken. "It's fine."

Sarah hadn't been so fortunate. Although the bullet that hit her had been stopped by her vest, the force of the high-caliber round had dislocated her shoulder.

The surviving LLA terrorists who had been swept up in the team's raid had been handed over to the regular army. They would be held incommunicado until King Kristof and the diplomats decided their fate. The documents the team had recovered from the LLA base would be analyzed by Intelligence before being turned over to the Ladavians.

The terrorist sympathizer within the embassy who had facilitated the kidnapping by giving the LLA details of the Vilyas family's schedule had turned out to be one of the embassy's chauffeurs. In his case, justice would be swift— he'd had the misfortune of being on Ladavian soil when the Royal Guard had caught up with him minutes ago.

Against all odds, Eagle Squadron's mission was a complete success. Only one final detail remained. They had to return Matteo Vilyas to his family.

Abbie laid her cheek against the top of Matteo's head. Jack had examined the boy before they had left the Mall and had determined he had no physical injuries that needed immediate medical attention, so there was no reason to delay his return. No physical injuries. What about the emotional scars? Was there any medical treatment for those?

The major slowed the SUV. Wrought-iron gates decorated with a crest of a falcon appeared through the rain. Guards with rifles slung over their rain ponchos surrounded the vehicle and jogged alongside as they drove into the cobblestone courtyard. They passed the embassy's main entrance and came to a stop beside a door in the side of the building.

"Look, Matti," Abbie said. "You're home."

The child shivered and refused to look up.

She rubbed his back. "It's okay. No one's going to hurt you again."

Flynn touched her hand as he gathered the child into his arms. "You'll be fine, Matteo," he murmured. "Come on, we're going to take a little walk."

Kate exited the Tahoe first and positioned himself beside the front fender, his gun held ready as he scanned the area. The Royal Guard formed into two lines to flank the path from the vehicle to the embassy. Abbie swung open her door and got out while Flynn slid across the seat with Matteo. With Major Redinger leading the way, Flynn hunched his shoulders to protect the child from the rain and strode forward.

Before he'd gone three steps the embassy door crashed open. Neda ran toward them, her arms outstretched. "Matti!"

Anton was right behind her. When he caught sight of his son, he forgot his dignity and his diplomatic training and whooped.

Flynn was engulfed in the Vilyases' embrace. Abbie knew the image would stay with her forever. Less than an hour ago this tall, black-clad warrior had swooped down from the sky with his gun blazing to rescue her from certain death. Now he stood in the rain with a child in his arms and grinned.

He *grinned.* Oh, God. How was it possible to love him more?

At the sound of his parents' voices, Matteo's face crumpled. He launched himself into his father's arms and started to wail. He was still crying when they reached the ambassador's quarters, but the sobs were punctuated by words. English mixed with Ladavian as the horror he'd endured finally came pouring out.

The formal sitting room with its chairs upholstered in

Ladavian blue and its dark wood carving and silver samovar rang with the sounds of emotion that needed no translation. Matteo might be fourth in line for the Ladavian throne, the pawn in a terrorist plot, the focus of a secret mission and an international crisis…but at this moment he was merely a little boy.

Abbie used the corner of her blanket to dry her eyes. She stood by the door with Flynn and the major, unwilling to intrude on the family reunion but somehow unable to move away.

Flynn slipped his arm around her shoulders. "Matteo's going to heal."

"God, I hope so, Flynn."

"We've got specialists who are trained to deal with this kind of trauma," Major Redinger said. "One of the top child psychologists in the country is on her way here."

"I'm glad." She looked at Matteo's ragged hair. "He's been through so much."

"He's already getting the best therapy there is," Flynn said, nodding toward the family group. A sleep-rumpled Sacha had just joined them and was holding on tightly to his big brother's hand. "His family loves him. That will get him through anything."

She turned her gaze to Flynn. She understood how seeing the Vilyases' emotion must stir painful memories of his own childhood. The pain was still there—she could see it in the lines around his mouth. Was it her imagination, or did something other than pain gleam in his eyes?

Neda approached them, her smile radiant, as if she didn't notice the men were still wearing their assault gear and Abbie was cloaked in a blanket. "How can I thank you enough for what you did, Abbie?" she asked. "You saved my Matti's life."

"The team saved him, Neda," Abbie said. "I was never really alone."

"Yes, they are all brave men. And you are a brave woman." She kissed Abbie on both cheeks. "I will be forever in your debt, Abigail Locke. If we were not constrained by the need for secrecy, we would honor you and the team publicly in the manner you deserve."

"Seeing Matteo reunited with the people who love him is all the reward I need," Abbie said.

Neda stretched to kiss Flynn and then the major. "My uncle sends his regards. He also is in your debt."

Redinger's face softened in a rare smile. "I'm sure our president will think of some way your uncle can repay us once the treaty between our countries is ratified."

Neda laughed. "Yes, I am certain he will."

"But we'll leave that to the diplomats," Redinger said. He dipped his head in a formal bow. "The Royal Guard will see to your safety now. On behalf of our government, I wish you and your family well, Princess Neda."

And just like that it was over. The mission. Abbie's reason for being here. Everything.

Flynn took her arm. "It's time to go home, Abbie."

Chapter 15

Abbie felt the last of her strength dissolve the moment she took out her keys. It was such an ordinary thing, taking out a set of keys. She had done it countless times, and could probably do it blindfolded. But as she rubbed her thumb over the beaded key ring her nephew Josh had made her at camp last summer and heard the familiar, homey clink of brass against brass, reality finally hit. And her hand shook too violently to fit the key in the keyhole.

"You look ready to crash," Flynn said, taking the keys from her fingers. He opened the door, scooped her into his arms and carried her inside.

She wanted to cling to him, but she shouldn't. "I'll be fine, Flynn. The major and Rafe are waiting for you downstairs."

He kicked the door shut with his heel. "I told them not to. They went back to the command center without me."

"Why?"

"Matteo has his family to talk to, but you can't tell

yours what happened. Rafe and the major agreed that you shouldn't be alone right now.'' He didn't put her on her feet. He took the blanket from her shoulders and tossed it aside as he carried her straight through to her bedroom.

The bed wasn't made. The bedding was still in a tangled heap the way it had been left yesterday. He laid her in the center of the mattress and tugged off her shoes. Then he unzipped her pants and started to tug them off, too.

She put her hand on his arm. ''Flynn…''

''Don't worry, Abbie. I know you're tired. You've been running on fumes for the past hour. I want to take off your pants because there are bloodstains on them.''

She had almost forgotten. She didn't look. She lifted her hips to help.

He pulled up the sheet and tucked it around her. ''Do you need to use the bathroom?''

She shook her head.

''Okay.'' He withdrew several ammunition clips from the pockets of his jumpsuit, dropped them on the floor and sat on the edge of the bed to discard his boots.

''What are you doing?'' she asked.

''All I want to do is hold you, Abbie.'' He stretched out on top of the covers beside her and opened his arms. ''Please, let me stay with you until you fall asleep.''

The longing in his gaze was her undoing. She'd been wrong. She could love him more. With a grateful sigh she moved into his embrace and put her head on his chest.

His arms settled around her back. He exhaled slowly. ''Damn, that feels good.''

She listened to his heartbeat, soaking in his strength and his familiar scent. She felt drained, completely boneless. Every overloaded nerve in her body was crying for rest. But she needed Flynn more than she needed sleep.

And she needed to talk. The horror had to come out.

Now that she was safe in Flynn's embrace, she could let it go. "Part of me can't believe this was all real."

"It will fade after a while." His voice was a soothing rumble under her ear.

"The Vilyases thought I was brave. I wasn't. I was terrified."

"You did well. By ramming that car, you saved Matteo's life."

"There was nothing else I could do after they shot Sarah. They were going to kill an innocent child."

"Yes."

"Why? How can people do things like that?"

He stroked her hair. "They didn't see him as a person. All they could see was their political agenda."

"They wouldn't have surrendered."

"No. That's why we had to shoot them."

Red light flashed behind her eyes, an image from the nightmare. Pencil-thin beams from laser sights piercing the car windows. Explosions of glass. The air filled with hot wet splatters. Her breath hitched.

"It's all right, Abbie," Flynn said. "It's over now."

She remembered the sudden silence. The smell of blood and death. Limp weight pinning her in her crouch. *Dead* weight. Oh, God.

"Abbie, it's over," he repeated firmly. "You're safe."

She exhaled hard and focused on Flynn's strong heartbeat. The nightmare faded. "I wish I could forget," she said.

He continued to run his hand over her hair. Long, calming strokes, the warmth of his touch drawing her back from the memories. "We have people who can help you deal with this. After a mission, a lot of men need support. I can call someone."

"No, Flynn. I didn't go through the kind of trauma Matteo did. I don't need a psychiatrist. I just need…this. I need you to hold me.''

"You got it. As long as you want."

She knew he didn't mean that. He would have to get back to the command center eventually. Until he did, though, she was going to treasure every minute.

He'd tried to warn her. So had Sarah. His world really was too different from hers. How could she ask him to open his heart? Now that she'd experienced what he had to deal with, she understood why he would need his distance to survive. If she really loved him, she would want what was best for him, wouldn't she?

But she wasn't some heroic commando, she was just an ordinary woman in love. She still wasn't ready to let him go. She curled her arm around his waist. "What time is it?"

He twisted his wrist to look at his watch, then slipped the watch off and laid it on the bedside table. "Just after three."

"Is that all? Are you sure?"

"Seems longer, doesn't it?"

"The past week seems like a lifetime."

"Time takes on a different quality during a mission. Speeds up and slows down whether you want it to or not." He spread his fingers over her back. "It felt as if the chopper took years to get to you."

"I knew you would come, Flynn."

His chest moved as he swallowed hard. "I shouldn't have left you, Abbie. I shouldn't have let them put you in danger."

She could feel the tension gathering in his body. His muscles quivered. He was squeezing her to him so tightly it was verging on painful. She lifted her head to look at him. "It was nobody's fault. Life doesn't always go according to plan. You've shown me that. There aren't any guarantees, even in my safe, ordinary, normal world. I could get hit by a truck when I cross the street on my way to the library next week.''

He cupped her head in his hands, his gaze suddenly fierce. ''Don't say that.''

''It's true. I see now that you were right. All we can count on is the moment.''

He looked at her mouth. ''When I heard you had been taken, I wasn't thinking about the moment, Abbie. I was thinking about all the moments yet to come.''

''Flynn, will you kiss me?''

''You need to sleep. I'll hold you, that's all.''

''I can sleep tomorrow.''

''You're exhausted. You've been through hell.''

''Kiss me.'' She stretched on top of him and brought her face closer to his. ''Then I'll be able to go to sleep.''

''Abbie…''

''Don't you want to kiss me?''

He tunneled his fingers into her hair. ''Oh, Abbie. I want to do a lot more than that.''

She rubbed her lips over the cleft in his chin. ''Please, Flynn,'' she whispered. ''I'm afraid of what I'll see if I close my eyes now.''

He hooked his leg over hers and rolled to his side. He started with her forehead, brushing aside her hair to trail tender, featherlight kisses to her temple. He kissed the line of her jaw and the hollow at the base of her throat.

She moved against him, trying to stir the passion that she knew he could give her, hoping that desire would shut down her brain. She reached between them and found him already hard. With the back of her fingers she traced his arousal, welcoming the answering throb that started between her legs.

He slid further down the bed, easing himself out of her grasp. ''Not like this, Abbie.''

She reached for the zipper on the front of his jumpsuit. "Please, Flynn. I want—"

"I know what you want." He caught her hand and brought it to his mouth. He kissed each of her fingers, her palm, her knuckles. He took her other hand and breathed lightly on the bandage that wrapped her wrist, then dipped his tongue in the crease of her elbow. "You've told me exactly what you want."

"What are you talking about?"

He pulled aside the sheet he'd wrapped her in and pressed a lingering kiss to her hip. His cheeks moved in a smile. "When I figure it out, you'll be the first to know."

She gave up talking then. It took too much energy to form a thought. Flynn kissed the curve of her ribs and the underside of her chin. He rubbed his lips over the bruises she'd gotten when she'd been thrown from the van. He sifted his fingers through her hair as tenderly as when he'd removed the shards of glass. Then he stripped off his clothes and used the heat of his body to caress her from her toes to her neck.

He didn't touch her breasts. He didn't kiss her mouth. He kept his hands away from her thighs, yet by the time he pulled her on top of him, she was trembling with the need to join her body to his.

They flowed together between one breath and the next. It was gentle, amazing. Precious. He took her in his arms, shifting his hips in a slow, sure rhythm that bound her to him even while she soared. When she finally closed her eyes, she didn't see blood or death. She saw candles. Tall, thick and glowing with warmth. She held on to Flynn and basked in their heat.

It was almost dawn when Flynn awoke. He was spooned around Abbie's back, his arms crossed over hers, as if even in his sleep he hadn't wanted to let her go.

He should head back to the command center soon. The mission was over. He had a duty to his team.…

But he also had a duty to Abbie. She had been so generous, giving emotional support to everyone else throughout this mission, that he couldn't imagine leaving her until he could be sure she was all right.

He took her good hand and twined their fingers together. Who was he kidding? He couldn't imagine leaving her at all.

The thought should have jarred him, but it didn't. He breathed in the scent of Abbie's hair as he looked around the bedroom. Her bloodstained clothes lay on the floor next to his black assault jumpsuit, her lace underwear draped over his discarded boots.

We've had different lives, but we still want the same things. I can see it in your eyes, Flynn. I feel it in the way you hold me.

That's what Abbie had told him the last time they'd been together on this bed. She'd told him she loved him. What did she feel when he held her now? She hadn't mentioned love at all.

She hadn't needed to. He had seen it in her gaze and felt it in the way she clung to him even in her sleep. He closed his eyes and listened to the sound of her soft, even breathing. The last time they'd been on this bed, he'd been so hot for her he hadn't wanted to waste much time sleeping. The sex had been better than anything he'd experienced before. Yet tonight he would have been content just to hold her.…

His lips quirked. Again, who was he kidding? From the moment he'd pulled her out of that car and into his arms, he'd been pulsing with the need to reaffirm her survival in the most primitive way possible. But she deserved more than battlefield lust and adrenaline. She deserved her dreams.

Something creaked in the living room. Flynn's eyes snapped open. He was instantly on full alert. He focused his senses on the shadowed doorway to the hall. There was no further sound, but a current of air stirred Abbie's hair against his chin.

They weren't alone.

The dead bolt he'd installed last week should have kept out a run-of-the-mill thief. Could the intruder be some left-over LLA dreg who had somehow escaped the sweep?

He assessed his options as he eased out of bed. He had ammo, but he hadn't brought any weapons into Abbie's apartment. It made no difference—if someone tried to harm Abbie, he would kill them with his bare hands. He moved to the bedroom door and listened.

There was a faint thud, followed by a whispered oath.

Flynn padded silently toward the living room. In the predawn glow that filtered through the sliding glass doors to the balcony, he saw two large male figures. He knew who they were—he was well accustomed to recognizing them in the dark. He let his muscles relax and reached for the light.

Rafe was sitting on the arm of the sofa. He had cleaned up and changed from his jumpsuit to army fatigues. "You're slipping, O'Toole. Took you almost five seconds."

Jack stood beside the avocado plant. Like Rafe, he had donned fatigues. He squinted against the light as he brushed leaves from his green camouflage-patterned shirt. More leaves littered the carpet at his feet. "What is this thing, anyway?"

"Abbie's intruder alarm," Flynn muttered. He went back to the bedroom, checked to make sure Abbie still slept, then grabbed his shorts and closed the bedroom door. He pulled them on and returned to the living room. "What the hell are you two doing here?"

Rafe gave him a loose salute. "Taxi service."

"Mother Hen ordered us to pick you up before you annoy the major again," Jack said.

"I thought Sarah was in the hospital," Flynn said.

"She is. She's supposed to be sedated, but these Yankees don't know her. They gave her a phone."

"How's she doing?"

"Her prognosis is excellent if she follows orders and takes things easy." Jack chuckled. "Which is unlikely. Do I need to look in on Abbie?"

"She's sleeping. I want you line up a trauma counselor for her, just in case."

"You got it." Jack glanced toward the bedroom, then looked at Flynn. "She did well. The men all admire her courage."

"So do I."

"Ironic, isn't it?" Jack said. "She saved the Vilyas boy three times. Twice by messing up the drop, the third time by bad driving."

Flynn wasn't sure he'd ever reach the point where he could laugh about it. The memory of what might have happened would haunt him to his last day. He rubbed the back of his neck and looked at Rafe. "Any more news on the LLA?"

"Plenty. Some of the documents we found at the LLA base that were in Ladavian turned out to be future plans. Names, places, dates. The Royal Guard is already moving in to round up the cells in Ladavia."

"That's more than we'd hoped," Flynn said.

"Yeah." Rafe gave him a long look. "Funny what we can find when we aren't even looking, isn't it? Have you thought about it yet?"

"About what?"

"The mission's over." Rafe pointed to the apartment door. A flowered tapestry-patterned suitcase rested on the floor beside the closet. "We packed up Abbie's stuff for her."

"She'll appreciate that."

"We had to pack yours, too," Jack said. "The warehouse is cleared out. The transport's loading to take us back to Bragg."

Flynn had known this was coming. The men would have started disassembling the command center the moment Matteo had been delivered to his parents. The tent, the folding cots, chairs and tables, the weapons and electronic equipment, everything that had comprised their home for the past week would be packed up and loaded into the vehicles that had brought them here. Nothing would remain in the warehouse to mark their presence except some footprints on the floor.

The mission was over. He should be on his way to Bragg with his team, analyzing the details of this mission and anticipating the challenge of the next. It was what he did. It was the only life he knew.

Or it had been, until Abbie had come into it. Flynn walked past Rafe to pick up the phone.

"What are you doing?" Jack asked. "We don't have much time."

"I'm not going with you. I'm calling the major." He punched in the number of Redinger's cell phone. "I need to request an emergency leave so I don't go down as AWOL."

Jack moved quickly to press his finger over the disconnect. "Don't do it, son."

"Keep out of this, Jack."

"Your duty here is done. Abbie's going to be fine. She doesn't need you anymore."

Flynn knocked Jack's hand away from the phone. "Maybe not. But I need her."

Jack stared at him. "You're serious."

"Damn right. I need that woman. I—"

And suddenly it all became perfectly clear. He had the answer to the question that had been circling his mind for days. He smiled.

"I don't like the look of that smile," Jack muttered.

"Yeah, I'd say he thought about it, all right," Rafe said.

Flynn dialed the major's number again. When he heard Redinger's voice, he squared his shoulders, prepared for a fight.

But someone had beat him to it. He listened, stunned, as the major confirmed a short leave had already been approved. He was told to report to Fort Bragg in three days time.

Rafe was grinning as Flynn hung up the phone. "The captain's been busy."

Flynn felt off balance, as if he'd just thrown all his weight against a door to break it down only to find it was already open.

"The three-day leave was Sarah's idea," Rafe continued. "Lately she's been getting into that touchy-feely stuff, said you and Abbie deserve some more time alone. Jack, can you give him anything for those hives?"

"Last chance, O'Toole," Jack said. "You can still come with us."

Flynn took a pace back.

Jack muttered another oath and reached into his pocket for his wallet. He counted out five twenty-dollar bills and handed them to Rafe. "Looks like you win, Marek."

Rafe chuckled as he folded the money. "I had an advantage. Ever since I found Glenna, I can recognize the signs." He stood up, reached behind the sofa and tossed a duffel bag toward Flynn. "Well, since you're staying, you're going to need this."

Flynn caught it and looked at the name on the top. It was his own.

"Your helmet's in the closet by the door," Rafe said. "I left your bike in the visitors' lot. Your keys are in the duffel bag."

Jack was still muttering as he walked to the door. "I thought it was a sure bet."

"It was," Rafe said. "You just chose the wrong side." He punched Flynn's shoulder as he went past. "Good luck, buddy. We'll see you at Bragg."

Flynn locked the door behind them and stared at the bag in his hand. Rafe had known all along that Flynn would want to stay. More than that, he'd suckered Jack into betting against him. Flynn wondered if Abbie's family was anything like his family, the members of Eagle Squadron. Probably. And oddly enough he was looking forward to meeting them. Shaking his head, he turned toward the bedroom.

Abbie stood in the bedroom doorway, her eyes puffy. Pink sleep wrinkles pressed into her cheek from the pillow. Her hair was a tangled mass of curls. She clutched her robe closed at her throat and looked around. "Flynn? I thought I heard voices."

How could he have thought she wasn't his type? He'd never seen a woman look more beautiful.

He put his bag beside her suitcase and walked toward her. "You did. Rafe and Jack were here to drop off our things. They're on their way back to the base."

"The warehouse?"

"No. It's been cleaned out. They're going home."

"Oh. But why are you still here?"

He stopped when his toes nudged hers. There were so many things he could say. Too many unformed explanations whirled in his head. It wasn't easy to change the habits of a lifetime, but right now—this moment—was where it would start.

So he gave her the simple answer. "I'm here because I love you, Abbie."

She blinked. The hand that held her robe closed trembled.

"I love you," he repeated. "Damn, I've never said that to anyone before, but do you know something? It gets easier the more I say it."

Abbie let go of her robe and touched her fingertips lightly to his face. She must be dreaming. Walking in her sleep and fantasizing.

But he was real. His jaw prickled with the start of his morning beard stubble. His dimples deepened beneath her thumb. He was no fantasy. Somehow the man she loved was standing in front of her and saying...

"Say it again," she whispered.

He laughed. "I love you, Miss Abigail Locke."

She smiled.

"That's the one." He lifted her up so her face was level with his. He looked at her mouth. "I sure hope your smile means what it did yesterday."

"Yesterday, today and tomorrow. It won't change, Flynn." She wrapped her legs around his waist. "I'll always love you."

He kissed her nose. "How about the day after tomorrow?"

"Yes."

He kissed her chin. "And the day after that?"

"Yes, yes!"

"Good, because I only have three days before I have to be back at Bragg. Do you think we can get married by then?"

She looped her arms behind his neck as her head started to spin. "Married?"

"I thought that's what you wanted."

"It's so sudden. We've only known each other for a week."

He swung her to the side and nipped her earlobe. "What's the use of waiting around once you've made your choice?"

"Flynn, are you sure?"

"Yes. I want to stay."

There was something about the way he said those words that made her pause. She grabbed his head in her hands so that she could look at him.

He was no longer smiling. There were no barriers between what he kept in his heart and what showed on his face. And what she saw made her catch her breath. It was pain mixed with courage. Caution tangled with hope. Longing. Certainty.

"I want to stay," he repeated. "Whether it's here or at Bragg. Where we live doesn't matter, as long as we're together. I'm through standing on the outside looking in. You've shown me what true courage is, Abbie. This time I'm not going to leave."

She knew what this must be costing him. She understood the scars of his past were only beginning to heal. But he was willing to take this risk, and she loved him all the more for it.

"And I know I'm not the man you had in mind," he said. "But I'll trade in my bike for a station wagon if that's what it takes to make your dreams come true."

"Oh, Flynn." She smoothed his too-long hair and pressed a kiss to one of his dimples. Someday she would take the time to think about fate and karmic birthday gifts, but not now. She pulled his head to hers. "You're all that I could wish for. I don't want you to change a thing."

* * * * *